DEN

Hope Bolinger

illuminateYA
fiction

DEN BY HOPE BOLINGER
Illuminate YA Fiction is an imprint of LPCBooks
a division of Iron Stream Media
100 Missionary Ridge, Birmingham, AL 35242

ISBN: 978-1-64526-266-4
Copyright © 2020 by Hope Bolinger
Cover design by Elaina Lee
Interior design by AtriTex Technologies P Ltd

Available in print from your local bookstore, online, or from the publisher at: Shop-LPC.com

For more information on this book and the author visit: www.hopebolinger.com

This is a work of fiction. Names, characters, and incidents are all products of the author's imagination or are used for fictional purposes. Any mentioned brand names, places, and trademarks remain the property of their respective owners, bear no association with the author or the publisher, and are used for fictional purposes only.

All scripture quotations, unless otherwise indicated, are taken from the Holy Bible, New International Version®, NIV®. Copyright ©1973, 1978, 1984, 2011 by Biblica, Inc.TM. Used by permission of Zondervan. All rights reserved worldwide. www.zondervan.com. "NIV" and "New International Version" are trademarks registered in the United States Patent and Trademark Office by Biblica, Inc.TM.

Brought to you by the creative team at LPCBooks:
Bradley Isbell, Tessa Hall, and Kelsey Bryant

Library of Congress Cataloging-in-Publication Data
Bolinger, Hope.
Den / Hope Bolinger 1st ed.

Printed in the United States of America

Praise for *den*

Hope Bolinger is an author to watch! She skillfully weaves a retelling of the biblical book of Daniel into the modern-day drama of an American high school. The cast of characters is relatable and deep. Fans of Young Adult fiction will not be able to put this book down—except to start Book Three!

~ **Rachelle Rea Cobb**
Author of *Follow the Dawn*

In this extraordinary sequel to *Blaze*, author Hope Bolinger continues Danny and his friends' quest for truth and justice, taking readers into even darker and more treacherous, twisted, and mysterious times for high school students at King's Academy. As pressure mounts against him, like Daniel in the Bible's Book of Daniel, will Danny survive this modern version of the Lion's Den? Beautifully and thoughtfully written details bring all the characters and the setting to life, making this story a riveting read for anyone, although especially relatable to young adults.

~ **A. L. Kent**
Author of *A Journey of Three Degrees* and *360 Degrees Home*

Den by Hope Bolinger is an immensely satisfying read about four Christian teens struggling to adapt to a new secular boarding school. This tale incorporates the tools of fine writing—from metaphors (like a caged bird), to attention to all the senses ... The story is very timely and relevant, dealing with issues around fitting in, social media, and teen suicides. It abounds with intrigue. I'll anxiously await the third book in this series.

~**Doug Cornelius**
Award-winning author of *The Baker's Daughter*

Contemporary, gritty, and stouthearted, author Hope Bolinger observes the nuances of life with an artist's eye. Bolinger's current series boldly reinvents an ancient epic as a modern story, examining what people do, why they do it, and the timelessness of truth. Bolinger is an author to watch.

~ **PeggySue Wells**
Bestselling author of *The Slave Across the Street* and *Chasing Sunrise*

Hope casts a new young Daniel into a den of perils in the modern world. Despite the dangers, fears, and feelings of abandonment that today's youth fear, the new Daniel follows his namesake, always doing the right thing when others do not. A good read for YA crowd.

~ **George Cargill**
Author of *In the Grip of God: Journey into Corinth*

Den provides a unique, modern-day spin on a familiar Bible story. Hope has written a sequel that will appeal to fans of "Adventures in Odyssey." I'm curious to see what she'll think of next!

~ **Olivia Smit**
Author of *Seeing Voices*

Den takes readers through a journey of unspeakable tragedy and consistently raises the stakes, asking the reader to have as much courage as its characters. Truly engaging!

~ **Leah Jordan Meahl**
Author of *The Threshold*

This series by Hope Bolinger is a treasure and I feel blessed to have had the opportunity to read an early version of *Den*. The story is crisp and raw and riveting, all in one, and offers a contemporary twist on a Biblical story. Daniel and his friends are "real," and deal with not only the usual teenage angsts and concerns, but also with topics that are relevant to our time—pregnancies, shootings, prejudices, the challenges of faith, the bonds of friendship, etc. The characters are unique, the drama high, and the story telling paced perfectly.

~ **D.L. Koontz**
Author of *Crossing into the Mystic* and *What the Moon Saw*

No YA novel is complete without gritty realism and characters you can't help but root for. *Den* passes with bold, blazing, red colors. From gut-twisting anxiety to heartfelt heroics, Hope Bolinger continues her retelling of Daniel with all the teen angst and sensory-laden detail you've come to expect, and a dash of humor thrown in for good measure. *Den* is honest and doesn't shy away from the hard issues, but Tweets them head-on, in the light of faith. It's sure to draw you into the *Den*... and end with a bang.

~ M.N. Stroh
Author of the *Tale of the Clans* saga

After reading Bolinger's first book, *Blaze*, I was fascinated with her engaging storytelling and the concept of Daniel in the lion's den meets modern-day teens. I couldn't wait to read the second book, *Den*. And let me tell you, it did not disappoint. The likable and relatable characters continue to develop as the plot thickens with twists and turns that kept me up much too late. Readers are sure to be captivated once again!

~ Beckie Lindsey
Author of the *Beauties from Ashes Series*
Editor of SoCal Christian Voice

With a distinct and captivating voice, Hope Bolinger interweaves the biblical story of Daniel into her second young adult contemporary novel, *Den*. Her ingenious use of humor and rhetorical devices brings new life to this Old Testament tale.

~ Tara K. Ross
Author of *Fade to White*

Bolinger gives fresh, new meaning to Daniel in the lions' den. Mysterious suicide attempts and related deaths provide key conflicts in a plot that offers plenty of twists and turns and leaves readers guessing. Often funny and witty, *Den* took me back to high school days, fraught with coming-of-age angst, interpersonal struggles, and identity quests. Danny's rocky world is no different, but he has a cast of fascinating characters along for the ride. Providing an entertaining yet gritty glimpse into the challenges of today's high schoolers, the novel sucked me in and left me wanting more. Don't miss this read!

~ **Adam Blumer**
Author of *Kill Order*

Den fueled my imagination from the first page. Hope Bolinger reveals the tension and fury of youth with clever twists and wicked characters. Through the unspeakable circumstances, *Den* will have you asking, "What could Danny possibly go through next?" and when you think you've turned a corner to take a breath, Ms. Bolinger ignites action and intensity once again. Written with grit and determination, this page-turner will leave you craving the next book. WELCOME TO THE DEN.

~ **Kass Fogle**
Author and blogger
Podcaster at The Introverted Believer

With the skill of an older wordsmith, 20-something Hope Bolinger has created an intense young adult trilogy entitled *Blaze*. Book 1 (also entitled *Blaze*) presents the scenario of 16-year-old Danny who just wants to survive high school, while a constant barrage of unsettling and dangerous circumstances keeps him aware he needs to watch his back. Unsure who he can rely on, he wants his friends safe—but can they all be trusted? *Den* (Book 2 in the series) picks up where *Blaze* ends and heightens the intensity of the mysterious plot. Bolinger is a fresh voice in the young adult market. It's a voice that will likely be well-received by many fans of young adult fiction.

~ **Elaine Marie Cooper**
Author of *Scarred Vessels* and *Fields of the Fatherless*

Reading DEN is kind of like biting into a piece of tiramisu. Each chapter introduces a new flavor, taking the reader deeper into real life issues, like regret, anxiety, social media pressures, drinking, teen pregnancy, and suicide. Just when you think you have the plot or person figured out, there's a twist that keeps your mind sprinting toward the next chapter. But it's not just entertaining; the way Hope deals with mental health issues is complex and refreshing—showing that people aren't necessarily all good or all bad, but a complicated mix of the two. Despite some of the darker topics, the takeaway is about being loyal to your friends and staying true to yourself. My two faves are Hannah and Danny. She's so quirky and fun, and he stands out as that friend you can always count on. Five stars, and I can't wait for book 3.

~ Dianne Bright
Author of The Soul Reader Trilogy and *Moms Kick Butt*

The beloved Danny is back and this time, things aren't just heating up. Hope Bolinger cleverly weaves a tale of intrigue and surprise, making *Den* a page-turner that you won't be able to put down.

~ Bethany Jett
Award-winning author of *The Cinderella Rule*

To Alyssa and Sonya,

Thank you for bearing with me.

Blaze *and* Den *would not have existed without you.*

Chapter One

"IF YOU DIG ANY HARDER, DANNY BELTE, YOU'LL SNAP the spoon in half."

Bel Graves' dark eyes twinkled at Danny as she glanced at him from underneath sticky black bangs. She swiped them with a hand covered in cookie crumbs, a customer-favorite topping.

He returned his gaze to the customer on the other side of the counter, a girl in pigtail braids. She eyed the ice cream tubs, tongue flicking out. Danny followed her stare to the container with the neon green dessert dotted with chocolate chips and half his scoop.

She shifted her eyes to a phone in her fingertips. Just before she flipped it around, he spied a little blue bird on the screen.

"Mint chocolate chip, please." She added the last part after typing a tweet.

Oh, mint chocolate chip always froze extra hard in storage. He eyed the clock—two minutes until his shift ended. He bet she was already waiting outside.

"Large size you said, kid?" He released his grip from the handle to massage his wrist.

"Uh-huh, I want the biggest one you got."

The girl could've worn the large container as a hat. She returned to her tweet.

Sweat brimmed on his lip, and he nuzzled it against his pink Fro-Yo Zone Ice Cream Shop T-shirt. Leaning closer to the glass case, he sighed as the cool air blew over his face. Too bad the freezer behind him radiated more heat than a King's Academy dorm. And people thought those working indoors had it lucky during the summer, especially a hot July like this.

"Don't forget the line of about ten customers behind her." Bel's soft voice carried just above the radio speakers nestled in the corner wall above the containers of various frozen chocolates and cakes. It blasted "Frosty the Snowman" just in time for Christmas in July.

"I can see the line," Danny growled, wincing at the pains in his wrist as he moved the scoop in an S-motion. He dislodged a green sliver and dropped it into a bowl and held it up for Bel to see.

Bel paused from loading fresh maraschino cherries into a bin to swipe her forehead with the back of her arm. With her other hand, she clutched at her stomach and grit her teeth.

At first, he thought it was a smile, but then she doubled over.

"You doing all right?" After she motioned for him to move away, Danny returned to the tub to dig up another find from the Ice Age.

"Just dandy. Also, *morning* sickness is a myth. The nausea gets worse in the afternoon, especially in the second trimester."

Yeah, Danny knew all about nausea from this last school year. Luckily, his mother purchased some anxiety meds after receiving reports of his stomach sickness from the school nurse.

"I'm sorry to hear about that. my brother's wife says it goes away the further along you get."

"Uh-huh, I've heard that too." She grit her teeth again. "As my biological mom would say, 'Serves you right for following in my footsteps. Pain means consequences, sweetheart.'"

Both Danny and Bel winced at this.

After two more scoops and a second chorus of "Frosty," Danny slid the large pink bowl to Bel, who rang up the price at the register. He went to swab his lip with his fingers but paused when they stuck together with green liquid. With ice cream in several other places on his body he didn't know could be dressed in the frozen treat, he wasn't exactly prom-ready.

Ah, prom. No one wanted to think about that.

"Next customer." He removed his scoop and dropped it into a bin full of warm water. As he fished out another one, he felt his shoulder relax as some of the ice cream glued to his fingers released into the brown water. They never said the place was sanitary.

He turned around and faced a pair of large eyes. His stomach dropped as he scanned the ceiling for any snowflakes he hadn't secured with hot glue before remembering the Winter Wonderland dance happened months ago.

"Hi-ya, Danny, didn't know you worked here."

"Ah, Valentina. Get a new hairdo?"

Valentina combed a finger through a bright-pink haircut that just reached her scrawny shoulders. The hair and her rosy dress fit in with the walls and the ice cream honeycomb balls hanging from the ceiling. If she doused herself in strawberry perfume, she would blend right into the place like a milkshake. With her free hand, she motioned to the figure beside her, a boy with very dark skin, dark curly hair, brilliant blue eyes, and a very, very stiff posture. Danny could smell his cologne halfway across the shop.

"Meet Reuben Benjamin, my boyfriend. You two might know each other. You used to attend Emmanuel before it burned down and all." She said "Emmanuel" as if someone had stuffed her mouth with lemon sherbet.

Also, why did she have to mention that? The whole your-school-burned-down-last-year-and-you-had-to-attend-your-rival-school thing? It had almost been a year.

Also, also, what was she doing dating an Emmanuel student? His fiery-haired friend Hannah Shad got enough flak last year from classmates about going to prom with his roommate Duke, a King's student almost in every sense.

Stop thinking about prom, dude, you've been having more flashbacks than when your dad died. Let's go back to Valentina nuzzling her nose in Reuben's pin-straight neck.

Ugh, why did they have to come back to that?

At least Valentina stepped up from her last obsession, his other roommate, Dean. AKA, the definition of King's Academy. He'd overheard her talking to her friend in the dining commons about the split, on the last day of school.

"I need to stop dating guys who treat me like how I feel about myself, you know? Ever since I got drunk at that party my freshman year and Hunter went farther than he should." She shook her head and plopped a pile of mashed potatoes on her red plate and sighed. "Am I always going to feel like I don't deserve better?"

Even if it was Valentina, Danny thought, no one deserved a Hunter or Dean.

"You might also recognize Reuben from our student council meetings last year." Valentina dislodged her nose from her boyfriend's neck. "Met him because he upvoted just about every bill I proposed. If you Emmanuel students hadn't transferred to King's Academy, I would've never met him."

Although not remembering more than a blurry face in a memory somewhere, Danny twitched his lips into a smile to suffice a greeting. Dagon, there was sticky ice cream on his cheek too.

"I'd shake your hand, Reuben, but you'd get all sorts of nasty stuff on it. Don't want to ruin that nice shirt either."

Reuben glanced down at his red polo, expressionless. He clashed horribly with Valentina. "I'm sure you'd break my wrist anyway, getting all buff with scooping that ice cream."

Monotone, he sounded like a dictionary mixed with some tasty trigonometry.

Danny shrugged as he heard Bel dump something soft and hard at the same time into a bin. Cookie dough? "Too bad I only use one arm to scoop because the other one looks like a noodle. Good thing I do cross-country in the fall and not football." Dean did football. "Enough about me, what can I get both of you today?"

Valentina squinted at the bright-green menu behind him for a moment. She turned to Reuben. "Babe, I'm craving a milkshake. How about you?"

Danny's stomach soured as his lips sagged almost to his chin. The only thing worse than scooping mint chocolate chip ...

"Sure, Valentina. Chocolate, right?" He allowed for a small smile, if you could call it that, at Danny after his girlfriend nodded and nestled her head into his shoulder. "Two chocolate milkshakes with no added toppings."

Throw a little bit of robot in there, and you had Reuben's voice.

Bel smirked at Danny as he grabbed the silver cup for shakes. She asked for the next customer, motioning for the happy couple to scoot to the side by a tip jar. The thing had only a couple bucks and some spare nickels. Probably didn't help the label on the jar read, *Don't be afraid to CHANGE the world*, a pun that would've earned Danny a Nerf gun shot to his face from his brother, Judah.

After depositing enough chocolate scoops into the cup, Danny tipped it at an angle as the machine groaned along to "All I Want for Christmas." Bel hovered beside him, hobbling back and forth between a pair of black tennis shoes.

"Your customer ordered a milkshake too?" Danny lurched forward to readjust the cup. It nearly spattered his shirt with chocolate soup ... wouldn't be the first time.

"Popular pick today." Bel sighed, then groaned.

"You need to sit?" He assumed she was clutching her stomach again but couldn't tear away his eyes from the swirling machine. When Bel asked what he'd said, he repeated himself louder.

"I'm fine, Danny."

"You sure? I can handle the line. Been here for a year ..."

"Sound just like my brother."

"You have a brother?" He clicked the machine off and emptied the contents into a thick Styrofoam cup. He'd heard only about her biological mother. She didn't seem to like to talk about family much.

Bel handed him a lid, and he spotted her eye roll amidst a sea of dark-blue eyeliner. She rubbed a thumb on her cleft chin. Maybe to flick off some ice cream that stuck to it.

"Yeah, I have a brother. You're roommates with him at King's."

Danny shuddered, eyes widening. "Dean?" He caught her eye, and it could've been his imagination, but her jaw sank into a gape as if she had forgotten how to breathe. She sealed her lips and scooped some loose nuts from the countertop into a trash bin beside her.

He reached for his scoop and mined the chocolate ice cream tub. Lucky he didn't have to wash out the milkshake cup since the couple ordered the same flavor.

As he clicked the cup into the machine, he saw Bel over his shoulder, fingers clawing at her stomach again.

"Not Dean, I meant Duke's my brother. I heard you two were friends, at least, as friendly as you can get for roommates."

Well, he wouldn't call it that, but at least the puffy-eyed Duke didn't drive fishhooks into people's noses.

"Oh." Danny frowned. "Are you and Duke both adopted?" He focused his concentration on the shaking metal cup. Even with the machine shrieking, he still heard a growl lodge in Bel's throat.

"He's not."

"Oh, neat, where are you adopted from?"

"Were you going to guess China? Everyone always guesses China. Look, just because I'm Asian—"

"I was going to say Mexico." A smile stretched across his sticky cheeks.

"I'm *fostered* from Kentucky, if you must know."

"Makes sense why you and Duke don't share a last name. I have a brother adopted from Israel named Judah. He's home this summer."

His coworker didn't appear to hear or care as she fished another silver cup from the warm water bin and turned to the glass case to fill it with some other flavor than chocolate. When he finished churning the soft serve, emptying it into a cup, and wishing the couple a nice day, he groaned when he saw a French braid and tennis dress approach the counter. Why did everyone from King's Academy come visit this ice cream shop? Today of all days.

"Hey, Julia." He kept his gaze on the pink-and-green tile floor. Some places had muddied to brown with all the dropped ice cream incidents. "What can I get started for you?"

He raised his eyes to the glass case to see her hands plant on her sharp hips. Her purple tennis dress was splotching with sweat.

"How about a small blueberry frozen yogurt? And I mean *small*. Your coworker messed it up last time. You must've been on a break or something."

She pointed behind him. He looked over his shoulder at Bel, who had splattered a white milkshake on her shirt.

"Sure thing, Julia." He glanced back. "Were you playing tennis outside? It's burning up out there."

He winced and bit his tongue. Good ol' Danny boy could've described it any other way. Now, a dark building licked in tongues of red and yellow fire danced across his vision for a moment. He shook these thoughts away and began scooping.

"Yeah, my stepdad and I hit ground strokes every day. Thank God those college recruiters saw me my junior year before your friend Michelle Gad schooled me in tryout last year."

"Pittsburgh U?"

"Mhmm, it's like, an hour away from here, not a terrible drive."

Gotcha, not too far from King's and a certain special someone.

She gazed at an ice cream–shaped clock on the wall opposite Valentina and Reuben on pink barstool seats. Danny glanced over as the small silver spoon hand touched the ten-past-three mark. Why hadn't his shift replacement arrived?

He bit a salty lip. "How are you and Dean doing? I saw you post about your one-year anniversary."

On Twitter, no less; didn't the dude at least have an Instagram?

He winced at the thought of Dean taking an artsy photo flushed in some filter, #wokeuplikethis #withafishhookinmynose #thanksDean.

She flicked a blonde eyebrow as if annoyed by the question. "Yeah, well, he was supposed to meet me up here but has bailed the last two dates because of work, so ..."

"No toppings?" Danny stared at the sad blue blob in the bowl and jiggled the contents. The frozen yogurt always ran runny.

"No, and Danny"—her eyes softened—"Dean and I wanted to say sorry about what happened at your friends' dorm in May. We would've said something earlier, but you kind of bolted from King's after that."

He doubted Dean wanted to say anything of the sort, but he accepted it anyway. Maybe the big beefy roommate did have a heart buried in all the muscle somewhere.

"Yeah, well, good ol' principal Ned let me go home early. Mind you, he sent the exams in the mail, so he didn't let me off as easy as everyone thought."

Bel grabbed the small cup of yogurt he slid to her, and the ring from the register blocked out his call for the next customer to step up at the counter. A girl in an Afro tied back with a headband approached, smelling of sweat. Danny leaned into the display case to fumigate the scent with orange sherbet.

Oh boy, head count from his school today. Let's see if Danny boy could keep track:

- Valentina (with the pink hair)

- Reuben (with the robot voice)

- Julia (French braid)

- and now ...

"Hi, July, how are you this July?" He chuckled.

July raised an eyebrow and tossed a *seriously?* kind of look at Danny. Nevertheless, she fanned herself with a hand and her lips quirked into a smile. "Hot."

"Agreed."

"What do you mean, agreed? You work in an ice cream store. That's, like, the coldest place you could be during a Pennsylvania summer."

"It's hotter than you would think back here."

"Hotter than breaking up sidewalk with a sledgehammer for your neighbors?"

July's parents weren't letting her off easy this summer, either. He jabbed a thumb over his shoulder at the large silver freezer. "Not that extreme, no, but that thing keeps blasting heat to keep all the good stuff cold inside."

"The ice cream tubs?"

"That and all the mistakes. If we mess up an order, we put it on a shelf in there and eat it after our shift. So, please, give me a very complicated order."

July let out a good-hearted laugh. Perhaps a little too loud and forced because she winced right after as "Silver Bells" began to play.

"Just salted caramel with caramel drizzle as a topping." She adjusted her headband.

"Oh no"—Danny gripped his head and moaned—"too complicated." No applause or laughter from July, but at least she had more of a sense of humor than Reuben, from what he could tell. He'd seen her dad once or twice, and the guy cracked more jokes than Tim Hawkins. "So July, don't tell me you're killing yourself with doing soccer already." He nodded at her sweat-stained T-shirt. "Thought tryouts didn't start until mid-August."

"They don't. Just thought I would go for a run today since Coach makes us do a timed mile for tryouts." Her eyes widened as she puffed a sharp exhale. "Also, I heard you might be signing up for Arabic too? You're the only one I've heard is in the class. Think they'll cut the program if there's only two of us?"

"Maybe. Figured it looks slightly more impressive on a college application than Spanish. What else did your advisor suggest you take?"

"PE, precalc, chemistry, AP Euro—"

"Me too. Maybe we'll be in the same classes." He moved to the caramel syrup container and pumped the red nozzle.

"Great. Can finally be friends with my friends' friends. Rayah was one of the only people on the soccer team to stick around after our season."

Ah, Rayah Abed. The Paul Rudd of all friends, you couldn't help but love her. Too bad Paul Rudd and friends were flammable, especially when you locked them in a fiery room.

He rubbed his sticky hands on his black pants. To the register July went. The bell to the shop dinged, letting in more customers to the already trailing line. He grimaced as he gazed at the clock again. When Bel went to storage to retrieve more chocolate chips, he tapped her on the shoulder.

"Bel, my shift ended over fifteen minutes ago. Any chance I can hang up my hat?" He tapped his visor.

Her eyes crinkled as she observed the line of customers over his shoulder. "Any way you can wait until that thing dies down? I saw who's supposed to come to your shift, and she's almost always late. Who knew three o'clock Thursday would bring in everyone and their mothers?"

Sigh. "Sure, just, I was going to meet up with a friend after this. She's probably waiting outside now."

"Why doesn't she come into the AC?"

"Because she'd feel obligated to buy something. Next customer p—"

He froze as a man with a square chin, red beard, and suit jacket approached. The man looked just like his principal, except twenty years younger ... and with glinting green eyes.

"Recognize me?" He smiled. Unlike Ned his voice didn't sound like thunder, more like a bull, a slightly higher register. "Dad talks about you all the time. You work on his Advisory Council or whatever, right? Telling my old man how to run the school and all?"

Danny clenched his mouth shut when he realized his jaw was sagging. "Uh-huh."

Ned's son shot a hand across the counter. "Name's August."

He'd have to get an attendance sheet soon.

Roll call: Valentina (pink), Reuben (robot), Julia (braid), July (soccer), August (beard). Got it? Got it.

"August, huh? Like the month?" Danny's eyes flicked to July's table as she peeled open a book for AP Language, *One Flew Over the Cuckoo's Nest*. Dagon, he needed to get on that summer homework. "And I've got sticky hands. You don't want to shake them."

August's eyelids narrowed, but he still wore a grin as he drew his arm back. "August like the first emperor of Rome. My parents just cut off the 'us' part at the end of it."

Parents liked to do that. "Oh, nice. So you want to order something?"

"Listen, my dad still feels awful about what went down in May."

"The fact he trapped Michelle, Rayah, and Hannah in a burning room? Yeah, I was pretty bummed out about that too." Danny bit his tongue as his cheeks flushed. A customer was a customer no matter what family they came from.

For a second, August bobbed back and forth to the beat of "Last Christmas." Shooting pains attacked Danny's soles as he glanced at the clock again. He returned to August, who had a large hand on his thick neck.

"Like I said, my dad feels terrible about it. Did you get the invitation to meet at our house on the second?"

"Of August?" They met eyes for a moment, and Danny coughed to suppress a chuckle. "I did. Same day as our first meeting with the cross-country team, though, so I might stain your floors with sweat."

The grin hid underneath all the red hair of the beard. "You can wash up beforehand. We don't plan to meet until seven, and it would be a really good time for him to reconcile about the fire in Suanna dorm and all."

"Sounds just peachy. Now do you want to order something?"

A tinkling of the bell caught his attention as a small figure waved at him from the door. Short hair, dark-skinned, and the most beautiful brown eyes to ever belong to a human being.

Danny signaled back with a half-hearted hello. "Be out in a moment as soon as I get through this line. I promise."

Rayah nodded, wiped a sweaty hand on her blue bandana, and disappeared behind the door.

Chapter Two

"WHAT ROOM DID THE SMOKE COME FROM?"

She shrugged, the orange strap on her prom dress sliding down her shoulder. With a jerk of the chin, she gestured to a girl crumpled on her knees, who had melted into a mascara and blue dress bubble. "She knows."

He placed a hand on the girl's arm. "Please, tell me what room."

"The–one–next–to–mine ... 315."

315. Rayah, Hannah, and Michelle's room. The doors locked from the outside.

The wind knocked out of him, and Danny clenched fistfuls of grass.

A hand clapped on his shoulder, and he stiffly glanced up at the giant figure of Ned in a disheveled suit and fresh tears streaming down his face into his knotted beard.

Then he spotted it, the lighter fluid in his beefy hand. Yellow, the casing glinted in the warm glow of the firelight from the building. With his mind in a haze, it took him several moments to put two and two together. Ned, fire.

And then it clicked like a pistol.

How could he let this happen? He had to protect them, keep Rayah safe. Danny knew the principal would punish them for not saying a pledge of loyalty to him in front of the school, but this?

He'd failed them. Just like he couldn't save Zai all those years before. He promised himself he wouldn't let anything happen to any friend after that.

"Danny," Ned began.

Click, bang.

A hot flash of adrenaline pumped through his veins like a shot. He jerked his shoulder and stumbled toward the building. Nails dug into his skin as Ned clenched harder, pulling him back.

Danny thrashed around shouting a combination of "no" and "murderer" between grunts. Ned pinned his shoulders to the grass, the principal's cheeks glistening. He couldn't tell if Ned smelled like smoke or if the scent came from the dorm building blazing fifty feet away. Nearby, he heard someone's phone beep three times, perhaps to dial the fire department.

Good luck calling them with the horrible cell service at King's Academy.

Ned pressed a knee to Danny's stomach to stop him from flailing. "Please let me explain."

With his remaining strength, Danny kicked his legs up and propelled himself forward, knocking back the principal. As Ned tumbled backwards into a patch of grass near girls in their pajamas, Danny staggered to his feet and lurched into a lopsided run until he caught his balance.

He gripped the arm of a nearby girl with dark hair and Tinkerbell tank top. "I need your keycard."

"The building is on *fire*."

"Uh-huh, and I'm going inside it to get my friends out. Keycard, now."

Her dark eyes burned into his for a moment before she reached into the pocket of her short Pink brand shorts. "It's your funeral."

He glanced at her and then squinted at the plastic card. It read her name, *Bel*, next to a picture of her with much longer hair.

"Thanks, Bel."

He leaned forward and broke into a sprint the way Coach had taught him in track. Sweat poured down his face the closer he approached. Clutching the keycard like a baton, he barreled through a crowd of girls who parted for him.

His feet burned as they slammed against the concrete path toward the gray dorm door. Dress shoes were not meant for track runners. With a quick swipe through a blinking key reader, he waited to hear the beep and click from the door. Just as he reached for the metal handle, two arms grabbed his and yanked him back. He tripped and stumbled as the figure who nabbed him continued to force him backwards.

"You're not yourself. We need to get you to a hospital." The low rumble of thunder sounded in Ned's voice as he whispered in Danny's ear.

Danny continued to thrash but to no avail. His arm muscles ached from the effort, but he continued to push through the fire. He'd make it inside even if he incinerated upon entry.

"Let him go!" The voice sounded like a growl with a distinct hint of girl. A girl in an Afro and a pastel T-shirt ran forward to meet them where Ned had successfully dragged him, by a scraggly evergreen.

He recognized her from Rayah's soccer games, a friend and a month.

"Miss *July* Jackson, your friend here tried to run into a burning building, a suicide attempt at best. We need to get him some medical help before he becomes a risk to himself and others. I suggest you stay at least one hundred feet away from the building as well."

"Danny's best friends are up in that room. *Of course* he'd try to rescue them."

Ned yanked him further until the pine needles stabbed his neck. "You aren't concerned that he'd willingly take his own life and likely die before he reached the third floor?"

"That's what friends do. He's more mentally there than most of us at the moment."

How could she sound so calm at a time like this? She was friends with Rayah too.

"Take him back to his dorm, Miss Jackson. If he shows any signs of resistance or suicidal actions, I want you to dial an ambulance."

"Yes, sir." The "sir" came out with an eye roll.

With a sharp exhale, Ned released Danny with a shove. No sooner had he tripped into July than she gripped his hand with dry, rough fingers and pulled him toward the direction of Phrat River, his dorm.

He waited until they were out of Ned's earshot. "You need to let me into Suanna."

"Try to stay calm. Someone actually reached the fire department, a miracle with the service here. I guess with about a hundred of us calling them, one was bound to reach their office."

A blaring horn sounded in the distance. He stopped, despite July's firm tugs, and watched as the red spinning lights whirled somewhere in the distance. They'd just made it to campus.

"Danny, Ned might check to make sure you made it back to your dorm. You don't want to mess with adults and hospitals. Make one wrong move, and they'll lock you up for months."

He remained put. "Why? You have personal experience with that?"

"No. Your friend Hannah does, though."

Ice surged through his veins as he envisioned his friend's fiery red hair, the only thing not bound by a straitjacket. When did that happen? After her parents' divorce? When she had worn long sleeves during the summer and joked about popping the pills from her mother's cabinets?

Another tug from July, and the fire truck's siren sounded louder. Fine, he would go back to Phrat River and wait in the lobby downstairs.

"Y-you will t-tell me if th-they make it out o-okay?" Suddenly his tongue and lips felt very thick, and he wanted to collapse onto the grass and sleep for ten hours.

"Of course. Now, come on. I'll knock on the doors when I hear anything."

They stumbled through a rocky path that wound to the squat concrete building with no windows. Danny reached for his keycard and accidentally pulled Bel's out instead.

"I borrowed this from—" he began, showing the plastic card to July.

"I'll get it back to her. She lives a door down, and we signed up to be roommates next year, so there's no way she won't get it back."

He nodded. His brain bobbled about a million miles away. After retrieving the correct keycard, he slid it and heard a clicking sound. Before he could swing open the door, he gave a soft "oomph" as July collapsed him into a hug. Felt sort of awkward, like she wasn't usually the huggy type.

"Don't worry. I know it's stupid to tell you that right now, but fire departments get to these things in minutes." She clapped a hand on his shoulder. "The Lord is a refuge for the oppressed, a stronghold in times of trouble."

"What's that from?" He'd heard it in a song before. The lyrics scrolled through his head.

"Psalm 9:9. Favorite verse. If it helped me get through my dad's cancer treatments, it can help you. Repeat it to yourself, kid. I'll knock when I hear any news, OK?"

Cancer treatments. It was amazing how her dad could still have such a good sense of humor. Emmanuel and King's both needed more families like that.

"OK. Thanks, July."

She winced a weak smile. "Sure thing. Emmanuel students gotta stick together, no matter what."

July vanished around the corner of the building. Danny had to re-swipe his keycard and entered through the glass doors by the lobby. He collapsed onto a couch that smelled of musk and distracted himself with whatever he could make out in the room.

With the lights off, one could just barely catch the scattered glass beer bottles and wilted petals from corsages and boutonniere arrangements.

Just over an hour before, he and his friends had pumped their arms on a sweaty dance floor with paper hibiscus flowers dangling from the ceiling.

By the end of the night, most anything hanging had been torn down.

He had taken the small Rayah into his arms as they swerved left and right to "Fooled Around and Fell in Love." As they swayed back and forth in the small space allowed them, he told her how Ned couldn't hurt her there. They watched a disco ball spin near a painted wall that read *WELCOME TO THE DEN*. He said if Ned tried to take her from his arms, he'd send a pack of lions on him.

If only they'd stayed on the dance floor.

He needed to think about something other than prom.

Glancing at the lamps on small side tables in the corner of the room, he recalled how he and Rayah spent several hours that past semester studying for Mrs. Burgess's impossible English tests. Rayah couldn't point out a symbol to save her life. Danny, on the other hand, seemed to have the opposite problem. He saw the signs everywhere.

No, he couldn't think about Rayah, not now.

He considered racing upstairs to grab his phone to distract himself. But the effort it would take to ascend two flights of stairs in a non-air-conditioned dorm seemed not worth the risk. Besides, what if July came back and he missed her knocking on the door?

One more chance to amuse himself with the items in the room.

Take, for instance, the television situated in the far-right corner. Michelle had him watch *Spotlight* with her for her journalism class. Never would say no to a Rachel McAdams film, considering *Mean Girls* was his second favorite.

No, couldn't think about Michelle. He had to get out of this room.

Head pounding, he rose and paced by the front desk near the glass doors. Movement could distract him. He passed by a bulletin board with pictures of guys in Phrat River who had won various "accolades." A photo of Dean frowned next to a heading that read, *Most Messy Resident*. A boy with white hair and a Los Angeles Angels hoodie was pinned next to the award for *Most Likely to Disappear*.

Gabe Adams.

How his friend from track managed to escape Ned's mandatory assembly that required all students to say a pledge of loyalty to the principal beat the whims of even an Agatha Christie. After all, Ned had stationed guards blocking the school entrances, and with the cameras positioned everywhere around the school ... it simply was not possible.

The only way Danny had avoided saying that pledge—he clutched his stomach as he thought about how much he vomited in the school's medical center until Ned let him stay behind. A fresh wave of nausea overtook him. The fact he couldn't retrieve his meds from Hannah's room, where he'd accidentally left them, seemed to catch up to him now.

His heart beat into his vision, eyes pulsating against their sockets. An acrid aftertaste filled his throat as he collapsed onto his knees on the dirty tile floor.

Breathe in the nose, out the mouth, repeat.

He rubbed his hands up and down the smooth tile to put his mind on something, anything. Clenching his eyelids shut, he envisioned the few, the proud calming images the year had produced. A walk with Rayah in Ned's favorite garden where the weeping willow bounced her branches playfully and he could taste the warmth and sunlight alongside the babbling brook.

No, stop.

Danny gasped as he realized he'd been hyperventilating. He arched his neck toward the water-stained ceiling and gulped in air. Nothing seemed to come. Corners of his vision blurred black as the darkness encircled his eyes. As his temples throbbed and mouth filled with saliva, he scanned the area for a trash bin. The nearest one was in the kitchen, about fifteen feet from the front desk.

He pressed his hands on his knees, but his arms wobbled; no chance in getting up now. He'd have to vomit on the tile and mop it up with a towel later.

Choking out breaths, he repeated the verse July had told him best he could.

A cold hand clapped on his sweaty shoulder. The figure walked around him until they faced each other. Even in the dark lighting, which Danny's eyes had adjusted to, the person seemed to have a glow about his face.

Gabe Adams knelt with his hand still on Danny's shoulder. "How are you?" Somehow it seemed more like a statement than a question. His friend smelled like smoke.

"Gabe, w-where h-have you b-been?"

"Do you believe in angels?"

Before Danny could respond, lava-hot liquid launched up his throat and out his mouth. Everything went dark for what seemed like a moment of silence and nothingness. Then a sharp rapping of knuckles against glass woke him up.

He was confused at first about why it was still dark outside and inside. As he tottered to his feet, he about slipped on the puddle of vomit on the floor. His dress shirt stuck to his body, and his stomach soured at the thought his mother had paid full price for the thing.

The knocking continued.

"C-coming," he slurred, shaking off whatever puke he could from his shirt. Unfortunately, some landed on the bulletin board and hit Dean's photo.

July's silhouette tapped an impatient foot as he swung open the glass doors. "Danny, they're fine. They're sending them to the hospital as a precaution, but no terrible burns from what I could see."

The words stung him like a BB gun pellet. Sharp but not hard enough to sink into his skin. Friends, safe, from fire. "How?"

"Don't know. The fire should've consumed the room with it being padded in carpet and all, but it stopped short of the closet. They'd climbed to the top bunk of a bed, according to a fireman I overheard. They were just huddled there in prayer when the firemen broke into the room."

"Th-they're alive?"

"Yes." She wrinkled her nose at his shirt. So much for another hug. "Get some sleep. You should be able to see them when they return to campus tomorrow."

Right then and there Danny believed in angels.

Chapter Three

"REMIND ME AGAIN WHY YOU CHOSE LASER TAG AS OUR first date."

Rayah swerved around a slushy vendor on the sidewalk near the ice cream shop. Someone held a paper cone nearby that smelled like blue raspberry. In the bright summer sun, Rayah looked odd wearing long black pants and a dark tank top to match the outfit Danny'd changed into after his shift.

He watched a pair of turtle-decorated swim trunks on a mannequin as they passed a shop. "Figured since we can't afford cars, we might as well try a place within a five-minute walk from where I work."

"Right. And with twenty or so shops and restaurants en route, none of those sounded appealing?"

As he twisted his head to face Rayah, he caught a twinkle of sun in her dark eyes. She slipped her hand into his and leaned close enough for him to catch a whiff of her cinnamon perfume.

Realizing his hands were sweaty, he wiped them on his pants before regripping.

"Well, I also figured that these restaurants don't have a five-dollar-a-game deal to shoot your girlfriend with lasers on Thursday, now do they? Besides, it's three. No one eats dinner at this time."

She laughed. "I like laser tag. It's just unexpected for a first date."

They paused as a woman in a green apron outside a fudge shop offered free samples on toothpicks. Danny swiped a melting maple walnut cube and popped it into his mouth. He discarded the toothpick into a garbage bin by the shop as the nut in the fudge dissolved in a pool of saliva.

"Bet you give out free samples all the time at work." Rayah's tongue probed the corners of her mouth for any remains of the mint chocolate sample she'd tried. They continued their amble up the sidewalk, dodging cracks and mothers' broken backs.

"Oh, don't even get me started. We have, like, forty flavors, and I swear some customers try every one, and they don't buy anything."

"Bel looked overwhelmed when I swung open the door."

"Lucky we spotted my shift replacement when I got out of the bathroom after I changed. She shows up late to everything, and our manager won't hire anyone new."

Rayah snapped her fingers. When he looked down at her, her lips sank into a frown. "Forgot to ask Bel about the AP Economics packet we got in the mail. I'm stuck on one of the charts."

They broke apart to let a family with a corgi through. Danny observed them for a moment as the youngest, a girl with a pink bow, tripped over a pair of shoes two sizes too large.

Danny interlaced his fingers with Rayah as they continued their trek uphill to the sound of car horns and wheels skidding into parallel parking spaces. "AP Econ, huh? Sounds like a nightmare."

"It's worse."

"Your fault for staying at King's Academy. Remind me again why you three did so after the principal freaking set your rooms on fire."

She drew in a long sigh, giving enough time for them to hear a dash of a conversation between two women eating outside at a Mediterranean restaurant. His mouth watered at the scent of pita bread and cooked onions.

Maybe he should've taken them out to eat instead.

"Didn't exactly have much of a choice, did we?" She pulled Danny toward a pot of yellow flowers she wanted to sniff. He avoided joining her as the leaves bounced beneath the weight of bees. She rose. "Single mom doesn't have time to homeschool two kids, and no other school in the area will ever be as good as King's to her. She's already thinking about sending Trevon to King's next year."

"Sorry again about your parents' divorce. It's crazy it happened in May when, well, when everything else seemed to turn upside down too."

Disasters always seemed to love company. Zai and Danny's father both passed in the same summer.

"It's fine. Hannah's been a great go-to. Most of the time, when we talk about divorce, she doesn't suggest killing off my dad in fan fiction. So that's a plus." She smiled weakly before they continued toward a dark-gray building in the distance.

They reached a crosswalk and clicked a stick-figure man on a rusted button they were certain didn't work. A woman with a Labradoodle sidled next to Rayah, and the girlfriend asked to pet it. Up went the corners of her lips as she scritched its curly head. A shrill beep sounded from the crosswalk, and they made their way across the hot black pavement.

"You're really good with animals, Ray. That dog almost rolled onto its back, you made it so happy."

"Guess working with Hannah doing pet sitting pays off."

"Yeah, I would team up with someone if given the task to watch seven dogs in one house. Has she murdered any of them yet?" The girl did seem to like to kill a lot of dandelions ... they reminded her too much of her time at the ward.

"No, she actually does really well with animals. I think they love her more than me, to be honest. Probably because they, and Hannah, hate people."

When they arrived at the parking lot, Danny noticed how some of the metal letters had fallen off the *Tagged* on the building. Now, in proud blue, it read *Ta d*. This reminded him of Phrat River, which had missed the *r* in Phrat. *Ph at River*.

As they squeezed between two minivans parked close together at the front, Rayah fanned her face with her free hand. "I'll be happy to go inside to air conditioning. Bet you'll miss it when you go back to school."

"Yeah, I tried to slip my name into room draw for one of the air-conditioned dorms, but they had no available slots. Guess who's stuck with Duke and Dean again?"

They nodded to a worker who puffed on a cigarette outside. He scrolled on his Twitter feed and didn't nod back. They swung open the heavy dark-glass doors. A strong burst of AC caused him to shudder as he entered the dimly lit room with various arcade games buzzing and some old techno music blasting out of speakers. Somewhere to the right, he heard the click of plastic. Over his shoulder, he saw a boy, no older than eight, swear as his opponent scored on him in air hockey.

"Speaking of room draw"—Rayah gestured to some free lockers for bags and fiddled with the strap on her purse—"Bel texted me saying she had to move out of Suanna into a single in Kading. Apparently, King's has a rule that anyone pregnant in their second or third trimester can't room with another person."

"Weird. Any idea who the father is?"

The locker creaked as Rayah swung it open. She winced. "I'd rather not ask. It's not really my business anyway."

His cheeks flushed. "Oh, right, sorry. Michelle's been texting me a lot about it. I swear, if she doesn't go into journalism, something has hijacked her brain."

With a grin and one soft laugh, Rayah shoved her bag into the one-by-one-foot locker and clicked it shut. She traced the number with her index finger. Eighteen. "You said they lock these up when you pay for a game, right?"

"Yeah, just give them the number at the front desk."

Synthesizers from the speakers masked their footsteps as they proceeded to wait in a line, or a clump really, of children in birthday party hats.

Danny whistled. "Man, we're gonna ruin some little kid's exiting-the-womb day when we get the top scores in this game."

"Exiting-the-womb day?" Rayah shook her head as she picked off a piece of lint on the center of her tank top. It showed up better in the blacklights hung around the room. "And, Trevon once had a birthday party here when he was ten. Trust me, we're the ones who should worry about getting low scores."

A shriek from one of the partygoers, who wore her hat like a unicorn horn, interrupted a pause in the music. How in the world was Bel ready for kids? He couldn't imagine bobbing a baby on a hip while studying for an AP Econ exam. The worker's dark eye bags hung long as they approached the front counter, which was spattered with neon orange paint, much like the rest of the room. The man smeared a hand across a five-o'clock shadow and gave a groan. Maybe his shift replacement arrived late too.

"Two for how many games?" His voice came out as lively as a corpse. Still, it rang slightly more alive than Reuben's, less robotish.

"Two, please." Danny dug into his pocket for a wallet. "We also have locker eighteen, but I want to stick this thing into it before you lock it up."

"Not a problem, sir. We lock them right before the game starts. Usernames?"

Rayah's knees crackled as she bent to read a list of custom user-names, for those non-creative, non-literature-loving types. She settled on GHOST, since she didn't know half the superhero names on the pa-per. Hannah would be ashamed.

"And you, sir? Username?"

"Yourself." Danny's high laugh that accompanied this cracked in his throat.

The worker gave him an eye roll for the joke and handed each a pink oval-shaped chip card to plug into the laser gun when the game start-ed. "These will assign your username to that gun so you can easily view your scores out here." He gestured to a television hanging above the air hockey table that read the scores for the current game. YOMAMA had the lead with 5,680. "Next game starts in five."

They passed a cluster of mothers clutching presents as they sank onto a bench against the wall. Rayah rubbed her hands up and down her knees. Sweat, maybe, but in a cold building? Danny tilted his neck and saw her forehead crease as her tongue glazed her lips over and over again.

"You doing OK, Ray?"

Her eyelids squinched. "Yeah, just heart's going really fast. Haven't done this in a while—laser tag, I mean."

For a moment, her eyes flicked to a wall with neon orange flames painted beside a huddle of green aliens with guns. Her gaze dropped to her black tennis shoes.

Oh, Dagon, maybe he shouldn't have taken her here for the date. The number of ways this one could go wrong flashed through his head. The dark room, the so-called attackers, the eerie music.

He swung an arm around her and felt her shake just slightly. "Listen, we can go someplace else if you want."

"No, you already paid twenty dollars. I remember having a lot of fun doing this as a kid. Besides"—she nodded at a boy who clutched a Pac-Man controller with a fist covered in cake—"they're just kids. What harm can they do?"

She pushed against her knees and forced herself to sit as straight as she could against the wall. "So I saw you talking to Ned's son in line at the ice cream shop."

Wow, what a segue. "How do you know he's Ned's son?"

"He stopped me in the parking lot and talked about the dinner happening in August. You planning on going?"

Mothers clutching the presents filed into a room with dark paint on the walls and a red table with a cake just cut off from Danny's vision by the door.

He squinted at the sign above the room and realized it doubled as an escape room. "Even if I said no, my mom got a hold of the invitation before I could toss it in the trash. She still loves Ned, you know. I never told her."

First day after the Suanna fire, he wanted to call his mom first thing in the morning, but even when his texts went through, she didn't respond until late that evening.

> MOM: Horrible thing happened at Judah's school, check the news.

He checked it. No use in fraying his mother's nerves twice that day, and she didn't seem to recover any better throughout the summer.

"None of us told our parents about what happened in May," Rayah said. "Couldn't bring myself to say anything to my mom after her divorce."

"Yeah, and Hannah doesn't really speak with her parents about anything. Any reason why journalist Michelle didn't spill?"

"About the fire? I think she wanted to look into taking Ned to court. She'll tell when she has all her ducks in a row, when she's figured out who can represent us and all that."

"Why wait?"

"Well, her dad also seems to love Ned as much as your mom. Probably would shut down any idea of a lawsuit and suggest they just let the adults handle things."

A red light above a gray door flashed in circles. As the door slid open, a worker in a dark shirt and khakis called for anyone with a pink chip card to come into the debriefing room. Danny was wearing *boxers* (not briefs) that day, and he made the joke to Rayah, who quirked an eyebrow at him.

Inside the dark room speckled with neon paint in black lights, the worker informed them that no running, kneeling, sitting, or using foul language would take place inside the arena. Considering the group of partygoers committed all four crimes in the debriefing room, Danny had his doubts.

Through another sliding door they went to retrieve their green glowing vests. The couple inserted their chip cards, and the guns beeped when they registered them. *Welcome, YOURSELF.*

"Welcome, Danny," he whispered to himself. "See, there? I did what it asked. It told me to welcome yourself, so I did."

Hand in hand, with the free ones holding the holsters of the heavy guns, the couple sought a hiding place in the dark room. They scaled the ramp to a second level, passing several mirrors as a countdown clock let out a sharp ring every second. At last, they stood behind a pillar near a ledge that overlooked most of the arena. Green vests dodged in and out of barriers below just as the beep-beep-beep sounded from an overhead speaker, followed by synthesized music that would've fit well in a spy or alien movie.

"So why did you choose Yourself as your username?" Rayah whispered, checking over her shoulder as footsteps pounded up the metal ramp.

"Easy, because of this." He aimed his gun at her chest sensor and squeezed the trigger. A red laser hit the plastic casing and caused all the trigger points—the shoulders, stomach, and back (he assumed)—to light up red. *Merry Christmas in July, y'all.*

"Hey!"

"Look at your gun. It should read, *You've Been Tagged By Yourself.*"

She peered at her gun as several laser blasts sounded from below. Danny adjusted his stance on the metal grate flooring as beams jutted through.

Rayah sighed, lip trembling. "Fine, but you have to let me tag you. It's only fair."

He sprawled out his arms like an Emmanuel eagle. "Go right ahead, m'lady."

Took her five timid shots to strike true, but when she hit his left shoulder, the whole suit vibrated for five seconds. He recalled the instructor in the debriefing room mentioned this meant he'd been disabled and couldn't shoot until the thing stopped shaking.

When it did, and his skin felt numb, he peered over the ledge and aimed a shot at a girl hiding behind a neon orange column.

"You can see everything up here, Ray. Seriously, we got our points made."

"Uh-huh."

"And these kids like to travel in packs, so we can pick them off easier. The only problem with making alliances, I guess."

Pounding steps grew louder up the ramp. The enemy still had several twists and ledges to pass before they'd reach them. Still, he felt a soft tap on his shoulder where the suit and skin met.

"M-maybe we sh-should find s-somewhere less e-exposed."

"Less exposed? Rayah, this is the most guarded place in the whole arena. Judah and I played here all the time as kids. Look, we got those two exits there, and that pillar hiding us nicely. You can't get anywhere safer than here."

An onslaught of laser shots cut off the "here" as a group of mostly boys surrounded the alcove, blocking off both the right and left exits.

No sooner had Danny aimed his gun to shoot when his suit buzzed from a direct hit, and then another, and then another. And then the kids in the green suits inched forward, steering the couple toward the gated ledge.

"All right, guys," Danny shouted. "You got us. Now go pick on somebody else."

Beside him, Rayah gripped his arm, shaking. She sank to the floor, still latched on as a kid in the firing squad yelped, "No sitting!" Most of the group now directed their beams at her, shooting so much the sounds of lasers blocked out any music.

Danny knelt beside Rayah and clasped her shoulders as her suit shook almost as much as she did. Even in the darkness, he spotted a glazed look in her eyes. She released her hand from his arm and clasped it to her head as if trying to block out something.

"All right!" Danny shrieked, voice crackling in his throat. The kids guffawed. "All right! Guys, you got her. Now, quit it!"

They continued to shoot.

Protection Mode: Activated

Friend Needing Protecting: Rayah

With a grunt, Danny thrust himself in front of her as the ambush continued. His suit buzzed against her as he shielded her from most of the shots. The footsteps drew nearer as the kids, with their non-gunned hands, clawed at him to pull him away from her.

He peered through the metal gate below and watched the supervisor yell at a kid on the lower level for running too fast. No way he could get his attention from this far back.

"Ray, we gotta get you out of this suit. Maybe that can help you stop shaking."

Her lip trembled, and she didn't seem to acknowledge any of his words. He fiddled with the strap at her hip, but this opened a barrier for the kids to hit her shoulder. The thing vibrated again.

"All right, fine. Let's get out of here, then."

One arm slipped around her waist, and with the other, he cradled her legs as he grunted, swooped her up, and disappeared down the right-hand ramp, racing against a trail of red beams.

Chapter Four

"THAT'S ENOUGH SALT ON YOUR FISH, JUDAH."
Raising a dark eyebrow, Judah stared at his mother for a moment across the wobbly kitchen table. Danny didn't tilt his head to watch his mother's expression beside him. Judah and his wife, Faith, exchanged an amused glance. Then he caught Danny's eye, winked, and set the glass salt shaker on the metal surface with a hard clack.

The brother gripped his knife and fork and tore into the white flesh of the tasteless cod. "Just turned thirty-one yesterday, Mom. You'd think you'd let me splurge on my sodium. Guess I don't get that privilege until I'm fifty."

Faith snorted into her steaming broccoli, almost bumping her dark-haired head into the low-hanging light over the table. Danny noticed she'd removed her ruby nose ring. He eyed her cow-patterned maternity dress with pockets in the front and bet she kept the jewelry in there whenever she met with his mother.

Back when Faith was wedding dress shopping, his mom nearly tore apart the veil when she heard Faith wanted to wear a sari-style gown instead of a plain ol' Baptist long sleever drowning in lace. Judah, of course, made everything worse by suggesting they kick the wedding Jewish style with a chuppah or huppah or something that ended in an uppah.

The cat clock ticked when his mother cleared her throat. "Faith, how is the apartment hunt?"

Her dark pupils met her husband's before flitting across the table. "Fine. We found a nice two-room in Nanna Apartments. Jude"—she placed her hand on his shoulder, her wedding band catching the glint of the afternoon sun through the windows—"did they say it was named after some woman who ran for city council or something?"

"It's a very nice place, Mom, about a fifteen-minute drive from here. Of course not as chic as those granite countertops you have in the kitchen, but at least it has a decent signal for Wi-Fi, so Faith can do her freelance editing."

Even King's couldn't boast as much.

Danny's mother wrinkled her nose at the steam wisping off her fish, which had one too many douses of black pepper. "I already looked into those apartments, terribly cramped. They could fit maybe two, but not an entire family."

Judah placed a hand on Faith's belly as if shielding it.

"We'll be fine. If you remember correctly, Faith and I met at Taylor University. If we could share rooms with two or three people, we can handle two bedrooms."

Following a huff and a sniff, Mom muttered something that sounded like "downgrade" and "not as big as the last place," but Faith's snorts from Judah whispering into her ear blocked Danny from hearing the rest.

Danny shoveled a forkful of fish into his mouth and chewed slowly. Not as bad as King's dining commons, but he gave it a C-minus at best for lack of taste.

Glowing, the sun laid a beam on an orange pill bottle in the middle of the table. Almost forgot about those. Danny unscrewed the white cap and swallowed the white pill with a gulp of milk. Like the fish, it also could've used a bit of seasoning.

Brushing a wrinkle in the stained tablecloth, his mother cleared her throat. "Any luck on interviewing with schools for a job, Judah?"

The smile fell from his face as he turned from his wife to his chipped plate. "A few sounded interested in meeting with me. But we haven't heard back from most."

"Still? Several schools start in the next couple weeks." His mother rubbed wrinkled hands over her rosy cheeks.

Judah scooped up his plate and reached to grab Faith's, which she'd barely touched. She winced and managed a weak smile at him as she clutched her stomach. Her husband kissed her on the head and ambled to the kitchen sink.

"Problem is no one's hiring. Washington County doesn't exactly have a cornucopia of schools, especially not for high school history teachers. And with Emmanuel burning up last year, that takes up another opportunity."

"Should've thought about that before you moved back here instead of another state."

His mother tilted her crooked chin back and emptied the rest of the grape juice in her cloudy glass cup. Too bad the dishwasher broke down when Faith and Judah took residence in the guest room. Add dish duty to the growing list of chores the adults didn't seem to want to take part in.

At least they had their driver's licenses. Maybe now Judah would make the hike up to King's to take Danny to church, if they could afford the gas.

While Danny's brother returned to the table to wait for everyone to finish, Danny swallowed a cold bite of fish as Faith asked him about cross-country. He forced the morsel down with the remainder of his milk, which had grown lukewarm.

"Season technically starts tomorrow." He shuddered as the glop of fish swam down his esophagus. "Coach is having us run a couple laps around campus and everyone's going out for ice cream afterwards. Except, I have to skip the last part because of"—another swallow—"Ned's thing."

"Oh right!" Faith palmed her forehead. "Forgot to write that in my schedule. What is that for again?"

"He said the four of us—me, Hannah, Michelle, and Rayah—won some award or something and he wants the families to be there because sentimentality or something." A lot of somethings. "At least, that's what I read on the invitation."

With a half-hearted motion, he gestured to the island in the middle of the kitchen where a stack of envelopes and old newspapers consumed most of the granite countertop.

"And Ned's the new guy at King's, right? Not the last dude who let students get away with horrible rites for visitors, right?" Judah rubbed the bridge of his nose with a knuckle.

Danny didn't know which question to answer because neither were terribly correct at this point in time. Ned led King's for a good decade, and as for the King's students sticking fishhooks in the noses of Emmanuel students ... Let's just say old habits died never ...

His phone vibrated on the table in the designated cell-phone area, the fifth seat, which his dad used to occupy during meals. Reaching across his mother and scooping it into his hands, he saw the picture of a girl with dark cut bangs before he read the name.

"Bel? She never calls."

"Can you take it later?" His mother flicked her eyebrows so fast they could've swatted a fly.

"Never leave a pregnant woman hanging." Faith grinned and hid her lips underneath a napkin Judah had forgotten to collect.

Danny skidded his chair back and it slid off the circular rug onto the hard floor. Pressing the phone to his ear, he darted toward the stairs to the sound of his mother's protests.

"What's up, Bel?"

Up the green carpeted steps, dodging brown sticky stains, he rounded the corner and dove into his room.

"Danny, is there any way you can cover my shift tomorrow? It's a nine-hour one, and I'm super sorry about that, but I don't know if I can do it, and no one else will pick up the phone."

His knees cracked as he bent on the floor to lie on his back and face the *Gladiator* movie poster on the ceiling. No, he was not entertained by the idea of nine hours of work.

He rubbed his fingers through the soft white carpet. "Bel, I normally would say yes. But tomorrow's the cross-country practice and I'm meeting at Ned's house."

The groaning from the other end of the receiver stung his ears. He rolled onto his stomach and faced the sliding-door closet with his stained prom shirt hanging loosely on a hanger.

"Again, I'm really sorry, Bel. Trust me, I would love to switch with you. If you want to cut your hair to my length and grow about six inches, maybe you can go to Ned's house and pass for me."

An exhale that resembled a dying laugh tickled his ear. "No, thanks. I don't want to go back to that house again."

Again?

Another moan from Bel that reminded Danny of a beluga whale, or at least whatever the large fish was he'd watched a documentary about for his biology class. "I can try calling the others again. You know me, when do I miss work?"

"Yeah, even the day you were throwing up every fifteen minutes. What happened now? Is the morning sickness coming in ten-minute intervals?"

Sigh. "Puking doesn't work like contractions, Danny."

"I know, but why do you want to switch with someone tomorrow?"

During a long pause, Danny twisted onto his side to stare back at the folks in eyeliner on his Red band poster. When he squinted, he saw a small spider crawl across the lead singer's bald head.

By the time the spider reached the band member's nose, Bel replied in a low voice, softer than most of the serve sold at his shop.

"I've been really down lately. Like, the kind where you can't roll out of bed and you swear someone replaced your blood with lead. Things, like, get physically darker. Everything literally looks like you put a gray filter on it. You know what I mean?"

"No, but I know people who do." To the right of his band poster hung a painting of a Venus flytrap eating a man, Hannah's dandy work.

"And I know it sounds stupid to call off for something like this when I've worked with the morning sickness and all. But Danny"—she broke off, choking on a sob—"n-never mind, I-I'll find a sh-shift replacement. H-have a n-nice day."

Three beeps from the phone indicated she'd hung up. He pulled the device off his ear and stared at the sweaty screen, which read *Call Ended*.

"She never cries," he whispered to the members of the band poster. They gaped back at him in a silent scream.

The dark ended call screen disappeared, and his green text message bubble indicated he had missed three messages during his lunch downstairs. With a clammy thumb, he clicked on the bubble, expecting them to be from Bel.

Instead, all three came from Rayah, each spread apart by a minute.

RAYAH: Danny, had another panic attack today. Happened when I was watching The Dark Knight with Trevon and his friends. I don't think they noticed, but it's getting harder to hide this from my family.

RAYAH: Been trying to get a hold of Michelle to see if she's made any progress on how we're going to sue Ned. The sooner she gets that, the sooner we can let our parents know what happened in May.

RAYAH: Is this what you went through last year? All the times you had to throw up and your heart went fast? How do you breathe during it, Danny? How do you breathe?

He chewed his lip so hard a layer of skin ripped into his mouth with the sheer force of the pull. His tongue probed the tasteless cells before he swallowed and typed back.

DANNY: You don't. You just hope your lungs remember their job. They will, though, they always do.

After he clicked the send arrow, he scrolled through the messages he'd sent her the past week after the laser tag incident. He'd sent funny memes and screenshots of her favorite comic, *Calvin and Hobbes*, which appeared to calm her down. At least, the smiley emojis she sent back placated some worries.

A knock on his door caused him to drop his phone. It landed on the carpet with a soft thud.

The door squeaked open a few inches as Judah popped his head in, giving the appearance someone had dismantled that part from the rest of his body.

"Can I come in?"

"Do you have a rule against cell phones?"

"Only in my classroom, and this certainly is not a place of learning."

"Step into my office."

Dimples bored into Judah's dark cheeks as he smiled. He slid past the narrow opening of the door and shut it with a click to prevent any more invaders.

"My oh my, little brother, you're missing a riveting discussion about socket testers and how they pertain to apartment searches. Apparently, Mom's an expert."

"Oh darn, too bad I'm missing out."

Judah wheezed as if trying to prevent laughter from reaching any of the inhabitants downstairs. He straddled the corner of the bed and bounced up and down, the springs groaning from the effort. So much for the people downstairs not hearing him. Judah never had a history of being quiet. Whenever they would play the Quiet Game as kids, he would always shout, "Oh shoot, I guess I lost," right when the game commenced.

"You know what I think we should do?" The bed creaked as Judah announced this.

"Act our age? Do all the thirty-year-old teachers do this?"

"No, and only the best ones do."

"What should we do?"

With a jolt, he bounded off the bed and darted to the closet. With impressive speed, he wove his fingers in and out of drawers and boxes. "Fishing!"

"Fishing?"

"Yeah, I thought vegetarians still ate fish. You just did earlier."

After watching that documentary in eighth grade about slaughterhouses, Danny never touched farm animals on a plate. "Anything in the creek in the backyard probably has died from runoff or pesticides. We do live close to farms, you know."

"Then that'll make them easier to catch. Where'd you keep that fishhook?" By now, he'd unleashed the sock and underwear drawer.

Danny slid open his desk drawer and pulled out the rusty hook. "Don't tell me you're trying to get a nose piercing to match Faith's. Mom'll never approve."

"Ha, no, thank you. Would rather not do that again." Judah twisted and spotted the hook in Danny's fingers. He reached for it, but Danny pulled his hand back faster.

"You mean you want to go fishing with the thing King's students jabbed into your septum?"

Then again, what else would they use? Their family had disposed of all previous fishhooks after Judah's "welcome" to King's.

His eyelids slamming shut, the images of the initiation rite flashed across his vision. The black spurting blood of Kim's son, the cold night air filled with the sounds of crickets and screams. Thanks a lot, photographic memory, he definitely wanted to replay that one over and over again.

He opened his eyes and caught Judah's knowing gaze.

"Danny, the thing happened way over a decade ago, almost two, really. I figure we put this bad boy to a good use. Can't just let him sit and rust in your desk."

"Sure we can."

"How 'bout this. If you don't go to the backyard with me to fish, Mom'll wonder what's taking you so long and force you to join in the conversation about suitable Internet providers."

"Let me see what I can use for a fishing line."

He unstrapped his laces from a ratty pair of tennis shoes and looped them through the eye of the hook. Thundering down the stairs, they raced for the front door so they wouldn't have to pass the kitchen. On their way out, they passed the *I'd Marry You Again* hanging cross-stitch. Not quite the same assurance of July's favorite quote, but it came cute in pastel-pink cursive.

Danny heard his mother remark about unreliable drains in apartment complexes.

Mugginess of the outdoors clung to Danny's socks, and he tore them off to run into the backyard barefoot. Along the way, he hoped he wouldn't step on a wasp in the grass.

The hook stopped bouncing against his thigh when he reached the surging brook. Everything smelled of dirt and beer from the cans the neighbors had dumped into the water.

They sat on the ledge and dipped their toes into the cold stream. Danny plunked the hook into the water, and it caught on a rock covered in algae. He shuffled closer to adjust it, and his soles pressed into the spongy bottom of the stream. Gagging, he launched backwards and nearly lost the hook when the tennis shoe lace knot undid. He retied it.

"Don't lose that thing." Judah shifted in his spot in the grass. "Faith might need to use the hook after she escapes the conversation with Mom. Heaven knows the hole in her nose closes up after a couple of hours."

"Yeah, remind me again why Mom let her wear a nose ring for the wedding?"

"Because we didn't get married inside the house. Trust me, she tried to adapt whatever she could. Got rid of a lot of traditions and family legacies, you know. Never knew someone could throw a fit over geraniums as a flower choice quite like Mom. I don't even know what geraniums are."

"They're a flower."

He shoved Danny and rubbed a rough hand through his younger brother's mop of hair. "Thanks. Glad to see even the younger generations are here to educate the older ones."

"Yeah, well, Mom likes to get whatever control she can. She felt like she lost so much with Dad gone and everything."

"No, no, I get it. It was rough on her because he couldn't attend and everything. Probably killed her when the DJ played the couples dance at the reception."

They repositioned themselves further upstream because Danny's toes kept touching the slimy rocks and a large oak tree shaded the deeper part of the river. Despite Judah's warnings that a leech was certain to come and gnaw on Danny's feet with its sharp teeth, Danny sank his legs as far as they would go before he'd slip on the ledge and fall in.

Water rippled as they plunked in the hook, and after a few minutes Judah asked if they'd caught anything.

Danny reeled in the hook and held it up, bits of rust and mildew-scented water running down his forearms. "Nothing."

"Keep trying. You'll catch something eventually if you keep trying."

That sounded like a mistaken mantra.

"What we need"—Danny traced the Eagle Claw logo on the hook before dropping it into the brown waters—"is a better hook."

"Good luck convincing Mom to buy you that. Looks like she splurged on the granite countertops with the money she saved with you going to King's for free."

"*You* could always get some new fishing gear."

"With my teacher salary? We're still living on ramen most days. It's too bad your birthday passed a couple weeks ago. We could've gotten you some nice fish bait along with a ticket to a rated-R movie."

Yeah, good luck convincing their mother of the latter.

Judah dipped his toes in once more before pulling out his feet and drying them on a patch of grass. "Guess we won't catch any today."

"Seeing that we were out here all of ten minutes, I'm thinking patience isn't your strong suit. I mean, you couldn't even listen to Mom's exciting discussion about apartment plugs."

"Listen, bud, I sort of lied to Mom at the table. I do have an interview at a school, tomorrow actually. But with her nagging Faith about the apartments, I didn't feel like giving her the satisfaction."

Danny wound the wet shoelace around his hand as he pulled out the fish hook. "Secret's safe. Where you interviewing?"

His brother stared at the hook for a long moment before his eyes met Danny's. "King's Academy."

Chapter Five

"ALL RIGHT, BOYS, WE'LL START YOU OFF EASY TODAY." Coach thrust his hands onto handlebar hips, hidden mostly by a blue-and-white-striped shirt. "Run five miles and meet back at the parking lot to do some core exercises. Grab a running buddy who goes at your pace and ask them about their summer."

Five miles—Danny knew that meant a lap and a half around the school.

"Easy?" He bent to tie his new neon orange shoes as another pair, white and unscuffed, stood next to him. "Five miles? Haven't run since May."

Gabe snickered and bobbed back and forth on his shoes as Danny reached to knot the other one. "You shouldn't have signed up for cross-country, then. A race is a 5K, you know. That's 3.1 miles."

Another pair of shoes, with tightly wound gray laces, approached them. Danny rose and spotted Reuben tearing off a matching gray shirt with armpit sweat stains. He crumpled it into a ball in the grass by a rusty red jeep. Judah's car. Reuben eyed it, nostrils wrinkling. "That thing looks like it could drive right into a museum."

Wow, the robot voice had a bit of disdain today.

"Thanks." Danny leaned forward and tapped the burning back of the car with his hand. "It's my brother's. Luckily his job interview today doesn't require him showing Ned his car."

Protection Mode: Activated

Friend Needing Protecting: Judah

Brothers counted as friends, most of the time.

"Oh. Sorry." Reuben didn't sound like it. "You guys have room for one more running buddy?"

Why? Last thing he wanted to hear about was Reuben's summer. Probably spent most of the time kissing Valentina, and he got enough of hearing about that with Dean last year.

"He did say you could have two running buddies." Gabe ran his fingers through his white hair, a bead of sweat trickling down his neck. Nothing like a hot August afternoon. "But Danny boy here runs like he's on fire, so you might have trouble keeping up."

Reuben set his jaw and then relaxed it. "Track and cross-country are completely different sports. As a qualifier for the state cross-country meet last year, I would know."

Fighting his twitching lips, Danny squatted to retrieve his water bottle from the hot pavement. He tilted his head back and took a long swig of the lukewarm liquid. Tossing it onto the grass next to the pile of T-shirts, he nodded at the cobblestone path surrounding the school. "Shall we?"

They ran on the grass that lined the path because of the spikes in their cleats. Reuben informed them about how he once sliced his hand on the shoes during a meet the previous year.

"Happened when I tried to attach a tracker to one of the laces. When you pass under the finish line, it lets out a beep sound. You guys have those in track?" He plowed ahead and continued to run upright.

Forget robot, his voice sounded crisp, like some teachers when they felt the need to treat high schoolers like sixth graders. He emphasized each word with a dose of spit.

Gabe waved at a student stationed on a ladder outside the administration building. He was busy touching up the golden painted lions on the side of the building. "Someone at the finish line has a stopwatch and taps it when you pass."

Reuben bolted even farther ahead of Danny, just enough for him to spot a nostril flare. "Seems inaccurate."

Darting toward the patch of what used to be Ned's favorite garden, they stopped and spoke with some of Gabe's friends who were out mowing the lawns. Along the way, Danny checked the grass for any mangled frogs. He spotted none. Perhaps the students took better care of the lawns than the adults had last year.

Gabe waved down his friend on the red riding mower, and she shut off her buzzing engine. They hugged while Reuben jogged in place.

"They gave you outside duty today, huh?" Gabe asked her.

Green grass shavings spattered her calves. "Yeah, didn't even get to pat mulch around Ned's special little tree. He gave that job to someone else." She pulled out her headphones, and Danny heard faint drumming and an electric guitar.

"Tree?" Danny kicked up a patch of dust that formed an anthill. "Ned trying to replant his garden or something?"

"Something like that." The girl returned to her riding mower and straddled it. "If you wanna see the thing, Ned planted it at the entrance of the old garden. Heard he had it shipped in from someplace fancy." She turned the key and the machine rumbled to life again as she sped off toward an unruly patch of grass.

They detoured to the garden, which had been reduced to a rectangular block of dusty land.

In front, where the weeping willow used to jive, a singular tree sat with its ancient bark climbing toward branches that looked like they had caught a green fire. Spiky leaves covered green baubles that had harshened to a reddish brown. Danny hazarded a guess at olives.

He stepped forward to take a closer look, but a three-foot-high iron gate coated in a bronzish color blocked him from entering. Lifting his leg like a hurdler, he shoved his foot onto the top of the gate to leap over, but a voice hidden behind the twisted trunk called, "Wouldn't do that if I were you."

A girl with thick glasses and overalls cut mid-thigh peeped out. She waved a hand caked in mulch, shooing Danny backwards. He unhinged his foot, and she returned to patting mulch around the stump. A bird in a nest on one of the higher branches poked its red head out to drill a few angry chirps their way.

"We just wanted to get a closer look, Maggie." Gabe leaned forward and pressed his palms on the gate. He hissed in pain and pulled them back—too hot.

"Maggie?" Danny squinted at him in the direction of the sun. "Do you know everyone who's working at the school this summer?"

Gabe shrugged. "People fascinate me." He turned back toward the trunk that hid Maggie. "Yo, Mags, wanna explain to my friend why he can't go near Ned's tree?"

A sigh and another chirp from the bird. "Didn't you guys read the sign?"

"What sign?" Reuben scraped some dirt caught in his spiked shoes with his finger. Then he resumed jogging in place.

"The one behind me."

The runners rounded the gate, which, Danny estimated, had to be about a ten-foot diameter. A terrible guess at best; Rayah was better at math. They stopped at a placard etched in the same kind of bronze as the rest of the gate, highlighted by a black background.

TO AMY REZZEN: A WIFE OF ALL WIVES

MAY THIS TREE LAST AS LONG

AS MY LOVE FOR YOU

*Do not touch this landmark.

Violators will be prosecuted.

Danny spotted a wire buried in a crevice on the trunk that wound up to a branch. Following the line, he spotted a camera at the end of it. Of course. Ned had those posted all over campus—why not here?

"Let's hope Ned's marriage is stronger than most of my other friends' parents'." He turned to Gabe and Reuben. "We should get back to running. We're probably ten minutes behind everyone else."

They murmured their assent and loped toward the academic buildings, back to the path.

"Danny, what position's your brother interviewing for?" Reuben kept ahead of him at least a foot. Wouldn't want the track star showing up the long-distance runner.

"History. He likes anything ancient, which explains his love of museums." He thought back to Reuben's comment about the car.

Reuben dodged around a green beer bottle planted in the grass. Guess those working at the school hadn't gotten to it yet. "Where did your brother work before?"

"At a school in Maryland." Why did he have to say Maryland? He could've said Virginia. That was just as close. "Right at the tip by the water. Been there during the summer. It's nice."

"Huh, why'd he move up here? Maryland schools probably pay more."

His cheeks flushed. Grateful Reuben ran ahead of him and couldn't see this. "Oh, well, Faith, his wife, is having a baby soon. I guess they wanted to settle close to home."

"Sure, but you can have a baby anywhere. Why would you quit your job when a couple with a new child needs money more now than ever?"

With the teachery tone and all, why did he like to ask so many questions? Michelle and Reuben would've made a good pair at investigative reporting.

They jogged in the shadows of the large buildings they passed, peering in the windows of empty classrooms, some devoid of posters and photographs on the slate-hued teacher's desks. Back at Emmanuel, the administration would sometimes force teachers to change classrooms, switching the foreign language rooms with the English once, and so on.

They ran in silence for what seemed like ten minutes. During this, Danny listened to the marching band play spy-themed tunes. He heard *James Bond, Mission Impossible*, and a tune from *Get Smart* before they reached the halfway point of the loop around campus.

A slight tap on the shoulder stung Danny for a moment. He craned his neck over his shoulder and saw Gabe doubling into his stomach. "Want to take a break inside? Not used to using my legs this much."

"Come on, Gabe." Danny swatted at him and laughed when he missed. "Don't tell me my angel friend gets exhausted when he can't use his wings."

"Angel friend?" A vein bulged in Reuben's temple as he hocked a loogie. "That because he has white hair and pale skin?"

Gabe stopped at the entrance to the Lebab Language Center (LLC), a pencil-shaped building, and leaned against the door. The word *Welcome* was listed in several different fonts and languages on the glass pane. Sweat glistened off Gabe's back as he ducked inside. Danny followed as Reuben continued around the loop, sprinting at full force as if making up for lost time.

Upon entrance, a cool blast of AC froze Danny's sweaty face. He exhaled as he slid down the white wall with a globe mural painted on it. His head touched Antarctica as he glanced across the way to see a shiny poster that read: *¡Que prosperes mucho!*

No idea what that meant, but the excited speaker used an exclamation point. It was probably important.

"Guess you chose the right wall, Lion Tamer." A puffy eye emerged from the corner of the hallway. The boy it belonged to gripped a paint can with his white-splattered fingers. Much of the eggshell-hued stuff had found its way onto the roommate's fingers. "We were planning on getting that wall on Monday."

Duke rubbed at his bulging eye.

Danny leaned his head back against the wall and felt the wet of his hair seep onto it. The Antarctic Ocean would get a whole new kind of global warming. "At least they give you the weekends off." Unlike certain ice cream shops. "And Lion Tamer? That's a new one."

"Sure, since you stood up to the King's Academy lions last year, you earned a new nickname, Lion Tamer."

"OK. But getting sick and avoiding that school-wide pledge doesn't really sound that epic, dude."

"Eh, everybody likes someone who can stick it to the man. Or, I guess in your case, *sick* it to the man." His lips twitched. Maybe some of Danny's love for puns rubbed off on him last year. "'Sides, got tired of sharing the same nickname Dean gave you. You don't really look much like a Princess."

With a smirk, Duke set the paint can on the white tile. He ambled over to Danny and sat across from him on the opposite wall. He smelled like a combination of body odor and paint.

"Sorry." Danny glanced at the trail of dry dirt his shoes had left from his entrance to LLC. "Didn't mean to pull you out of work."

"Eh, could use a break. We go for eight hours straight five days a week, you know. They pay worse than most other places, but we do make a bit more than you guys at the ice cream shop."

"Believe it or not, the building's cooler than the one we work in with the burning freezers and all." He sneezed, good ol' pollen season. "Also, poor Bel. She's about to get bombarded with the whole cross-country team after our practice."

Yes, Bel, the girl Duke forgot to mention was his sister. Probably because they didn't have many heart-to-heart talks last year, not with Dean ousting him with a sock on the doorknob every night.

Duke nodded at an old round clock hanging above a room with a German sign. It ticked the same in any language. So did the green stick figures on a wooden sign with an arrow pointing to the left. So that's where Gabe went.

With his paint-dried fingers, Duke rubbed his neck. "Yeah, she mentioned she couldn't get a shift replacement. Good thing school starts soon. She's dying at that place."

"We all are wherever we work. Even Hannah gets tired of pet sitting after enough weeks. You two still going strong?"

"Strong as the energy drinks. Last date, I took her to a paintball range. Little worried about how into it she got." He pulled up his green shorts to show a large purple welt.

Good ol' Hannah, keeping all those admirers in their place.

A toilet flushed somewhere nearby, and Gabe emerged, pinching his nose shut. "Does anyone clean those things over the summer? Smells like a skunk died in one of the stalls." He spotted Duke. "Oh, sorry."

"'S all right, man. They put me on paint duty instead of bathroom cleanup or heavy lifting, no idea why." He flexed a bicep, which swelled. "Probably because our supervisor, Mrs. Quercus, felt sorry about my eye and all."

Danny rose and motioned to the round clock. "We should get back to Coach. Whole team'll meet up in the next five minutes."

The two threw a wave at Duke before charging through the glass doors into the humidity. No need to worry about looking like they'd worked out because sweat beaded on their foreheads faster than a crab apple tree producing fruit in August. When they returned from their sprint, Danny slapped his palms on his knees and wheezed, focusing his blurry vision on the two lion statues guarding the road into the school.

He spotted Reuben's shoes and followed them up to his hands on his hips and then to his tightened jaw. He flared his nostrils once, twice as if to say, *Thanks for giving me a lack of a workout.*

When the rest of the stragglers reached them, Coach moved them to a patch of itchy grass that the lawn mower had given far too deep a trim.

In the dry grass, they completed crunches and burpees. Prickly blades proved too much for Danny and a few of the others, so they retrieved their shirts and pulled them on to complete any more exercises that required lying on one's back.

Heavy wooden doors to the administration swung open midway through the two-minute plank exercise. Danny's abs burned as he squinted at the steps to get a look at his brother. He wore a gray suit with a slightly crooked blue tie. Emmanuel blue, no one within a mile radius could mistake it.

"Proud of you, bro." Danny grunted into a dandelion the lawn mower had missed. If Hannah were here, she'd pluck it right away.

"Thirty seconds!" Coach called from behind him as he paced up and down the rows of runners, forcing some to angle their butts downward to feel the burn of the exercise more. "Time."

In a collective movement, they slumped to the grass and let out a sigh of relief. A green scent filled Danny's nostrils as he inhaled, too stiff to roll onto his back. Forget about ice cream; even if he didn't have Ned's thing and was going with the team to the shop, he couldn't even down a sherbet with how much his abdomen seared.

Judah's slick shined shoes approached Danny to the sound of jingling keys. With a groan, Danny forced himself to rise and accompany his brother to the car. Too bad the AC didn't work inside the vehicle.

He slid into the passenger seat and pulled off his shirt. He used the fabric to grab hold of the hot seat belt and clicked it into place.

"Sorry, bud." Judah jabbed the keys into the ignition and the engine sputtered to life. "I wanted to park where there was shade, but there are not too many trees in this area."

Danny's mind flashed back to the olive tree at the entrance of the garden. To the way the bronze placard glinted in the sunshine, already looking ancient and tarnished. For some reason, he wondered what the tree would look like on fire. Its spiky head in an orange-red glow, olives plummeting to the ground like fallen stars.

"How was your first cross-country practice, bud?"

He shook his head and winced at an oncoming headache. "Quick. I ran with Gabe and Reuben, the dude who's dating Valentina. Reuben's … well, he can run fast."

"What's wrong with him?"

"Besides the fact he sounds like a dictionary? Or that know-it-all kid every middle school seems to have? Don't people grow out of that by high school?"

"Ah." Judah reversed the car and pulled up the smooth pavement. "And no. Most people don't grow out of anything. Maybe he feels like he has to prove something. We had a version of Reuben in my class. I think he won *Jeopardy!* twice."

"Were you friends with him?"

He shrugged. "No, but he came from a family of geniuses, and nothing he ever did seemed to impress his parents. And I *know* you have a friend like that."

Right, right, no one could ever forget Michelle. Danny didn't know much about Reuben's parents, but plenty of students at King's never could match their parents' expectations.

"He was asking why you'd moved all the way up here to teach when you had a good job in Maryland." When Danny faced his brother, he saw his shoulders tense. "Don't worry, I didn't tell him about the shooting."

"Good."

Judah clicked on the radio and flipped to a calming music station. Two commercials in, he shut it off. "Interview went well today."

"You get the job?"

"I think so. Did they ever tell you what happened to the last history teacher?"

Danny frowned at a bone-dry wheat field as they passed it. "Got an email a week ago or so. They said he was in the hospital for something. Mr. Peterson, right? Didn't he used to work at Emmanuel?"

Craning his head to the left, he saw his brother's features darken.

"It was an accident," was all Judah said for the rest of the car ride home.

Chapter Six

"LEAVE YOUR SHOES AT THE FRONT DOOR."

Right as they passed through the wooden door, an incense odor punched Danny in the nose. He kicked off the dress shoes he'd forced his wet feet and socks into and swiped a damp bang toward his ear. No chance to blow-dry his hair at home following the five-minute shower after practice.

Soft piano music played on a speaker nearby. Danny located the speaker as well as the camera beside it. He wondered if Ned monitored the rooms of his house as much as King's.

He caught a glimpse of the low-hanging chandelier by a winding staircase. It coiled down another level to, Danny presumed, a basement. Dim lights gave no more than a faint glimmer against glass beaded balls. He tilted his head, following the copper wire holding the thing all the way up to the ceiling.

When Ms. Belte followed suit and dismounted from her fraying fabric heels, she turned to a beaming Ned. Even in the warm brown glow of the lights, one could not mistake the silvery tint of his beard. Much of his hairline had withered into the middle of his wrinkled scalp. Crazy how the man could age ten years in two months.

Brushing down a sleek black suit with his fingers to find some invisible hair, Ned jerked his head over his shoulder. "The others already arrived. We'll have announcements after you've had a chance to eat."

They followed him down a slick dark hardwood tile toward a left-hand room with a glow dimmer than the front. Danny eyed a dark wood table with glass trees sprawled across the deep-purple fabric covering it. In the light, they reminded him of transparent veins.

The kitchen greeted them with the scent of deviled eggs, bacon, honey, and other smells that couldn't form under a single identity, odd mixtures of sweet and spicy.

He spotted Hannah in a wrinkled dress speckled with flowers, which clashed with her curly red hair. The dark fabric didn't do much for her super-pale skin. Probably took a great deal of coaxing into it. She popped a stuffed pepper into her mouth and hiked the dress where it sagged around the chest area.

Beside a long glass table, Rayah's and Michelle's moms discussed something with a wine glass in each of their hands. The two daughters hung out by the kitchen sink, Rayah throwing a polite wave at her boyfriend before returning to Michelle's wide hand gestures and eyebrow movements. Michelle paused and flipped her short blonde hair over her shoulder to wave at Danny.

Judah and Faith reached for plates and scooped piles of cheese, one of Faith's most recent cravings. Hannah's dad stood awkwardly to the right by a side table with glass birds. He every once in a while bent to whisper something in Hannah's ear. This happened whenever she adjusted her dress or chewed with her mouth open.

Recovering from his cross-country practice, Danny's stomach groaned a hollow tune. He reached for the closest finger food, a cheesy glob of something. Shoving it into his mouth and chewing, a hot earthy juice spilled over his tongue—mushrooms.

His hand tingled as his mother smacked it with a clear plastic plate. "Remember your manners."

"They're called finger foods, Mom. If they were meant for plates, they'd be called plate foods."

She leaned in closer, hissing, "In a house like this, finger foods do not exist."

He caught Hannah's eye across the table as her father angled in once again to whisper. Danny suspected it had to do with the fact she spilled shrimp cocktail sauce on her dress. Hannah marched forward and grabbed Danny's forearm. "We're going to explore the house."

Pulling him back into the hallway toward the front entrance, she swerved right into an office. A computer glowed white with a background used for King's Academy email servers. In the corner of the room, a small blue bird cradled a bar in a cage with its black feet.

Hannah released his arm, and he reached to massage it.

"Sorry to take you away from your girlfriend, but I had to get away from Dad. One more 'Hannah, your principal is going to think you're a hobo,' and I would've lost it."

"Nah, you saved me from a similar treatment from my mom."

Like Reuben and Michelle, they all seemed to disappoint their parents in one way or another.

The bird seemed to perceive the two strangers in the room and chirped something high-pitched yet sad. Perhaps because the notes came out slow, as if it took a great amount of effort to sing each one. He wondered how often Ned let it out of its cage.

"Sounds like a poem from English class." Danny bumped into a bookcase near the entrance of the room and perused the titles.

Hannah shuffled behind him, socks against a well-vacuumed carpet, as she whistled back at the bird. Her tune sounded familiar. Took him a while to figure it out, but eventually he recognized "Mad World" by Gary Jules.

Epic of Gilgamesh, Code of Hammurabi, One Thousand and One Nights, The Republic, Metamorphoses—goodness, did this man read anything printed in this half of the millennium?

A shriek of metal replaced Hannah's whistling. Danny whipped around as she slid the bar open to the bird's cage.

He rushed forward and slammed his hand on the door. The bird blinked, or at least some sort of translucent eyelid passed over the black bead buried in its white and blue head.

"You can't open that thing. What would Ned do if you let it loose?"

"Come on, it would be fun. I really want it to poop on my dad's head."

"He's bald, so I imagine he'd just wipe it off. Now, let go of the lock."

She met his gaze with eyes that, for a moment, seemed to spark. Her shoulders relaxed, and her straps nearly slid off them. Adjusting her dress, she placed her hands on her knees to meet the bird at eye level.

She cocked her head to the side. The bird followed suit. "He says he wants to be released."

"Uh-huh, you notice he's not chirping now, so how could he tell you that? Also, how do we know he's a he?"

"No one likes a cage, Danny. Why do you think it was singing before? And I know it's a boy because it was stupid enough not to peck your finger when you stopped me from opening it."

"Says the girl who is dating a *boy*."

She grinned, chin buckling into her neck.

"Hope I'm not interrupting."

Danny tensed and twirled around to find a man with a red beard in the doorframe. August. He stepped in, thick shoes still on, and gestured to Danny. "Thought you might like to see our tech room. Heard you were a bit of a computer whiz yourself."

With three large strides, he marched to the glowing computer and clicked the power button. As the screen faded, an odd darkness filled the room. Not a darkness belonging to what was once light, but something that could be felt, like a cold stream of water in January or a warm blanket in summer.

"Interested in taking a look, Danny boy?"

Goosebumps rippled on his arms. "Sure." He turned to Hannah, whose fingers twitched near the cage. "Don't touch anything."

She crossed her arms over the shrimp cocktail stain. "Fine, but you can't stop me from singing."

He wouldn't dare, even if she didn't know how to stay on key.

Twisting back to August, Danny saw him laugh, flashing bright teeth. "The little guy's name is Obi. Short for Obi Wan or Obadiah or something. Mom and Dad couldn't agree what it's short for. Mom was the one who always took care of him. She'd be the only one to let him out of that cage."

Danny followed him to the staircase and around the winding railing. A moth darted from the glass chandelier and clinked in and out of the various balls. Passing a wall by the upstairs banister, he lost sight of it.

They ducked into a room filled with ghostlike glows, white and bright and something not right. August groped the wall and flicked on a switch. The room erupted with a wan light and, compared with the open spacing of the house, reminded Danny more of a claustrophobic cave made of old video game cases. Dust flooded his nostrils as he stepped in the direction of Ms. Pac-Man, thumbing off the gray dirt on the red toggle stick.

"Knew you'd find it interesting." August swooped to his left side and placed his hand on top of the machine, looking like a boy with a very tall girlfriend made of plastic. "You play any of these dinosaurs? Dig Dug? Tetris?"

"Yeah, our youth group had a basement full of these."

He laughed and turned to lean his back against the machine. "Mom was a fan of that church stuff back in the day. I do remember having fun at one event, a food fight or some other teen event."

This shocked Danny for some reason. He never thought the Rezzens went to church. "Where did you go?"

August shrugged. "Can't remember; it was almost a decade ago. Mom and Dad didn't really see eye to eye on that religious stuff. Anyways"—he tapped the machine—"Dad decided to turn the basement into an indoor garden, so these bad boys went in here. He likes to keep all sorts of crap in here. Family photos, juicers Mom never used, that sort of thing."

Now that he mentioned it, Danny spied various boxes sprawled throughout the room. In an absentminded stroll, he headed toward one by a Betty Crocker Bake and Fill box. He peered inside. All yellowing academic awards on top for August from King's Academy. "No, man, I get it. You should see our storage room in our house."

Athlete of the Year 2015. National Honor Society 2015.

August guffawed, a little too hard. "Yeah, parents can drive you crazy sometimes, or maybe they're driving themselves crazy. If you've seen my dad lately—ah, never mind, stress and old age, I guess."

Highest Grade in AP Government 2015. Man, that must've been a happening year.

"So, my dad says you're going into your junior year, that right? You look more like a senior."

Class President 2015. "Unless I failed last year and no one told me."

"You taking government class?"

"Yeah, just got my schedule emailed to me today." He paused when he found a photograph in a boxy wooden case. Made him think of the material a person would use on a birdhouse. In the picture, August had his arm draped around a Bel with slightly longer hair and a flatter stomach. She had mentioned visiting Ned's house before. Now it made sense.

"Fifth period?"

They locked eyes. "Uh, yeah. That's, um, a very specific guess."

August spread his arms as if inviting him in for a hug. "Meet your government teacher, fresh out of Penn State."

Danny stacked the awards over the photograph in the box and rose. Dagon, even leaning against Ms. Pac-Man, August still stood a few inches taller than him.

He cleared his throat. "My brother, Judah, was interviewing for a job at King's, too. He's the one in the wrinkled gray suit downstairs. Mom insisted on the striped green tie."

"Adopted, right?"

Like Bel, yeah. "Uh-huh, Mom and Dad adopted him from Israel." Well, Bel had said *fostered*.

"Dad told me about his interview. Did very well, but, as always, I am willing to put in a good word." His eyes flicked over the box with the Bel photograph before he winked at Danny.

"Um, thanks."

To protect his brother's safety into his new job or to protect Bel and ask about the photograph?

A large figure peeked in the doorway, and Michelle's pupils lit when she spotted him. She marched toward him as fast as her pencil skirt would allow and swept her arm into his.

"Wanted to borrow you. I thought you might want to look at the garden downstairs."

He breathed a sigh. "Yeah. You know how much I like botany. See you in class, August."

August wagged a finger at him. "Mr. Rezzen to you."

Oh boy, that thing had a sequel. All the worst things did.

They rushed out of the room, not too fast to catch suspicion, and wound down the staircase two levels. A punch of green hit his nose. Michelle dragged him behind a hibiscus bush in a full maroon bloom.

"Hannah told me that August had kidnapped you."

"Yeah, he sort of did." His ear itched from a large leaf on the plant tickling it. "Why couldn't you take me to the kitchen? There's safety in numbers, you know."

"I also wanted to give you an update on the suing Ned situation. Figured it would be awkward to bring it up in front of him."

"Good point, and?"

"Good news: found a guy. Bad news: works for a couple hundred an hour, and he goes cheap, apparently."

Danny sighed and leaned against a large ceramic pot holding a small tree. "Sounds like one hour with him takes my salary for two weeks."

"Yeah, and I'm sure most of that's going to college. Hannah says she would have to save for about ten summers to make up for her tuition."

Danny set his jaw and scanned the room to make sense of the jungle. If you took away the bright humming lights and the piano music playing upstairs and the lack of crickets and frogs chirping, you could almost travel a year back to King's Academy. He squeezed his eyes shut and tried to imagine themselves back in the old garden. Part of him wanted to dash upstairs and set the bird Obi on one of the plants down here.

His eyelids flipped open. Ah, reality, it smelled like mold. "I would offer everything I earned this summer. But that'll get us maybe ten hours with the guy. Doubt that would be enough."

It wouldn't.

"I'll keep looking, but maybe we should let our parents in on it." She held up a hand to block Danny's protest. "Yeah, not my favorite plan, but maybe they could help. At least financially." She bit her lip as his mind swarmed with thoughts about confronting his mother. With the shooting that happened at Judah's school and Faith's pregnancy, he didn't know if she could even handle the news. "We'll get him, Danny. He can only get away with so much crap for so long."

Her eyebrows knotted together. She turned her gaze to the tree behind Danny. "Did you see the new gift Ned put up by the school's ex-garden?"

"The tree with the placard to his wife about his undying love?"

Michelle rearranged her legs for a different sitting position. "Wanna take a bet on how soon that thing'll get chopped down?"

"Not particularly, why?"

She tapped her left ring finger. "Didn't see it when he reached for a napkin upstairs."

Soft footfalls hit the winding staircase, causing Danny's heart to thunder like Ned's voice. A silky suit and a silvery beard emerged around a palm plant at the base of the stairs. Danny eyed the walls for any camera, remembering the one by the front door. He hoped the principal didn't have any decent audio recording software.

"Oh, found you two. We're about to head upstairs for some brief announcements. Care to join?"

The two stood, a little quickly to avoid an eyebrow raise from Ned.

Michelle bent to brush off some dried leaves on her skirt. "Starting to get stuffy down here."

"Ah yes, not quite the same garden we had back at campus. Made that for my wife several years back." He rubbed his neck, forehead, and then exhaled. "Guess that's one legacy that won't live on as long as hoped."

That's how legacies tended to go, never long enough.

He moved to a ficus by the hibiscus plant and stroked the teardrop-shaped leaves, his left finger ringless with a tan line where a golden band once lived. He plucked off a leaf, stared at it for a long time, then let it fall.

"Before we go upstairs to announce about your academic achievements for the year, I wanted to run something past you." He tore off another leaf. This time he ripped it in half. In quarters. In sixteenths. "As you know, you four impacted King's significantly with your cafeteria reforms as well as your contributions in student council."

With a single step, he snagged a hibiscus flower and plucked it from a cage of leaves. He cradled it in his palm and stared at it as if it bore some invisible writing.

"I plan to offer you all positions on the Principal's Advisory Council. As you may know, I choose who I place on this board every year."

Michelle squinted at Danny for a moment before they both returned their gaze to Ned.

"As you two may also know, the position is accompanied with a five-thousand-dollar tuition reimbursement. Because you four have full rides, that will go directly to your bank account gratis."

Danny's heartbeat pounded in his ears. He realized the piano music had stopped upstairs and wished the bird would start singing again. Where was a cage when he needed one?

"Five thousand?" He furrowed his brow at a dead leaf, pinched it, and crumpled it into his palm. "It was two thousand last year."

"Yes, and that is the amount we will tell your parents, two thousand. But I highly appreciate your contributions to the school and want to compensate you for any troubles King's caused you in the past year."

Warmth rushed to his cheeks. He and Michelle shared a gape and a narrow-browed stare for a few seconds, eyes wobbling. Each shake seemed to let Ned's words sink in.

Shake. Money.

Shake. To keep quiet.

Shake. About the fire.

The hibiscus flower fluttered from Ned's fingertips and landed at Michelle's feet. She focused on it for a second and then stepped on it with her bare foot.

"Ned, we'll gladly accept your offer."

Chapter Seven

"WITH DEAN OUT OF THE ROOM, YOU WANNA TAKE THE top bunk? Doesn't smell like pee like the one you had last year." Duke leaned his arm against the doorframe before dodging around a long black power strip left at the entrance.

Arms wobbling from the weight of a heavy box, Danny dropped it on the floor and kicked it against the sweaty white walls.

He peeled off his T-shirt, which already stuck to his skin in the humid dorm. Lack of windows didn't help.

"Dean move to another room in Phrat?" Danny gazed at the extra space in the room without the beer cans and crumpled tissues decorating the floor. Hadn't had a chance to look at it before now with moving boxes for the past thirty minutes while his mother talked to Duke's dad outside.

"Yeah, Dean got a single on the first floor. Probably got annoyed having to keep his sock on the doorknob all the time. Now he and Julia can get a piece of each other in peace whenever she comes up from Pittsburgh U."

Oh dear, Danny didn't want to think about that in a hot sweaty room that made him want to faint and vomit at the same time. The memory of the rancid stink of puke filled his nostrils. How was he going to do another two years here?

Also, now that he thought of it, he knew too many people whose names started with *Ju*. Julia, Judah, July. With meeting so many new people, he had to start giving them nicknames, like his old roommates had called him "Princess" and "Lion Tamer."

He decided to differentiate Julia by calling her Frenchie for her frequent French braid and for her delight in the kissing employed by the French.

Ah, an attendance roster to remember and forget. Why did King's have to have a significantly larger population than Emmanuel? OK, fine, in alphabetical order:

- August (Ned's son with the beard who was once with Bel)
- Bel (coworker, preggers)
- Dean (ex-roommate who likes fishhooks)
- Duke (puffy eye, roomie, Bel's brother)
- Frenchie (Julia, Dean's girlfriend)
- Gabe (angel, albino)
- Hannah (friend, possible psychopath)
- Judah (brother, history teacher)
- July (soccer player, kept Danny out of a psychiatric hospital during the fire)
- Michelle (friend, future reporter)
- Ned (principal, murderer, arsonist)
- Rayah (girlfriend and the most gorgeous girl at the school in Danny's humble opinion)
- Reuben (teacher, robot, runner)
- Valentina (pink hair, Reuben's girlfriend)

Cool, all accounted for, let the class begin.

He crossed over to the pee-scented bed and collapsed onto the springy mattress. "Does that mean we get another roommate?" Oh great, that meant they had to add someone else to the roster. "If that's so, I'd hate to give the new guy this old bed."

"I think it does. Dean was on the waiting list for a single for a while, so they must've recently picked our guy." Duke kicked a box as he made his way to the lower bunk across from Danny. He ducked and collapsed onto his bed, giving an oomph along with the squeak of the frame. "You see the new tree by the old garden spot?"

Danny rubbed his hands against the mattress and stopped when he hit a crusty spot. "Yeah, didn't know you liked plants, Duke."

"I don't, but this one had graffiti on it."

Danny bolted up in bed, the heat that had risen in the room swirling around his head. "What'dya mean?" He blinked away some darkness coating his vision. Forgot to take his pills this morning.

"I mean some kid spray-painted some gang sign in white on the bark. Carved some initials on it too: KA."

Danny squinted at the orange open house hours sheet posted on the door, trailing his eyes down to the tarnished doorknob that locked on the outside. "Didn't they know Ned had a camera hooked up to that thing?"

Duke shrugged and craned his neck far enough out to glower at the boxes and heavy wooden furniture forming a crowded city within the room. He snapped his neck back at Danny.

"Lion Tamer, want to do me a favor and help me stack the dresser on that desk and shove it into the closet?" Veins bulged in his forearm when he motioned to the said items. "Could free up a lot of space."

He swallowed, throat dry with a distinct Cheerios taste. "Sure."

They stumbled out of their beds and shoved open the top drawer on the dresser to grip it from the inside. Danny grunted as his knees popped when he bent to pick it up. They heaved it onto the desk.

Duke pulled back his fingers, which the dresser nearly cut in half. "Didn't think I'd risk losing my hand twice today."

"Twice?"

"Yeah, I helped Bel move into her single. She and Dean got lucky, I guess. Won't have to deal with any roommates."

Danny didn't know if he should take offense, but as he thought about it, he wouldn't mind a single room either. Duke had mentioned earlier that day that he shared a room with Bel until he turned fourteen and his family upgraded from a two- to a three-bedroom apartment. Danny himself had roomed with Judah until he got his first job as a teacher.

"Lucky, huh? Is Dean pregnant?" Another push, another two inches. "Rayah told me that they made Bel move because of some weird trimester rule or something."

"No." Duke faced his bed and pushed the desk with his back. His corner sidled next to Danny's. "But maybe they found out that he got her pregnant."

Danny stopped pushing as the image of the photograph with August and his hand wrapped around Bel in a blue bikini flashed through his head. Thanks, handy-dandy photographic memory. "You sure about that?"

"Come on, keep going. The thing has a couple more feet into the closet."

Danny pressed his palms against the furniture and bent forward again. "Positive?" Dean and August both were large men with beards.

"Look, sometimes Dean would forget to put the sock on the door ... and let's just say I've walked in on a couple, uh, well ... a couple. I'd rather not relive it, OK? Now keep pushing."

Half a foot later, when they heard the clunk of heavy furniture hit the closet wall, they slid down the desk and leaned against it. Danny didn't mind the pain that came with his spine not lining up right with the siding.

"Leave our roommate to do the rest of the moving stuff?" he panted, rubbing his forehead against his knee so the hair could collect the moisture.

If they hadn't left the door open with frantic mothers holding mini fridges bustling past, he would've torn off his shorts and gone stark as Tony from *Iron Man*. Right as he considered rising to shut the door, a stiff figure in a red polo emerged in the entrance.

Reuben set down a shower caddy in the hall and consulted a white slip of paper. His eyes darted up to the top of the doorframe, perhaps looking for the number placard that read 207. Danny caught a whiff of his cologne from the far corner of the room.

The visitor stooped, picked up his shower caddy, and placed it on a desk, Danny's desk. Reuben's nostrils flared once, twice, and then he spotted the two others in the corner. He marched forward and shoved a hand under Duke's nose.

"Name's Reuben, your new roommate."

Ah great, Danny guessed stiff know-it-all was a step up from guy-who-likes-to-jab-fishhooks-into-your-nose-and-get-girls-pregnant. And, in honesty, didn't know Reuben well enough to shove him into a Hogwarts House yet. All the boy amounted to at the moment was good smells, fast runs, straight spines, and boring voices.

Duke ignored the hand. "Top bunk's yours. Lion Tamer here played nice and took the bed that smells like pee."

Reuben took back his hand and straightened his spine, leveling with the guards on the top bunk. Flicking his dark eyes once at Danny, his expression softened, almost a thank-you.

Then, he took a moment to scrutinize the room. "Any chance we could stack some of this furniture?"

Duke laughed and banged his head back against the desk siding. "Any chance you could move out into the hallway? Got some nice couches out there in the lounge area. Carpet's a bit burnt up though."

Reuben set his jaw. "Thought I'd ask."

A ping sounded from Danny's pocket. He pulled out his cell phone and wiped the clammy screen on his shorts. He slid open the text.

> MICHELLE: Wanna take a tour through the buildings to find our classes? Got some buildings on here I've never been in before.

Not a hard thing to accomplish at King's. They practically lived in a city.

> DANNY: Sure, Reuben's talking about bringing up his stuff from his car, so anything to get out of that. Miracle the school Wi-Fi is working huh?

> MICHELLE: Probs because Ned isn't fiddling with it. Someone told me he was out all morning, taking a mental health day. Shocker we now have cell service.

Stumbling down concrete steps and out the clicking door, he met Michelle by a group of boys sprawling on a futon outside Phrat River. Armed with a color-coded schedule in hand, Michelle reached out her front arm to give Danny a side hug. After, she tugged a strand of loose straight hair behind her ear and fanned herself.

"Does it feel hotter here than last year?"

"You're one to talk, Miss My-Dorm-Has-AC."

"Well, my dorm also has a wasps' nest in the ceiling tiles by the bathroom, so."

They ambled their way toward the LLC where Michelle had French in the mornings and Danny would take Arabic in the afternoons. He scrolled on his phone through his classes, turning up the brightness. "So, it looks like I've been in most of these buildings before. 'Sides, I know all the ones I've never been to. Remind me why we need to do this?"

"To A) get me out of helping July move in her closet—love the girl, no idea how she'll fit all those rompers into that tiny space. Only child, and her parents are both doctors, so makes sense why she has so much stuff. And B) to talk about our plan for suing Ned where he doesn't have audio hooked up like he probably does in the dorms."

Danny recalled seeing the images from cameras stationed around campus on Ned's laptop last year. The black-and-white pictures never emitted any sound, but better safe than dead.

"OK, so how we gonna sue him? Remember the money problem?"

He glanced at her as she smiled at the pencil-like building in the distance.

"True, but Ned just gave us three thousand each that our parents don't know about. That gives us dozens of hours with a lawyer. You know, they spend about eight to ten per case, not including court time."

A sharp rock hit his foot. He should've worn tennis shoes instead of sandals today. "Ned gave us that money to keep quiet and put toward college."

"Rayah's already volunteered to donate."

This paused him at the entrance. A group of girls behind them passed through the glass doors. He stared at the various Welcome signs, wondering if the أهلا بك would make sense after a couple days in class, and returned his gaze to Michelle.

"You can't ask her to do that, Mitch."

"And she's planning on telling her parents as soon as we head home for fall break, since lawyers usually have a problem with representing minors without parental consent. In two months, we're gonna come at him with all the fire we got."

"She needs the money for college. Take mine if you must but keep her out of this. Rayah has enough panic attacks without needing to add stress from debt."

Michelle's eyes rolled into her forehead. "*Bien.*"

Blonde hair stuck to her neck. She ducked through the glass doors and bent around the small hallway to the French classrooms. Danny found his room near the drinking fountain at the end of the hall. Everything smelled of Lysol and some other strong cleaner. Inside the classroom, he shook hands with a short man with a strong grip and wheezy voice, Mr. Parsin.

"Pleasure to meet your acquaintance." He blinked hard and shoved a pair of clear glasses up a dark thick nose. The English came out broken and slow. "You taking Arabic class with me?"

"Yes, sir. I heard we have a small class."

Mr. Parsin giggled into his white oxford. "Three." He tapped a slip of paper with his left ring finger, the gold band tarnished. Danny peered at the paper and read the roster for the class: himself, Reuben, and July.

Uncertain of how to feel about it, he met up with Michelle to venture to the history building, one that lay on the edge of campus with Grecian columns. But before they entered, they took a detour to stop by Ned's tree. Sure enough, white etchings of graffiti blotted the twisted trunk.

Michelle clicked her tongue. "Too bad. I kind of liked the new landmark. A nice reminder that history shouldn't repeat itself. Speaking of—" She nodded at the history building, and they backtracked.

Danny had government on the first floor and AP Euro on the second.

He ventured to the second floor first, enjoying an elevator ride, even though it rattled the whole way, lights buzzing and blinking. On his way out the sliding doors, he read the last time the elevator had a code check, ten years back.

In room 225 he ran into Frenchie (Julia) and Dean, who waited in a line of students and parents to meet the teacher, none other than ol' Judah himself. Michelle tapped Frenchie on the shoulder, and she spun around, sporting tangled pigtails today.

"How's tennis treating you at Pittsburgh U?"

A wry smile crawled up Frenchie's wet lips (either from ChapStick or a new makeup brand called Dean). Her boyfriend tugged a stiff arm around her and afforded Danny a curt nod.

Frenchie nuzzled his arm. "Not bad. It'll make up for my dad making me do tennis for three hours every morning, before both of us worked. Doesn't want me to lose a single match, but we did lose a lot of sleeping time, for sure."

Maybe Danny had gone a little hard on Reuben. If his parents resembled Frenchie's stepdad or Michelle's dad, he would earn his full sympathy. Maybe he should give grace to all King's students, even Dean. They were, after all, just trying to survive the Den.

After giving Judah a hug, Danny and Michelle headed downstairs.

Michelle waited in the hall as he ventured into room 166, which smelled a bit dustier than the room upstairs. Perhaps it had to do with the fact the teacher had drawn the blinds.

He faced a bust of Alexander Hamilton, or some dude with white hair and a white face. At the front of the classroom, August Rezzen wrote his name using an electronic blue marker and a SMART Board. Turning on his slick dress-shoe heel, he noticed Danny, and his eyes twinkled.

"Long time no see." His grin disappeared in the red beard. "How long's it been? Nine days?"

"Ten."

"Glad to see your brother got settled upstairs. Doesn't decorate his room as much as mine." He gestured to the walls filled with posters, memes, and newspaper comics about politics. "Heard about the terrible school shooting. I'm so sorry to hear about that."

He did sound like it. Ned did show, in the nurse's office last year, capability of sympathy. Perhaps Danny should believe the same in his son.

"Thanks, it's been rough on our family."

Eyes shifted to the SMART Board. "Hope he assigns lots of homework, because I won't give any. King's teachers grilled me hard during my time here, so I want to give you all a break." He winked and then his neck snapped at the door. "Ah, Dean, my man, hear I have you for fifth period too."

Great, he guessed the school wanted to make up for all the time they wouldn't be spending in the dorm together.

Dean cleared his throat as he lumbered into the room, arm over Frenchie as if he were a wounded soldier. "Actually, wondered if you could switch me to eighth. Tried to get the secretary lady at the front office to help—Ashley, right?—but she said the advisors were all out for lunch and I had to leave because Principal was having some sort of mental breakdown or something."

Mental breakdown? Like Rayah's panic attack?

August's face darkened as he clawed at his neck with his thick fingers. "Yeah, Dad's having a bad day with the divorce and everything. Best to keep him away from pill bottles."

Danny thought back to Hannah during her suicidal episodes when her parents divorced. Sympathy for August dripped in his chest like hot wax.

Then something else struck him hotter. He pulled out his phone to text Michelle.

> DANNY: Hey, just heard Ned might be having a mental breakdown, or something. Just had a thought, do you think the court will ignore our case if he claims to not be in his right mind?

The teacher slid out a rolling chair from his desk and slumped into it. "Unfortunately, I already have a waiting list for eighth period."

Purple crawled into Dean's face as August continued his explanation. Stepping away before the fire got at King's Academy level, Danny inched toward a comic on the wall that featured Abraham Lincoln as a fresh throng of parents and students flooded the doorway. His phone pinged.

MICHELLE: It's rare in real life. Lemme Google it.

Thirty seconds later.

MICHELLE: So, few cases like that actually succeed for the defendant. Ned would either have to have a history with mental illness or do something drastic.

DANNY: He's from King's Academy. He's bound to meet both those criteria.

He raised his head to see if he could make an escape for the door. A woman in a large sun hat caught his eye and nudged her husband to move over. Danny mouthed a thank-you and strode toward the door, stopped by a pregnant girl in a low-cut top and puffy eyes, the kind someone wore when they'd just finished crying.

"Whoops, sorry, Bel, almost ran into you there. Happy to turn in your two weeks yesterday?" He pumped his fist in the air. "No more scooping ice cream!"

She nodded, but as she glanced over Danny's shoulder, she locked eyes with something that caused her to freeze. He turned around and watched the veins bulge like snakes in Dean's neck as he balled his free fist. August continued to list the names of the students on the waiting list for eighth period.

When Danny returned to explain the situation to her, Bel had already disappeared.

Chapter Eight

"DANNY, WHAT WOULD YOU DO IF RIGHT NOW YOU WERE standing alone in the forest confronted with a mountain lion?"

Twenty heads swerved in his direction as he squinted at the Alexander Hamilton bust on August's desk. His cheeks grew hot and his heart beat faster than the ticking clock at the back of the room.

"Umm, well, I'd pinch myself because I was dreaming? Didn't mountain lions go extinct in Pennsylvania last year or something?"

Laughter rippled throughout the class.

Corners of August's eyes crinkled, and he waved a hand to silence the students. "Fine, say a mountain lion confronts you on the western half of the Mississippi." He leaned against his desk. "Tell me your game plan."

Danny's toes bent and unbent in his tennis shoes as the air conditioner unit kicked on with a groan. He swallowed, tasting the spaghetti and Alfredo sauce he'd eaten the period before. Of course, they had to put government in the building farthest from everything on campus.

"And he already saw me, right? Like, I can't play dead?"

"You didn't luck out with a blind mountain lion." In complete honesty, he couldn't luck out with just about anything.

"Umm." He clicked a mechanical pencil until it ran out of a stick of lead. "I'm not sure, sir." The sir tasted like a B-vitamin or his anxiety pills, bitter and hard to swallow. "Maybe back away slowly? Like, you'd still keep your eye on him, but you'd reverse." Like he'd learned with his mom in her car over the summer. No way she'd let him get a license before eighteen. The way she hyperventilated and gripped the side door the first time on the highway or when he tried to parallel park. Maybe if they'd gone driving any other summer than the summer right after Judah's school shooting, he'd have a better chance.

August laughed into the bulge of his stomach sticking out of his dress shirt. He rose from his desk and drew a stick figure on the SMART Board. He labeled it in green marker with Danny's name and put RIP next to it.

Oh, he hoped Hannah wouldn't give the eulogy. Would she read *Goodnight Moon* in her serial killer bunny voice?

"So Mr. Belte here passed tragically with his mountain lion encounter. Let's try another student." August perused the rows like Danny's mother did when inspecting watermelons at Save-A-Lot. Danny whirled around and eyed the clock, which was mostly buried in Garfield comic strips. Five minutes into class, and he already died.

"Miss"—August consulted a clipboard—"Bel Graves, tell me how you'd confront a mountain lion."

What about the picture he found in Ned's game room? That flashed in his mind once more. If only the photographic memory came with something useful, like an interpretation.

Danny frowned, looking over his shoulder again to exchange a bewildered glance with one of his friends only to find himself facing Dean. He whipped around as his cheeks grew hot. Whoops.

"You run as fast as you can." Bel wasn't looking up at August. She kept her gaze transfixed on her folded whitening knuckles. "It'll catch you, but at least you can say you tried."

He had a feeling she wasn't talking about a mountain lion.

The teacher took a moment to consider this. Then he reached for a red marker and drew another stick figure, with Bel's name and a gravestone epitaph.

"So, Miss Bel attempted to run and was brutally mauled. How about another try?"

Before he could call on the next student, Bel already had her maroon bag swung over her shoulder. She brushed at a tear spilling down her cheek as she darted for the door and slammed it behind her.

Danny knew from experience with Faith that pregnancy came with odd hormonal responses, but he couldn't seem to figure out why that would send Bel running. He recalled when he and Michelle had toured classes. Bel bolted then too.

Because of Dean? August? Her inexplicable hatred of Garfield the cat and the president?

For a moment, August watched after her, and then he consulted a world map with his hands on his hips. He reached for a golden water bottle tin on his desk and tilted his head back for a swig. Then turned back to the class.

"One last chance. You, Mr. Reuben. Tell me, man, what do you do when face to face with a mountain lion?"

Two seats to the right, Reuben straightened his spine against the red chair. "I read somewhere that you have to make yourself big as possible. Spread your arms wide and roar at it, and you'll intimidate the crap out of it."

August pointed at him with the red SMART Board marker still in his hand. "Correct. Reuben survived his encounter with the forest beast. Can anyone tell me why we started out our government class this way?"

The air-conditioning unit shuddered off, and the sound of students shifting in their hard metal seats filled the echoing room.

Leaning against the desk again, August smoothed out his red metallic tie. "I'll tell you. Government is like a mountain lion. If you don't know how to react when faced with it, it will destroy you." His eyes hovered on Danny for a moment before he reached for a Bill of Rights handout on his desk, right beside a golden lion paperweight Danny hadn't noticed before.

Last time he'd visited the basketball court, they had decorated the stands with papier-mâché palm trees and a surfboard attached to each basketball hoop. Everything stank of beer and sweat and sea-scented air freshener the chaperones would occasionally douse everything in. Now, it seemed odd coming here for class in his all-gray PE uniform with a black vector lion logo on the front.

He dropped his book bag on the floor. Why'd they have to make his history class so dang far away from the gym?

Upon entering, he spotted *WELCOME TO THE DEN* painted in red above the fan section. Lights flickered and hummed, giving the stadium an odd greenish sort of glow, which reflected on the shiny wooden floor. Last time, they'd covered the lights with blue tissue paper—a fire hazard, shocker. Gave the gym a nice underwater feel.

Now it reminded him of green, the color of his stairs back home. Zai had ridden a bicycle of almost that exact green before the accident. The color of the once-beautiful garden, an ashen ghost of what was once good and now decayed gangrene green.

He jogged to a cluster of students huddled around a whiteboard by the padded wall at one end of the court. Some kid doused his hands with hand sanitizer. Another one elbowed him.

"Martin, you're gonna make your hands bleed again."

"Just want to clean them one more time." He squirted another glob of clear liquid onto his palms and rubbed.

Danny elbowed past Martin and caught a glimpse of instructions left in maroon marker on the whiteboard.

Hey, Students,

Out for the day because of a family medical emergency. Please do the following outside, since it's a nice day. High of 83.

1. Jog a lap around campus. I realize this might be difficult for students with asthma. If needed, run half a lap. Grab a running buddy.

2. With your remaining time, do some core exercises, at least three. I recommend 10 push-ups, 30 crunches, and 20 jumping jacks.

3. Send me a one-page reflection of what you did and who your running buddy was.

Thanks. See you all in a few days.

"Running buddies?" A hand shoved him from behind. He turned, and Reuben bit a sweaty lip, panting slightly but still standing upright.

Danny scanned the clump of students as it disintegrated into pairs of students. None he recognized. Only knew one other name now, Martin, and his hands had just begun to bleed. "Sure, Reuben, I'll run with you." What happened to the sophomore days when he had Hannah, Michelle, and Rayah in classes? Now he had maybe one with each. But, although stiff and sometimes judgy, Reuben came from Emmanuel, and Emmanuel students stuck together, no matter what.

They strode past the *WELCOME TO THE DEN* sign and headed out the squeaky metal doors into a warm sunshine bath. *Bath* best described the wetness of everything. Danny pumped his arms and grumbled under his breath about how they should've run inside in the AC. Overhearing him two steps ahead, Reuben jerked his head as they jogged by a biology class, students cross-legged in the grass to hear a lecture about biospheres.

"Glad the teacher put us outside, that old gym creeps me out." Reuben shuddered.

Danny puffed out a pant once, twice. A bee buzzed past his ear and landed on a cluster of dandelions ahead. "Why, though? Sure, the lights flicker and everything's a ghosty green, but what'dya expect? They built the thing decades ago."

Reuben, as far as he knew, didn't have bad memories associated with prom in that gym. He had stood with the rest of the student body, said the pledge, and went home with no burns.

They rounded a cobblestone corner as they zoomed by a group of boys in polos playing an odd game involving tennis balls and golf clubs. Acid filled Danny's lungs and calves as Reuben continued to speed forward. A taste of dryness and vomit filled the back of his mouth.

Reuben glanced over his shoulder before charging ahead even faster. "It's not the oldness of it that freaks me out. We live in a dorm that's literally falling apart."

A student lighting the carpet on fire certainly didn't help with the overhead.

"What then?" Danny forced his feet to pick up the pace even though his toes stung against the hard rocky path.

"On your left." A biker in a neon pink shirt skidded past Danny and nearly ran into his running buddy. Taking advantage of the pause, he dashed forward and landed by Reuben's side as they continued to charge toward the bright afternoon sun. Seconds later, Reuben took the lead again by a couple inches.

Inch. "You know that teacher Mr. Peterson?" Inch. "The one who Judah replaced?"

An image of Judah after his interview flashed through his head. Beads of sweat had cascaded his cheeks when he muttered something about an accident and Mr. Peterson being in the hospital.

"Yeah, didn't know him personally, but heard of him. Didn't he work here last year and then quit in the middle of summer? He have a medical emergency?"

"Suicide attempt." Inch.

Danny stopped.

Reuben continued ahead past an empty metal bench. No one would sit on that in the baking sun. He veered on his heel and returned, running in place.

Swaying his head back and forth and letting the cool drops drip down his neck, Danny squinted at the sun, at Reuben, at his shoes. "They didn't word it like that in the email they sent to the students."

He dropped to the grass to sit a moment. Reuben's shadow hovered over him, blocking out the dandelion sun.

"Uh-huh, and they also didn't let people know that the reason Mr. Enlil, a government teacher, left the year before was because he'd sexually assaulted two of his students. They just said he 'retired,' that he wanted to spend more time with his family."

Yikes. His blood froze despite the eighty-degree heat. "What does this have to do with the gym?"

"That's where they found him, comatose. Mr. Peterson, I mean. Didn't Duke tell you? All the kids working over the summer knew."

"Never got around to it, I guess."

"He was here early to set up his classroom for the summer." He shook his head, sun peeking between his curly dark hair. "Got him to the hospital, but I don't know if he made it. They wouldn't tell us."

Danny's knees clicked as he stood. The grass had begun to itch his legs. "He could've attempted suicide anywhere, though. What if he collapsed in Phrat River? Would you be scared to go in there?"

"Do you believe in ghosts?"

"No, but I do in angels."

"You'd be smart"—he turned toward the sun again and began to pump his arms and legs—"if you believed in both."

They continued in silence as they headed toward the old garden spot. There, they would complete core exercises and call it quits. Danny stopped at the metal ring around the tree to catch his breath and rest his hands on something.

Mistake. He yanked his arms back and waved them, hoping for an afternoon breeze to cool them. The spiky leaves on the tree didn't rustle once. Dagon, he couldn't wait to get back to his sweltering dorm.

Seeming to ignore him, Reuben lay on his back beside the tree and began the thirty crunches, counting each one in a loud voice and accompanying growl. Danny bent down to join the number and catch up to the ten, eleven, twelve Reuben had already reached. But as he squatted onto the square patch of dirt that used to hold the garden, he spotted something odd in the lining of the bark. Leaning closer, he found it.

"Reuben, someone chopped the wire to the camera on this tree."

"Twenty-four, twenty-five, they what?"

"Seriously, they took a nice chunk out of it, even sliced off part of the bark. You see where it's light brown instead of gray?"

"Thirty-one, thirty-two."

"Dude, you're only supposed to go to thirty."

At forty, he rose, brushed off the dust from his gray gym uniform, and moved in Danny's direction to inspect the tree. Sure enough, the thin black wire missed part of its spine, the lower vertebrae. Wouldn't his biology teacher from last year be proud?

Stroking his chin, Reuben tilted closer over the metal circle protecting the tree. "A stupid thing to do, you would think. Ned'll expel whoever did this into the Dark Ages."

"Doubt it." Since when did Ned step in when it came to sexual assault, suicide, or arson?

Exhausting their curiosity, they continued the core exercises. Reuben waited while Danny toiled through his crunches. So much for having lunch fourth period. He'd have an offering for the old garden soon enough with the way his abs burned.

"You look pitiful." Reuben picked at something in his nails.

Said the boy named after a sandwich. Or dude who showed up in Genesis. Either way, he was letting down sandwich and Old Testament fans.

"You"—up—"try to"—down—"do crunches when"—up—"you have lunch"—down—"two periods before."

"Try having lunch during seventh period. I'm closer to cross-country practice, you know."

"Did you literally just pick me as your running buddy to feel better about yourself, man?"

"No." Reuben flicked an eyebrow. "I picked you because you run, and I need someone to push me to go fast."

"Why? This isn't a competition."

He laughed, once. "At this school, everything is. Welcome to the Den, Danny." Reuben squinted at the robin-egg sky, and the wrinkles on his forehead relaxed. "Glad it won't rain. Coach likes to run us inside when it rains. They made a rule against us using the academic buildings, so guess where we'd go."

The gym. Danny focused on his crunches.

"Twenty-nine, thirty." He collapsed on his back and let out a puff as the burning in his abdomen subsided. "So you have lunch after this? I got history. It's a light-year away from the gym."

He rose and rapid-fired his jumping jacks. Reuben joined along and, of course, swung his arms and legs like scissors, faster than Danny. He finished and dropped to start his ten push-ups, which he turned into fifteen.

"Got an eye on the time? I hear seventh period is the most crowded the dining commons gets."

Danny completed his jumping jacks. "Sorry, left my phone back in the gym." Dagon, he had to get his bag before heading to his next class.

He vowed to complete the push-ups on his own time. "I'll do it at cross-country practice. Don't worry." He sprinted toward the gym across campus. His gray shirt stuck to his skin as he scampered past a building where a couple made out underneath birds perched on the roof. The birds looked almost as blue as Obi and Twitter itself. Several minutes later, he arrived at the old gym and shouldered his way through the hot metal doors into the cool AC.

Savoring the cold blast for a moment, he eyed the hall that led into the gym and noticed not a soul breathed. Aside from the distinct hum of the Gatorade vending machine, silence filled the room.

He pushed into the metal lever on the door, and his shoes squeaked on the court as he jogged to retrieve his bag by the padded wall. He unzipped it and dug around the BO-scented thing for his phone.

Checked the time, he had ten till his next class. If he jogged, he could make it.

Another squeak caused his heart to hammer. He zipped his bag and swung it over his shoulders, collapsing under the heavy weight of textbooks. Then he spotted her, walking in a dizzying stupor toward him, clutching her stomach.

"You doing OK, Bel?" He paced a few inches her way and noticed how her flip-flops tripped over each other.

She bent over, bangs shielding her eyes as she unleashed the contents of her stomach on the gym floor. Everything smelled of burnt flour. Danny plugged his nose with one hand, speech adenoidal.

"Morning sickness? Need me to take you to Nurse Nintin? I think her office is about a five-minute walk from here."

Bel tumbled headlong onto the floor, fingers and legs twitching. Danny rushed to her side and shook her shoulder, the skin feeling cold to the touch. "Bel?" He rolled her over so she wouldn't drown in the vomit. Perhaps the green lights in the gym tricked his eyes, but her lips faded to a blue. "Bel!"

Something clacked onto the hard floor, dropped from her hand—three large white pills.

Chapter Nine

"*I WANT TO RIDE DOWN DEVIL'S BACKBONE TODAY.*"

"*Zai, that road's like a ninety-degree angle. Thing's got a crap ton of potholes.*"

"*Yeah, it'll be awesome. Pers says I can hang with him at Mills Springs Park if you film the whole thing.*"

"*I don't know, Zai. I've heard he and his group do some messed-up stuff around 2:00 a.m. down there.*"

"*You sound like your mom, Danny.*"

That shut him up. He wished it hadn't.

"My sister just tried to commit suicide yesterday, Lion Tamer. How do you think I'm doing?"

Duke scrolled on his phone, the glow highlighting the bloodshot corners of his eyes. Danny still had his knuckles on the door from knocking. His hand dropped to his side as the toy ghost in the Phrat River bathroom giggled from afar.

With a sigh, Danny kicked off his shoes and shoved them underneath the desk he and Reuben shared, next to a trashcan already littered with tissues. Although Duke was no Dean, his mess almost made up for it.

In his already-damp socks, Danny tiptoed to his bed and collapsed onto the squeaky mattress. Eau de Urine filled his nostrils. Reaching for his book bag by his pillow, he unzipped it and pulled out his AP Euro textbook: *Western Civilization Since the 1300s*. Leave it to Judah to assign homework the first day.

Good thing they canceled the second. He overheard some guys in the bathroom complaining over toothpaste-spattered sinks that the school would take it out of their allotted snow days.

Way to take a suicide attempt hard, guys.

He flipped open to the first chapter. It looked like a review of ancient times.

"Can you take that out into the hall?" The folds of Duke's chin gave him the appearance of a winking bullfrog.

"Sure, buddy." Danny shoved the book into his bag and fiddled with the stuck zipper. "I'll leave you alone."

"Thanks." The word died on the roommate's trembling lips, almost untraceable with the roaring box fan positioned by Duke's closet. Thing did nothing but spread dust and clog Danny's nostrils, but he liked to believe it brought the temperature in the room from a ninety-five to a ninety-four point five.

"Last question, man, I promise. You meeting with Ned today?"

Duke blinked at his screen. "An hour after you, with Dean, the guy who got her pregnant. Yippee."

Got it. Danny's eyes flicked up to the blinking smoke detector on the ceiling. "Any idea why they're making us go in two at a time? All the people who know her?"

"You said that was the last question." He huffed, kicking a brown sheet to the corner of the wall. "And probably because the school doesn't trust faculty to be alone with a student, not after the Enlil incident."

Dagon, did everyone know about that? And if so, why did nobody sue? Perhaps taking Ned to court was going to be harder than anticipated.

Swinging his backpack over his shoulder as he stood, he staggered into Duke's bunk bed railing because of the weight. He caught a watery glint in his friend's bulging eyelid.

Upon entering the hallway and clicking the door shut, he unpeeled a sock and placed it on the doorknob in case Reuben dropped by. He doubted anyone would believe Duke would fool around with a girl after yesterday's events, especially not Hannah, who was firm about waiting for marriage, but he figured he couldn't carve *Do Not Disturb* into the wood without getting fined.

He slumped into a chair in the lounge, the one right beside a burn mark left last year.

Pulling out his phone, he texted Michelle while perusing the flat world map in his book.

DANNY: Did you know the real reason Mr. Enlil was fired?

His phone made a doo-whoop sound, indicating Michelle had received it. What gave with the school's once-terrible Wi-Fi?

By the time he'd reached a page with a buffalo cave painting, he received her reply.

MICHELLE: Yeah, kind of had an icky feeling about him when I saw him in the hallways last year.

MICHELLE: Dan, we need to do something about Ned. With the arson thing, the letting teachers get away with taking advantage of students thing, and now the Bel thing, think we should talk to the lawyer before fall break?

DANNY: Maybe, but what do you mean Bel thing? He couldn't help that she tried to commit suicide. No one could.

Already his inbox that morning had flooded with letters from teachers encouraging the students to do kind acts, such as sit at an empty lunch table with lonely students because "you never know when a student is going through something hard." Talks of school counselors offering sessions popped into his email, but by noon that day, they'd indicated waiting lists.

Michelle's message scrolled down his screen.

MICHELLE: Ask July, but pretty sure Ned had something to do with what set Bel over the edge. Either that or his son, you know the apple never falls far.

DANNY: True.

MICHELLE: Let me know how the meeting goes. Talked with Hannah and Rayah, and we've decided to let our parents know about the lawyer thing. Gonna tell them after you meet with Ned. FaceTime in Suanna?

DANNY: Sure, but maybe do it outside where the cameras have no audio.

MICHELLE: Have you seen the school Wi-Fi lately? Ned's head is a million miles away. Probably got hit with too much at once.

DANNY: Life does work like that.

Zai and his father in one summer, the fire and divorce for Rayah, disasters always worked like that.

DANNY: See you at Suanna around four to FaceTime.

He wiped the sweat from his arm off the faux-leather chair and skimmed the maps of the Fertile Crescent and the Yellow River. Blues, greens, and light browns all blurred together. Five pages into the huge citadels of words and past the picture of the Code of Hammurabi, he checked his phone and realized he needed to head out for the meeting with Ned. With an absentminded leap from the chair, he ambled toward his room and reached for the knob. When his fingers grazed the sock, he scrunched his nose.

"Dagon. Left my shoes in there."

Thinking on his feet, one socked, one bare, he knocked on Gabe's door, the prickly welcome mat itching his foot. The friend retrieved a pair of Chacos. Danny thanked him and slipped the shoes onto his feet, discarding the other sock underneath the couch in the lounge. Black-and-white arrowed Chaco straps headed down the concrete stairs that echoed with each step.

He found July parked on a hard wooden bench outside Ned's office. She dangled her shorter legs off the side and swung them back and forth. Ashley Penaz, the secretary, clacked on her computer. She reached for the phone, bumping into the messy spattering of K-cups by her desk. Everything smelled of coffee, which churned Danny's stomach. Lucky he remembered his meds today.

"How you holding up, July?"

Sidling beside her, he noticed how her hands rubbed her dry knees. She reached into her bag and pulled out a nutty-scented lotion, rubbed. "Fine if people would stop asking me questions all day."

His cheeks flushed. "Sorry." He forced his attention on the signs slapped onto the glass windows. Homecoming Court elections were happening already? The dance wasn't for another two months. And for the play ... *Charlotte's Web*. He wondered if Michelle would go for the spider. Then again, tennis practice. Plus, most girls didn't react well when someone said, "You've got the body type of an arachnid."

A hand tapped his shoulder. He rotated and caught a withering smile from July. "You're curious. I don't blame you. I roomed with Bel last year, so of course I must know everything about why she did it."

Fire flushed his cheeks again. Poor Duke, already that day he'd had several text him asking for details about what went down in the gym. He remembered his phone had flooded with texts about Zai that summer, all from concerned Emmanuel classmates. Zai's classmates.

"Michelle says you know something about—" He jerked his head toward Ned's shut door. Behind it, he heard a soft moaning, maybe crying. Perhaps one of the meetings with the students had not gone well.

July slid the lotion into her bag, zipped it, and angled her chin at Ashley, then at Danny. "Not here," she whispered. "Maybe later."

Creasing the corners of his eyes, he nodded, mind swarming with possibilities. The clacking from Ashley's computer ceased for a moment.

She jabbed a purple fingernail at Ned's office door, then smoothed back a severe dark bun. "He can see you now."

Five minutes past their appointed time, Danny hoped so. He thought about the FaceTime call in the Suanna dorm afterwards.

They rose and approached, the moaning from inside growing louder. Danny knuckled the door once, twice, eyeing the golden placard with Ned's name. The moaning stopped and a weak "Come in" followed.

The second he swung open the door, a strong incense fume punched him in the nose and kickstarted the headache. Stronger than any of the smells of his previous visits. July also seemed affected as she crinkled her nostrils.

In the corner, wilting in a large red chair, sat Ned. His cheekbones jutted almost as much as his secretary's, and graying hair reminded Danny of feathers with the way it spiked. No, wait, it looked like the leaves of the olive tree by the old garden spot.

"Sit."

A wrinkled hand motioned to two seats in front of the desk.

They parked as Danny observed the chaotic state of the room, much like his mother's storage space in their house. Books lay overturned and open butterflied on the shelf. Crumpled papers littered the floor and desk. The trash bin to his right smelled of something rancid, but the incense disguised most of the scent. He peered at the desk, wondering if Dean took residence in there.

Then his eyes landed on pill bottles, orange and translucent, sitting empty on the desk. That didn't look good.

July cleared her throat, shifting in her red chair and rubbing her septum with a finger as if to block out the strong incense. "Mr. Rezzen, you called us in to discuss Bel? Since Danny was the last to see her before he called 9-1-1, and I was her former roommate?"

Ned winced, clutching his stomach. In the glow of Ned's laptop, Danny realized just how many wrinkles lined the man's face with the way his skin sagged off his chin.

"Mr. Rezzen?"

He doubled over and puked into his trashcan.

"Mr. Rezzen?" July rose, pounding her fist on the desk. "Do you need us to call someone? Are you feeling all right?"

"The tree." He gasped before retching again. "First Amy and now the tree, it's not worth it anymore."

Danny eyed the pill bottles once more. Although the labels blurred in the dark room, he remembered what August had said when he first visited his classroom, about needing to keep Ned away from medications.

Something encircled Danny's wrist with an iron grip. Before he had a chance to figure out what was happening, July swung open the door to the office and yanked him out with her. She released him and slammed the door.

"Ashley, call 9-1-1." July dodged around the front counter and slapped her palms on the desk.

The secretary didn't lift her eyes from the computer screen. "What for?"

"Tree." As Danny muttered this, the events swirling in his head seemed to funnel into one coherent thought.

As in the tree beside the ex-garden? What did this have to do with Bel?

"Call 9-1-1, or I will. Ned's suicidal. He had about twenty different pill bottles on his desk, and he's taken all of them, *all of them*."

Ashley grabbed her cell phone and bolted into Ned's office.

Danny glanced at July. "Should we stay and wait for the ambulance to come?"

She shook her head. "Like the Suanna fire, it might be best to stay back and let adults handle it."

Like always, he marveled at the calmness in her voice. Maybe he should use that favorite quote of hers more often. It seemed to help her a lot.

"I think I'm going to check out the tree, to see what he's talking about."

"By all means, go, before someone burns the evidence."

Danny burst out the doors and wound around the cobblestone path, knocking into a couple or two holding hands on their way to the dining commons. Darting toward the rectangular patch of dry land where the garden once stood, he stopped short when he saw the metal ring around—

"The tree."

Someone had chopped it, in two clean slices, it appeared. One higher, one lower, creating a seat in the twisted trunk. A throne, perhaps, like the ones in his AP Euro book. The carcass of the thing sagged on the circle that failed to protect it.

He approached it cautiously, scanning the area for any sign of an ax or of who felled the great thing. Nothing, no evidence, everything smelled green with a vague whiff of olives.

When he reached the placard, he read the *KA* spray-painted over the sign declaring Ned's everlasting love for his wife.

Ping went the phone in his pocket. He slid it out and turned up the brightness in the late-afternoon glare of the sun. Squinting at the lock screen background of him and Rayah posing for a prom pic, he read the message from Michelle.

> MICHELLE: You out of Ned's office yet? We want to get the FaceTime started soon. My mom's off to retail in thirty. Think you can make it here by then?

Stepping sideways down a grassy hill, he replied.

> DANNY: Coming, but Mitch, I think Ned just tried to kill himself. Ashley dialed an ambulance.

He quickened his pace, the sound of a riding mower in the distance blocking out his breath. Broke out into a jog. Might as well, cross-country practice got canceled today too.

The *wee-oo-wee-oo* of an ambulance sounded in the distance. They showed up even faster than they had for the Suanna fire.

He reached the evergreens shielding him from Suanna. Pushing past the sticky, prickly branches, he headed around the building and knocked on the front door. The front desk worker glared at him underneath a large pair of glasses but pressed a button that clicked open the door. Fresh AC cooled the sweaty spots underneath his armpits.

"Open house hours have been canceled today." She gestured to her computer. "Ned's secretary sent a message recently."

"Haven't had a chance to check my email."

"Too bad." She crumpled a Kit Kat wrapper and tossed it toward a silvery bin by the door. Missed. "I can send my friend to a room to get your girlfriend if you like." She gave a curt nod to a girl with blue hair on a stool by the desk. "And do me a favor and pick up that and put it in the trash."

Danny stooped to grab the wrapper. "If you could get them, they're in room 108."

Front desk worker whistled. "First floor, lucky them, don't have to move anything upstairs since elevators don't appear to be a thing the campus invests in."

Yeah, lucky them, you too can get a first-level room if you survive a murder attempt from your principal.

He jabbed a thumb over his left shoulder. "I'll be in the lobby waiting for them. That's neutral for guys, right?"

She rolled her eyes. "Correct."

Past a group of girls twisting their mailbox locks, he wandered toward a brown couch that, unfortunately, would receive many sweat stains from him. Collapsing into the cushion, he let out an "ah," masked by his fast-beating heart. Didn't realize he'd moved so hard to get here.

He gazed at the brown water stains on the white ceiling tiles, ignoring the glares of a group of girls working on a project on a couch nearby. Hearing the clip-clop of flip-flops, he straightened his spine against the seat, which had begun to eat him. Hannah approached with her fiery bush of hair forced into a ponytail, arms hugging her chest across a neon blue tank top.

"Check your email."

"The front desk worker told me about the open house hours thing. Figured we could do FaceTime outside."

She jerked her chin. "Check it again."

Pulling out his phone and swiping the screen, he turned down the brightness as he opened his inbox. A new message from Ashley Penaz blinked in bold.

"They've taken Ned to the hospital." Hannah sidled next to him, maintaining a foot of distance. "He's going to be there awhile."

"Is that what the email says?"

"No." She sucked in a breath. "It says he's no longer principal of our school."

Chapter Ten

"THANK YOU FOR TAKING THE TIME OUT OF YOUR morning classes to join us at this assembly. The revised class schedule is included in the packets the student helpers are passing out."

The lady in a pantsuit cleared her throat into the megaphone, knees knocking together in the early morning breeze. A student dashed across the football turf and handed her a purple jacket that clashed with the pink pantsuit. She muffled a thank-you, not out of the mic's earshot, and slipped on the coat.

Something tapped Danny's arm. He turned as Hannah whacked him again with the stack of packets. The student helper had already reached one of the top rows on the bleachers.

He snatched the thick thing, twenty pages deep, and passed it along to Rayah beside him, wondering how many trees the school murdered for the Wednesday morning meeting.

As the helpers weaved up the rows, he scanned through the packet, skimming the headings.

I.   School Counseling Center Information (p. 1)

II. Suicide Warning Signs and Prevention (p. 2)

III. The F.R.I.E.N.D.L.Y. Talk (p. 3-4)

IV. Cyberbullying Prevention. See something. Say something.

Pausing on the third point, he flipped to page three and wondered how anything friendly could spring out of King's Academy. Rayah shivered beside him, so he tore off his orange hoodie and placed it on her lap; her knees stopped bouncing.

"Thanks." It came out as more of a whisper as she fumbled the hoodie over her head, messing up the yellow bandana.

"You'll want to tear it off in a couple hours. High temperatures all this week."

A weak grin spread across her face before she nestled into his shoulder. Ah, a little extra cinnamon lotion used today, nice.

They read the F.R.I.E.N.D.L.Y. Talk together.

As many students know, we can prevent student suicide if our fellow peers remain vigilant and responsive to those who are hurting and who need help. Before another incident can occur at King's, we ask that students read and implement the following tools:

F: Find a student who shows warning signs of depression or suicidal tendencies.

R: Reach out to that student. Remind them of the counseling center and suicide hotline.

I: If the student ignores you, get a school counselor involved.

E: Emergencies, such as finding a student in the middle of an attempt, necessitate 9-1-1.

N: Never carry the knowledge of a struggling student alone!

D: Don't try to counsel them yourselves. Professionals need to be involved.

L: Let administration know if school counseling appears to produce no improvement.

Y: You, and you alone, may be the only one to prevent this student's suicide.

Hannah growled, marched up to the top °of the stands, dodged around one of the helpers, and tossed her packet over the bleachers. Even from his seat below, Danny heard it flutter and land on the concrete.

She returned and huffed as she slumped into her spot. Behind him, a zipper flew across a bag at lightning speed. Michelle stuffed her packet into her book bag and muttered, "What a piece of trash."

"That's why I threw it away." Hannah hugged her chest. Dagon, girl. It was too cold to be wearing a panda tank top. "Those teachers who found the cuts on my arms and told my parents to send me to the hospital were anything but friendly."

Michelle snorted. "I'd at least like to recycle mine. Heaven knows how much this school has accelerated the earth's impending environmental death." She'd quit using straws that summer, at least from what he'd seen when she ordered milkshakes at his shop.

"Might as well do something to help," she had said while wiping a pink milk mustache off with a napkin. "You should see how much paper my mom destroyed this past year, directing at the local theater."

Danny's neck hurt from playing the tennis ball in the match back and forth between Hannah and Michelle. Rayah's head probably hurt too because it was still nesting in the crook of his chin and neck. He faced forward as the speaker on the middle of the field tapped her foot.

"Did you get to the F.R.I.E.N.D.L.Y. Talk, Mitch?" A ding from his left side indicated Hannah kicked some part of the bleachers.

"That's why I called the thing trash. They made it sound like students are the sole reason why other students get depressed."

"I could get past that if they didn't insist we tell the administration every time we thought about popping a pill that wasn't ours," Hannah said.

Danny wasn't sure if he agreed. His mother's voice, from that one summer, still rang in his ears.

"You knew about it. You could've prevented it. Now his blood is on your hands."

The speaker on the field nodded, at least from what Danny could tell in the tangerine glow of the sun. She raised the microphone to her lips, smacking them together and swallowing.

"Read through those packets and inform us if you know of a student who needs help or counseling." She raised a fist, the corners of her pantsuit wrinkling at her armpit. Even from far away, Danny could tell the thing needed ironing. "We will not let students suffer alone."

Hannah kicked the bleacher again. "You'll make them suffer in great company."

Dropping her arm, the speaker thrust her hand on a jagged hip. "Today the school will be blocking all social media sites as we highly suspect much of the *incident* was spurred on through an online forum."

Incident. That made it sound like a construction accident, or a tree falling in a forest.

Groans of various shapes and registers spread across the bleachers. Like a human wave in a basketball game, but this time, comprised of a ghostlike grate.

She raised a hand, smacking her lips again. "Privileges come with prices when misused. We will investigate the social media forums, question the students at fault, and then determine if we may allow you to access these sites again." She dropped her hand, not before checking her watch. "We've used up all the time for this brief assembly. Please follow the class schedule in your packets, section five, and resume your morning classes."

Michelle, before the speaker had finished, stood and barreled past Danny, knocking into his legs. She marched to the top of the stands, as those in the upper sections rose and filed out, and unzipped her bag. Retrieving the packet, she gave it one hard look before throwing it over the chain-link back of the stands. It too fluttered like a broken butterfly.

Swerving around students spilling down the middle aisle, she returned to Danny's row, wiping her hands on her billowing skirt. "Wasn't worth recycling."

The fifth-period bell rang as Danny approached Ned's office. Already, the administration had scraped off the name plate, which left behind a sticky yellowish residue.

He knuckled the door and the "Come in" caused the blood in his chest to freeze for a moment. It echoed just like Ned, except higher and not quite like thunder.

Turning the knob, he swung open the door to a faint incense odor. Now, a lemon fresh spray disguised the scent of its previous owner. Sunlight spilling from the window burned his eyes. August sat in Ned's seat, rummaging through one of the middle drawers. Danny cleared his throat but found the thing to be very dry.

August peered up at him, crumbs lost in the midst of a crimson beard. Eyeing the table, Danny found the culprit: a half-eaten blueberry muffin.

"You wanted to see me?" He found his way into a seat across from the desk before August had a chance to motion to it.

"Yes, figured you'd have time since I canceled our government class for today. A shame, we were going to go over the electoral college today."

They both had very different ideas of shame.

Slamming the desk drawer shut, the principal's son pulled out a crumpled sheet of paper, speckled in red ink on both sides.

"It seems"—he tossed the paper ball at Danny, who caught it—"Dad left you with the school." He chuckled, folding his hands over his belly and leaning back in the rolling chair. "And the bird."

Danny unfolded the paper and squinted to make out the markings. Looked like the bird Obi had dipped his feet in ink and landed all over the paper, attempting to create letters. "Umm, what?"

"Apparently, prior to your and July's meeting with him in this office, he appointed you as the successor principal of this school, as a last will and testament sort of thing." Despite his smile, he looked a shade too gray to be happy. "He also requested that you take care of Obi since Mom moved out already and didn't take him with her."

Wait, what?

Heart pounding, Danny set the paper on the desk next to a photograph of Ned and his son during a fishing trip. He swallowed; the taste of his anxiety meds lingered.

He shook his head, black tendrils of hair tickling his nose. "I don't understand. I haven't even finished high school."

"Don't worry. We're not planning on fulfilling his request. Hiring a principal takes a search committee, effective advertising, blind interviews, and all sorts of boring stuff they don't teach you in high school or college."

Seemed that list of "boring stuff" grew by the day.

Danny exhaled, all the tension releasing from his chest. His hand hurt. He noticed he'd been gripping the sides of the chair, knuckles whitening. He relaxed.

August glanced down at his beard and brushed the crumbs. "However, I do want to discuss the bird with you."

"The bird?"

"Yes." August slid open a drawer and pulled out a Polaroid of the small blue Obi. "Dad planned to commute back and forth between King's and home to take care of him before ... the incident."

He set the Polaroid beside the crumpled ball of paper. Right between the photo of him and his dad. "It put another considerable strain on him on top of everything else happening at school."

Licking his lips, he leaned forward. "Considering I need to help the school get back on its feet and help designate people for a search committee, they've tied my hands and feet for going back home most of the day. A lot of pressure for someone who just left college." He laughed, once.

Poor August, Danny thought for one brief moment. Even if he'd caused Bel a great deal of grief, he now had to deal with a suicidal dad and with running a school until they found a replacement.

"Plus"—August's tone shot up—"Obi does get separation anxiety. Most birds do."

Danny continued to stare at the paper, then the bird photo, then the picture of August and his dad. His brain felt as if someone had filled it with cotton.

"So." Danny focused on the picture of the bird. How its little black claws clung to the bar in its cage. How the old Polaroid washed out most of the color, making the blue feathers seem more like white, no longer the Twitter poster-bird. "You need someone to watch over it."

"Particularly you since Ned appointed you to do it."

But didn't Ned also appoint him to lead the school?

August continued, leaning in even closer. Danny could smell a faint trace of alcohol on his lips. "We'd pay you, of course, for all your help. Ned lives down the road from school. Or he did until ... We'd just need you to visit during your free period in the morning and right after school. I don't get home until six or seven most days."

He clung to the armrests on the seat again, nails digging into the wood. "I don't know the first thing about taking care of birds. What do they eat? Worms?"

"We have a mix we use, but you can occasionally treat him with fruit or cucumber."

Also, sure, he avoided eating animals, but taking care of them was a whole other matter. Especially caring for the bird of all Twitters.

"I think I'd be afraid of killing him, August. We don't have pets at home."

Once a goldfish his mother promised to feed. Like the wilted plants on the family room windowsill, the creature went many meals unfed. Killed Danny when the orange scales harshened to a pale corpse hue within a few days, kind of like Obi's feathers fading to white in the photo.

August interlocked his fingers, forming a pyramid. "Better you try than to let the thing die on its own. I could give it away, but when Dad gets back from the hospital ... he'll want to see it."

His mind flashed to Rayah and Hannah. They pet-sat over the summer, and with their money going toward the lawyer, they needed a little extra income.

"Would I be able to have some of my friends help? They could use a little bit of cash since there aren't a lot of jobs on campus."

"Absolutely, and we'd pay them for whatever hours they log."

A muffled bell rang. "I'll think about it." Just like he thought about everything since the Zai incident, a little too much.

Michelle groaned and slammed her laptop shut. "I can't even access Yahoo News. What is this world coming to?" She leaned back in her wooden chair, head landing on her triple-stacked bunk. Rayah inched back in her bed, knees hugging a notebook from one of her classes. Hannah, on the top bunk, kicked a poster on the ceiling from *Code Geass* with her bare foot.

Massaging her temples, Michelle groaned again. "The journalist in me is *dying*. I need to know everything about Bel and Ned. Now the school will let us access our email, and that's about it. I guess news websites count as social media."

Anything with a comment section, anyways. So much for tweeting a weekly verse, something he liked to do whenever one caught his eye. Zai had actually gotten him into the habit, back in the day, before he started hanging around Pers.

He'd been itching to post July's favorite for some time now.

. . . a stronghold in times of trouble.

Times of trouble seemed to take place every hour at King's.

The AC unit in the Suanna dorm kicked on with a sputter. Hannah dislodged the corner of the poster with her toe. "Should've thought about that yesterday and researched the crap out of everybody, Mitch."

With a slam, the chair bolted forward, Michelle out of it and pacing, making sure to dodge around Danny, who sat by the left-hand closet. "Not my fault my AP Econ teacher decided to assign a test the first week. Was at the library studying since somebody decided to blast Scream-O music from the top bunk." She glared at Hannah.

"It helps me relax." Another corner stuck out from the poster, the character on the front, dark hair, swooping cape, and purple eyes, now facing the door. "Besides, you're gonna have to use the library a lot more if you want to research anything, since they blocked most websites."

Mid-pace, Michelle slumped to the carpet after she brushed away a pair of heels lying on the floor. "But all those old articles aren't going to tell us squat about the Ned or Bel situation. We won't get anything done until fall break."

Rayah shuffled in her bed. Her notebook flopped onto the floor, and she bent over to grab it.

"Speaking of fall break"—Rayah retrieved the notebook and flipped to the proper page—"any possible way we can sue Ned now with his medical condition and all?"

Michelle leaned back to knock her head against the closet wall. "Probably not. Even if insanity cases don't survive much in court, you know he'd somehow wiggle his way out of it. With this school's track record and the law, especially with the Enlil thing—" She broke off and buried her head into her knees, purple skirt suffocating her sigh.

The female inhabitants of the room all appeared affected by this announcement. With one leg swing, Hannah freed the poster, and it spun in mad circles toward the floor. Rayah stared at her class notes, pencil wobbling in her hand, eyes not moving.

Neck bent toward the crusty carpet, Michelle tapped her fingers on a brown stain for a few moments before clenching her fists.

"I did scroll on Twitter last night when I finished studying." Michelle sucked in her cheeks until her cheekbones showed. "I checked five minutes before the library closed, but I tried to glance through Bel's feed. For any signs, since people let on often on social media if they're not feeling all right."

She swallowed and unrolled her fists.

"Trashy as the assembly this morning was, I did see someone post something about the pregnancy. Some kind of holier-than-thou crap about Bel sleeping around. Can't remember who did it. It was really late, and my eyes had gotten all dry and blurry by then."

Hannah rolled onto her stomach with a grunt and a moan from the mattress. "And?"

"And, the person who posted it went to Emmanuel. I do remember that. Because someone talked about that in the comments."

A door slammed down the hallway followed by a silence and the swallows of all four friends.

"So?" Hannah moved to her back, her red sheet coiling around her body like a snake.

"So, do the math, Han. Some religious kid from a religious institution. Add that to this person making fun of someone for doing something not religious. Then multiply that by that girl attempting suicide soon after. What do you think King's, an institution that hates religion, will do?"

Rolling her fists into bony balls, Hannah rubbed her eyes, smudging dark makeup all over her face. "Wish people would think before they tweeted."

No luck seeing that blue bird anytime soon. Wait a minute—tweet, bird, Obi.

He'd forgotten about his meeting with August.

Aligning his spine on the section of wall between the two closets, he explained what had happened in Ned's ex-office. During the whole conversation, Michelle cocked her head to the side, almost blocking Danny's face. He scooted to the right, bumping into the heater on the wall.

"So he wants you to watch Obi?" Hannah perked up considerably during the explanation and almost hit the back of her head against the ceiling.

"I guess so, but I asked him if you guys could help. He said he'd pay and all; not that we really need it since our money won't go to the lawyer."

Michelle's hand slipped into a pocket in her skirt, no doubt reaching for her phone buried in there. "Does Ned's house have Wi-Fi or a computer? Doubt he'd give us the Wi-Fi password."

Bet it was something like Emmanuelshouldburn or SettingStudentsOnFireIsFun!

Screwing his eyelids shut, he envisioned the room where Ned kept Obi. The bird's cage basked in the glow of a computer screen on the other side, the bright screen whiting out the blue bird.

"Yes, I saw one when we visited."

"Great, count us in." Michelle blew on her bangs to remove them from her forehead. "We're gonna use it to take the murderer down."

Chapter Eleven

RAYAH: Hi, this is Rayah Abed. Zai told me this was your number. What is the book we have to read over the summer? I'm new, and Zai said he had a different English teacher.

DANNY: Hey-o! Yeah, we have to read Where the Red Fern Grows.

RAYAH: Thanks! I've been texting my friend Hannah Shad like crazy, but she's not responding.

DANNY: Sure thing! And, Hannah Shad, you know her?

RAYAH: Yeah, we both do rec soccer, why?

DANNY: She seems kind of sad all the time, and also how does she not burn up in those long sleeves?

RAYAH: Well . . . her parents divorced recently, and she's not taking it well. I haven't heard from her in a while. She says she always tried to get good grades and do well in sports to make them happy and keep them together. Now that they're not anymore . . .

DANNY: Shoot, well, let me know any ways I can be of help. My parents are together, but with my dad being really sick, it's got me wondering what life would be like without one of them.

RAYAH: I'm sorry to hear. Let me know how I can be an encouragement. I get the whole no-family-is-perfect thing. Mine can be rough.

DANNY: Thanks for offering! I'll keep you updated on my dad, and you keep me updated on Hannah?

RAYAH: Sure! I mean, what I can. Hannah isn't an open book.

DANNY: Gotcha, well thanks, and let me know how I can encourage you. I'm sorry your family is rough.

RAYAH: It happens.

DANNY: I'm happy Zai sent your number my way. Maybe we can sit together in English class.

RAYAH: Sure but be careful. We might end up becoming friends.

DANNY: What's wrong with that?

RAYAH: Well, friends are a lot like family. If one goes down, everyone else does.

DANNY: Oh, mind blowing, but things at Emmanuel kind of work the same.

RAYAH: Yeah?

DANNY: If one student goes down, so does the school.

"Reuben, please tell your girlfriend to back off." July frowned at her worksheet, pencil pausing above the blank for number nine. She gestured at Danny, accidentally flicking the Israeli flag dangling above her head. "Danny, what's the feminine Arabic present tense for 'you write'?"

Clearing his throat, Reuben shoved his arms over his chest and eyed the empty teacher's desk. Bathroom break, they must not've told Mr. Parsin that teachers took those between classes. Either way, with a class of three, they were way ahead of the schedule anyway.

"*Tarsumeena*, and what do you expect?" Reuben crossed his arms even tighter. "It's been a month since the whole Bel thing, and the administration hasn't let up about social media."

Heat surged to Danny's cheeks. He glanced at the wall with the labels underneath the flags of various Arabic-speaking countries. Oh, he didn't know they spoke it in Mauritania. He couldn't point to it on a map, but change the letters a little bit, and his roommate Duke and ex-roommate Dean spoke that language all the time.

July pounded a fist on her desk. "I didn't send the tweet, OK? Heaven knows I haven't used a social media account in months. Don't have time to post at this school."

Algeria, Bahrain, Chad, Comoros, Djibouti, oh dear, that was an interesting country name. People seemed to favor that one a lot at school dances.

"Besides"—July's pencil tapped her paper, perhaps got stuck again—"it didn't come from my account. Even before it got deleted, administration caught the girl's name. They interrogated her in the office."

Egypt, Eritrea, Iraq, Israel—hey, Judah came from that last one!

"And the girl claimed she was hacked." The head of Reuben's chair creaked as he leaned back into it. Danny bet he looked rather odd bending backwards with how straight he stood. "She had received an email about unusual account activity."

"Danny, do you think I would go shaming my past roommate on social media when I knew she was clinically depressed?"

He returned to the paper and then met July's burning gaze. "I think we should get back to the questions before Mr. Parsin returns."

"Danny!"

Sigh. "No, July, you don't seem stupid enough to post something like that. Besides, you two seemed to work well as roommates last year." Images from the Suanna fire danced across his eyes.

She propped an elbow on the chair back and waved an eyebrow at Reuben.

With a growl, he aligned his spine, one vertebra at a time it seemed, until he was taller than the other two classmates while sitting. "That brings up another one of Valentina's points. You guys are *ex*-roommates. That looks suspicious."

"Oh my word!" July banged her head into the desk three times before running her fingers through her curly hair. "They *made* her move to a single because of the stupid trimester rule, and that's another thing." She jabbed a finger at Reuben. "She was barely on social media. If you want to know what made her depressed, ask the guy she slept with."

"I'm just repeating what Valentina said."

Danny's cheeks burned. *Don't get involved, man. You don't like conflict and you don't want to be like your mom when it comes to arguments.* She went haywire on Facebook comment sections.

"Whatever." July rolled her eyes. "But this is low for you, to assume I would say something like that. I thought Emmanuel students were supposed to stick together, no matter what. We have to in this God-forsaken school."

"Stop acting holier-than-thou. You stood up for that pledge."

"So did you."

Reuben's chair made known its rust as he squirmed in it.

He turned to the window, avoiding July's gaze. "So Danny, who's been watching Obi instead of you during practice?"

"Hannah, since she's the only one not doing a fall sport. Kills Michelle because she wants to do some hardcore investigating into the Bel thing but can't without access to the Internet. And with tennis practices and no free periods, the only time she could come over is when August is already home." He caught July's burning irises. "Don't worry. She thinks you're innocent."

"Good."

She unfolded a gum wrapper from her overalls pocket and placed a green wad onto the paper with her tongue. "You know"—she balled the wrapper, gooey present tucked inside—"she called me the other day. Bel, I mean. Not Michelle. We don't know each other that well." She pinched the ball. "They have limited time given to talk at that ward, but she sounds broken. And it wasn't just because the speaker came out all garbled. Something tells me the place is making her worse, not better."

And they wouldn't let you out till you got better. A Catch-22, no, wait, he was thinking of another novel.

Danny reached for his yellow Arabic folder and tucked the worksheet into the pocket. He unzipped his bag and placed it next to his copy of *One Flew Over the Cuckoo's Nest*. "How long can they keep her there? I thought people didn't spend more than a couple days at that place."

July rose and aimed the ball of gum at the trash bin, missed. It landed by a tile on the floor that hosted a centipede the other day.

"If you're bad enough, you can stay for months." She veered around Reuben's desk to retrieve the prodigal wrapper. "I hear they can keep you ninety days, even longer. And Bel isn't exactly improving." She stooped and grabbed the ball, placing it in the proper bin this time.

Danny wondered how long the hospital kept Hannah. Why hadn't they developed a closer friendship until freshman year?

A student in the hallway chattered excitedly with another in some thick-throated language. German? Goodness, how long did the teacher need to use the restroom? The two passed a homecoming sign with the word *dance* painted in various colors and languages. The theme appeared to be a techno night of some sort. At least the chaperones wouldn't march up and down the dance floor in grass skirts again.

July returned to her orange chair and question twelve. "Had any luck in hacking Ned's computer at home?"

Baile, Danse, Tanzen, with the *T* appearing more like a *J* with the way the blue paint dribbled on the white paper.

"Nah, we can't find the Wi-Fi password, so no dice with using our phones—thank you, parents, for not getting enough data. We also wanted to create a new User for his computer, but he or August would get suspicious when they returned home."

Something smacked the window, perhaps a bird.

"Let me know when you do. Valentina's convincing August to hop onto my trail. Heard he might be pulling together some sort of snitching team."

"That makes no sense with the rules of Quidditch."

"Danny, be serious."

"Might as well ask me to stop breathing."

Mr. Parsin poked his balding head into the classroom and issued a broken greeting and something about a clogged toilet. Made sense since they heard no flush. On to problem number thirteen, with plenty more questions to go.

"I believe July, but if I say anything, Valentina will kill me."

The running buddies jogged past the tennis courts, and Danny paused to watch Michelle slam a winner against a girl in a bright-orange tennis dress, at least from what he could tell through the billowing red windscreen. He shouted a "woot!" before a bystander on a bench, a mother with a fanny pack, hushed him.

"Why doesn't Valentina like July?"

"I think she kind of has a thing against Emmanuel students, since half of you took over the student council last year. She said I was an exception because I'm not like the others, apparently. Guess I'm less judgmental or something."

Huh, that was weird with his comments about Judah's car.

Also, the fact he upvoted all of Valentina's bills probably secured the seal of approval.

Although Danny couldn't entirely blame Valentina. His cul-de-sac used to have only seven houses with stretches of beauty land between each one. That is, until one year the Homeowners Association decided to double the number of homes in the neighborhood. Even the most extroverted person could get frustrated with new neighbors taking up precious yard space, especially neighbors like Pers who liked to steal bicycles and trim Christmas lights with garden shears.

Danny plucked only one bright moment from all those neighbors moving in—one of them was Zai, a stocky kid from North Carolina.

"You ask Valentina to Homecoming yet?" Danny resumed his jog, catching up to Reuben.

Reuben veered to the left to kick a pebble. "Yep, picked some flowers during practice and asked her afterwards." Another rock went flying into a patch of browning grass. "She said, 'Yes,' then paused, and then said, 'Dean'll be mad when he sees me grinding with an Emmanuel kid.'"

Danny focused on the dirt path, watching behind him as his spikes drove holes into the dusty ground. Only person who hated Emmanuel more than Valentina was Dean. Heard he grew up with three brothers, sharing one room. No wonder he hated more people taking up his yard space, so to speak. "You excited to go with her?"

"Dude, she's my girlfriend."

Didn't really answer the question, but OK.

Reuben's foot reached for yet another rock. He stopped mid-kick and brushed his forehead with his forearm. "Just kind of wish she didn't bring up the Emmanuel thing."

"Yeah?" Danny's abdomen released a series of shooting pains complaining about the lack of breaks in their run until now.

"Uh-huh, or when July brought it up in class earlier. That was sort of annoying. It's not who we are anymore. We've attended King's for a year. Can't they see us as part of them now?"

"I don't know if that's possible."

"Whatever, man, I'm used to it. Mom's white, and dad's black, so people tend not to see me as a part of anything."

Sweat burned as it dripped from his forehead into his eyes. Wow, he'd never even considered that before. No wonder Reuben felt the need to excel in everything, to prove he belonged.

"You ask Rayah?"

"Yeah, just did." He swallowed, mouth full of a spaghetti taste from lunch hours and hours ago. Something like a laser dashed across his vision. He blinked several times, stupid sun. "Last time, for prom, I threw up on her, so I figured just asking would be a step up. She doesn't really like grand gestures anyway."

"You excited to go with her?"

"Dude, she's my friend." He thought it was an adequate answer.

They carried the rest of the run in silence, listening to the music of campus on the way back to the tree where the team did their core exercises. Birds and tree bugs hummed in high rhythms as a scoreboard for a girls' soccer team blared to indicate they'd reached halftime. He wondered how Rayah and July did, but the orange numbers blurred too much from the distance they gained. They listened to the trumpet blare of the marching band and a group of students screaming and chasing each other for some video project for a class.

At last, they reached the tree to the music of grunts of runners midway through crunches. Half the team hadn't returned by this point.

"What should we start with?" Danny collapsed onto a patch of itchy grass underneath an oak tree. Edges of the leaves had been dipped in an autumn orange.

"Coach usually has us do ten different ones. I say we start with burpees, fifteen of 'em."

Danny's head thunked against a tree root, and his vision blurred for a moment. "Why do you always have to pick the hard ones?"

"Because when I make us do the difficult core exercises, we get the top scores. 'Sides, you and Gabe keep tying times neck and neck. Don't you want to pull ahead of him?"

The pale runner clicked his metal shoes against the sidewalk as he ran alongside a teammate with a buzz cut.

Pulling himself to his knees, Danny groaned, wincing at the tree root poking him in the behind. "We're not trying to beat our *own* team, Reuben. That's why we run against ten other schools at meets. Besides, aren't we supposed to focus on personal record times instead of the other runners?"

"They give out first place medals for a reason. Now, come on. Burpees. Fifteen."

His arms wobbled like jelly by the end of the first core exercise. When, by the third, Reuben suggested heading inside to grab weights to make planks more difficult, Danny joined Gabe's group as they completed their third exercise, penguins.

He giggled as he sprawled on his back and wiggled back and forth, touching his heels with his hands. "This thing does nothing."

Gabe exhaled as if someone just punched him in the stomach. "You're not doing it right. Tighten your abdomen."

"Bro, stop ruining my fun. I just got out of a torture session with Reuben."

Reuben had already headed toward the gym to the upstairs weight room, too distant to hear. Judah approached with a key ring on his left ring finger, right on top of the blue silicon wedding band. Had bought enough to match his outfits, today's harmonizing with his Emmanuel-blue tie.

He stood over Danny, blocking the bright haze of the sun behind the all-gray sky. "Want to grab some coffee?" He jangled the keys and pressed a button. The car behind him emitted a shrill beep.

Danny stopped after he grabbed his right heel for the thirtieth time. He cringed as his stomach erupted in a fire. Coffee was a bad idea. "Not really. I could always get it at the dining commons."

Judah hunched onto his haunches, looking like a frog. He placed a firm hand on Danny's sweaty shoulder. "I think we should get coffee away from campus anyway, just you and me. *Just* you and me." He craned his chin at a wooden light pole with a camera attached to the fixture.

His brother nodded, understanding. "Give me five minutes to change."

"Gonna finish that blueberry muffin?"

Danny slid the pastry across the wooden table to Judah, almost knocking his head into the low-hanging light. Judah's thanks disappeared behind the shrill grinding of ice and coffee for a Frappuccino order. He bet those were the milkshake orders of the coffee world, pure torture. Even if people, like Michelle, drank them without straws.

His tongue grazed the roof of his mouth, digging out blueberry residue from his molars. "So, you wanted to talk?" Asked this after the grating machine ceased, replaced by the soft tapping of piano keys on an overhead speaker.

Judah raised a blue mug to his lips. Coffee, black, he tipped it back. He set it down on the table and gestured to a painting on the wall. "Really like that, the starry painting, kind of like Monet. They really changed this place since I went here."

"You know, you had the whole car ride to tell me what you needed to. Don't think Ned buried a camera in your car."

The other shrugged. "Might've." He tilted the cup again and his Adam's apple bobbed as the drink went down. "Besides, couldn't take that horrible watered-down stuff from the dining commons. Stuff in the teacher's lounge in the history building isn't much of an improvement. I'll bet the coffee they use could actually be as old as some of the stuff we talk about in AP Euro."

In a corner booth by a bookshelf an acne-scarred student with lemony hair pressed his knuckles to his temples as he stared at his computer screen. Jeremy.

Michelle's boyfriend stuck a Pirouette cookie in his mouth like a long cigar. He beat his palms against the keyboard and then waved a fist at the sky, er, the wooden ceiling. "Come on, inspiration! I just need six hundred more words for this chapter."

Ah, he had mentioned writing books last year at Michelle's performance of *Julius Caesar*. Sent Danny plenty of links to his blog as well. If he just copied and pasted three entries, he'd have a whole novel.

Although he wasn't quite sure why Michelle ended up with him, when he asked her, she scrunched her shoulders and said, "The kid is impressed by me, and I never wanted to end up with someone like my dad, so I think I scored a win."

Danny scooted a little to the left so Judah blocked him from Jeremy's view. "So, again, you wanted to talk?"

He set the coffee cup on a coaster. The mug featured a design of a mother bird nestling a baby in the crook of her neck. "Faith's ultrasound didn't go well yesterday. Two months out, and they're thinking he might come early."

The Frappuccino machine cried again as it crushed up ice. Scents of coffee and burning milk sent Danny's stomach churning. After several moments, the noise died.

Judah blinked as a watery glaze covered his dark-brown eyes, lip trembling. "We're scared because, as you know, we lost the last one at fifteen weeks."

His brother nodded in a slow bobble, uncertain of what to say. He wondered how Bel was getting along with her pregnancy at the ward.

Judah puffed out his chest and squinched his eyes shut. Moments later, he reopened them and cleared his throat. "But I could've told you that at King's."

"Right, but people are listening everywhere. I'm sure there's some students or teachers you wouldn't want to know."

Setting his jaw, neck apple bobbing, Judah nodded. Then he shook his head and leaned forward over the coffee and coaster. "I wanted to talk to you about something else." The bitter coffee scent on his breath caused Danny to wrinkle his nose. He leaned as far back into the brown leather couch as possible.

"I don't see any King's people here, so we can talk like normal human beings."

Staying put with his arms on his knees, Judah clasped his hands together. "Something about August seems very off. I think he might have something to do with Bel's attempt."

"Why?"

"She left right after your government class and popped the pills less than an hour afterward. Doesn't that seem odd?"

His heartbeat accelerating, Danny eyed the painting on the wall. How the darkness swallowed up the stars, where it began as a large cluster on the top, and by the bottom, reached a black hole. "I mean, Dean was also in that class, and we think he got her pregnant. Maybe it had to do with him."

Judah's pupils resembled black holes. "Keep an eye on August. Those who have something to hide try to place the blame on others." Ah, everyone was targeting July, right. Maybe August had helped spur on that rumor.

July was no Rayah, but she came from Emmanuel, and he had to help her out. So he wouldn't fail like he had with his three friends in the burning dorm or with Zai.

"Find what you can about him at Ned's house. Find him before he discovers somewhere no one can get to him."

Chapter Twelve

A FLUTTERING NOISE GREETED DANNY AS HE ENTERED Ned's house. "Hannah, you're supposed to keep him in the cage."

"And you're supposed to be at cross-country practice."

Her voice bounced off the walls from a room in the distance. Danny kicked off his tennis shoes at the front door and placed them on top of the red-and-blue Persian rug. Edging past the glass trees on display in the hallway, he turned right and found Hannah upside down on a chaise lounge, scrolling through her phone. Her hair plummeted toward the waxed wooden floor. Perched between the Y formed by Hannah's legs was Obi, tilting his head at Danny. "Got canceled. Coach gave us the day off since we placed well at Saturday's meet." He wrinkled his nose. "Dagon, Hannah, did you spray all of the lemon fresh in here?"

She jabbed a finger in the air, pointing down from her angle. "Wanted to fumigate the incense stuff since it gives you a headache. And we no longer use Dagon. We've updated to Mazda."

"Mazda? As in the car company?" He realized how high his voice had gotten and dropped it.

"As in Ahura Mazda, the Persian god. Figured we'd evolve in our timeline each year of high school. We can pick a different ancient deity to curse. Next year we have Ancient Greece, so get your memorization skills ready."

"Yeah, well, I'm sticking to Dagon. It rolls off the tongue easier."

Sliding down the chaise, Hannah readjusted her position, causing the bird to launch into the air once more. It flapped in circles around the popcorn ceiling and a beaded glass chandelier before landing on Danny's hair.

"Put my hair in a bun the other day." Hannah bent herself in half, the redness that had surged to her forehead now draining into her cheeks. "Imagine trying to get those little claws out of curly ramen noodle hair."

"Which is why you don't let him out of the cage." He inched toward the sofa, feeling the extra weight on his head wobble.

Hannah sprawled out on the couch before he had a chance to sit. He settled on the rounded armrest, feeling much like a bird crouching on an egg. Hannah's feet near his behind didn't help much with the smell or the feeling of the room and furniture.

"Figured we'd give the poor little guy a chance to stretch his wings." She leaned forward and stroked the bird. Her voice rose an octave higher. "Isn't that right, little guy? Mean ol' Ned never let you out much. How about we go to the ward and peck his eyes out? Yeah, that would be fun."

Danny reminded himself never to get on Hannah's bad side.

A shrill chirp replied atop Danny's head before another flash of wings followed. He moved to fix his hair as Obi settled atop a large cherry wood TV stand, which took up half the room. Tail feathers ruffling, he weaved in and out of framed pictures and glass ornaments.

"I like how he has a blue splotch by his neck." Hannah leaned back, poking herself underneath her chin. "Makes me think he got stabbed there in another life and the mark stayed."

Did birds bleed blue?

White, the head bobbled up and down with the small bird's body as if it were dancing to some faraway tune. Now, Danny realized how silent the house seemed without soft piano.

Hannah slumped deeper into the chaise. "Speaking of stab wounds, I'm looking for speech pieces. Without any Internet, it's difficult to find anything online. Tried the library, but reading physical books takes so much effort."

"Yeah, what have you been scrolling through on your phone?"

"Photos I've taken throughout Ned's house. Michelle wants whatever *evidence* she can get."

"What evidence?"

She shrugged and lowered her arm to drop the phone on the floor, then paused. It was hardwood. "She doesn't exactly know what she's looking for. Just anything that can incriminate Ned or his son or just anything. I think the journalism and tennis practices are getting to her head." The phone clunked onto the floor, inches away from her finger-tips. "Hope she likes lots of pictures of Obi, though, our only evidence that Ned is human."

Something slid on the TV stand, like the sound of furniture scrap-ing across hardwood. A glass sphere paperweight with purple flowers stuffed inside approached the edge of the TV stand. In a flash, Danny bolted out of his seat and caught the thing right as Obi bumped it.

"Reason number two for why we don't let him out of the cage." He scooped a hand to pick up Obi, but the bird blasted into the air again and made several orbits around the chandelier. "Didn't you read the in-structions on the fridge?"

Ducking his way out of the family room to avoid the swirling bird, he ventured into the kitchen, socks on the cool tile. He reached for a list on the black steel fridge, removing the picture magnet of August in his white basketball uniform from Penn State. Returning to the family room and stooping again, he read the typed instructions, written in a blocklike font.

Hi, Danny and Friends,

Thanks so much for taking care of Obi. I'll try to do whatever I can around the house. We do have a cleaning lady who comes in every Tuesday, so don't come in those days. She knows how to take care of Obi.

Some ground rules.

1. Don't open the cage. I can let him out during spare mo-ments when I get home, but there's too many breakables around the house.

2. Feed him once a day. I don't know how you want to break it up, whether you do so in the morning or your friends

in the afternoon, but keep it consistent. I have further instructions on food by his feeding supplies in the kitchen. See the blue sticky note. Occasional treats are fine. I put them by his cage.

3. Don't place your fingers through the bars of the cage. He's not much of a biter, but he'll be tempted.

4. If he pulls his blood feather, call me immediately, and I'll come and pull out the appropriate feather. He'll bleed profusely otherwise.

5. Keep calm always and talk to him in low tones. Birds tend to mimic the noises of their environment.

Thank you once again. Don't hesitate to text me if you have any questions. God knows how much I text in class. No wonder I let the students get away with it.

He really did let students get away with that last one, the texting in class. Maybe he wanted to be as far away from the apple tree as possible when it came to Ned. Instead of rigid, he wanted to be the best friend of students.

Danny tapped the paper. "See? It was his number one rule. No opening the cage."

Hannah rolled her eyes. "You didn't have to read all of them. I got the point."

"Let's get him back to his cage. We can talk to him in there."

Right as he glanced up at the chandelier, he realized Obi wasn't rotating around the popcorn ceiling again. To his dismay, the noise of something else sliding off the TV stand caused his blood to freeze. He scooped the picture frame into his hands before Obi had a chance to send it to a plummeting death.

With a sharp sigh, Hannah rose from the chaise and stuck out a finger by Obi. She tapped his stomach with her index finger. "Up." The bird balanced on the new landing pad, and she carried him toward the computer room, crooning, "Yeah, is mean ol' Danny making me put you back in your cage? Yeah? We'll peck his eyes out, too."

So much for not getting on the bad side.

As he set the picture frame back on the mantel, the warm glow from the window glinted on the glass, unshattered from a near-nasty fall. Slanting his eyelids, he caught something he hadn't noticed before.

"Hannah, you know this picture from the day me and the Principal's Advisory Council did a couple hours at the soup kitchen?"

In the shot, Valentina, himself, and another kid by the name of Lawrence all posed with hands in plastic gloves and hair shoved into hairnets. Wow, would the new principal they were interviewing, or planning to interview soon, establish the same group? Or did Ned's five grand to all of his friends go to waste?

The friend returned, arms hugging a "Eat, Sleep, Anime" T-shirt. "Yeah, that's one of Obi's favorites to knock down."

"Ned has his arms around Ashley in this." He picked up the photograph and showed it to her. "It's hard to see behind the bin full of breadsticks, but you can see some of his fingertips on the hip of her white apron."

No one else in the picture had their arms wrapped around anything. The closest thing to humerus and ulna movement came with Valentina's arms making triangles on her hips as she attempted to block out the other two boys with her broad shoulders.

Hannah's lips curled, and then her face relaxed. She shrugged. "Not a shocker that his marriage fell apart then, is it?"

No doubt Hannah knew a thing or two about parents who had a few side Ashleys during marriage.

Without another word, she traipsed toward the computer room. Danny followed.

He entered to the tune of Hannah slapping her palms against the keyboard. A groan followed by a chirp from Obi's cage filled the dark room.

"Still haven't figured out the password to his account?"

"Or the Wi-Fi." She opened the drawers by the desk, each full of old receipts and electric bills. "Tried every drawer in this house."

A blue circle swung on the computer followed by a red *X*: Incorrect Password.

"I'd create a new user, but August probably uses this thing. He'd know, and without a Wi-Fi password ... so much for finding a speech piece."

"Or figuring out who the Twitter user was who framed July."

Her red eyes vacationed in her forehead for a moment. "Sure, or that. Tweet got deleted, though, so no luck in finding out what it said. Michelle sort of remembers."

A *clink, clink* came from Obi's cage as he banged his food dish against the bars. "You feed him?"

"He could always use a little more. I put a couple apple slices by his cage."

While Hannah typed, muttering her newest password creation, "King'sAcademyIsDaBest," he found a ceramic plate with browning apple chunks. He slid one through a top bar on the cage, careful that he didn't expose too much of his fingertip. Danny licked the sweet water droplets left on his thumb as Obi bit off a piece of the slice. Satisfied with his nibble, he bopped up and down again to an inaudible beat.

"King'sAcademyIsDaBestest?"

"OK, actually be serious, Hannah. It might kick you out if you guess wrong too many times." Obi chirped, fluttering around the small cage and beating against the bars. "Oh, I forgot about the bedtime story after the snack."

"Bedtime story?" Hannah raised her wrist as if looking at an invisible watch. "Isn't it, like, four in the afternoon?"

"I always read to him after a treat. It calms him down. Ned has so many boring books over here."

Moseying to the bookshelf against the wall, he touched the yellow fabric spine of *The Republic*. "Good ol' Plato, puts me and him right to sleep."

Groaning through her fist, Hannah hit the enter key with her free hand, a little too hard. Lucky she didn't break the thing at this point. "Could you not? Didn't have my coffee today. Can't fall asleep before I get this precalc homework out of the way." She gestured to a beat-up faux-leather book bag. Much of the black "leather" had flaked off, leaving chunks of browning fabric behind.

He perused the titles, noticing just about all except for *The Republic* had collected a layer of dust. Perhaps the cleaning lady didn't do extensive work. Or maybe August really didn't do widespread house chores on his part.

A ring of metal indicated Obi had begun chewing on the cage.

Back to the books, all had a coating of brown film, except for one.

"Hannah, you down for a *Code of Hammurabi* reading?"

Her head hit the keyboard. The blue circle spun on the screen again. "Kill me now."

"I'm sure there's some kind of law against that." Not that King's Academy would follow it.

He flipped open the book, a warm vanilla scent floating from the old pages. The scent was reminiscent of Rayah's lotion. "And this is the only one with a minor coat of dust. Just a little bit on the edges. Maybe August likes to read this one."

"If there's a little dust, probably not. Maybe Ned did, though."

"'When Anu the Sublime, King of the Anunaki, and Bel, the lord of Heaven and earth, who decreed the fate of the land, assigned to Marduk ...'" Danny shook his head. "Better get the Keurig machine in the kitchen running, Hannah. This thing'll put you out for a week straight."

She slapped her palms on the desk as she rose and huffed out into the kitchen. Smile crawling up his cheeks, Danny sat cross-legged beside Obi's cage. He flipped to another page, wanting to smell the vanilla scent again. When he reached the tenth one, an index card fell onto his lap. He raised it eye level and read it in the darkness.

"Hannah?"

A groan and high-pitched squeal from the Keurig replied. As the machine drizzled into a cup, filling the room with a warm coffee scent, Hannah replied a curt, "What?"

"Try Babylon as the password for Ned's account."

She shuffled into the room, setting the cup on a stack of papers by the printer. Typing the letters and entering, she caught a shriek in her mouth and swallowed it.

"Worked. How did you—?"

He flashed the index card. "Has his password for his emails, accounts, everything. There's gotta be about twenty listed on here. No wonder he needed an index card to keep track."

"Stupid." Hannah's spit doused a corner of the computer screen. She grabbed a crumpled tissue from a trash bin to wipe it off but stopped mid-smear. "He has a document open."

His stomach soured, gut burning. "Would it be illegal if we looked at it?"

"Is it illegal to lock three girls into a burning building?"

"Fair."

He rose and grabbed the edge of her rolling chair by the computer and read over her shoulder the document titled "Legacy." She read faster than he, so he had to ask her to scroll slower.

Ashley,

As usual with these documents I send, I expect you to keep them confidential. I have appreciated your unquestioning loyalty when, even at times, I know you'd wonder why I ticked a certain way. Last night surprised me when you asked why I'd done the school-wide pledge and the fire incident months ago. I hate to keep secrets from you, and this one has been particularly eating me alive. I feel as though I'm losing my mind every minute.

"When did he write this?"

Hannah upped and dropped her shoulders before checking the document information. "A couple days before school started. Before his incident and the whole Bel thing."

"Makes sense."

It all started when Danny explained the Photoshopped image that had made its way into my inbox. Some sender thought the school would take a downhill turn after I left. At first, I was ecstatic by the news, because of course, that meant no other principal could carry King's quite the way I did.

But then I realized, that meant my legacy I left behind on the school would disintegrate with whoever took over next. All those years for nothing.

Obi chewed on the cage again. Danny rose from his spot and slid in another apple before returning to read.

> I had to demonstrate to whoever sent that email that I had the school's legacy perfectly under my control. Attendance was up that year thanks to an "unfortunate" Emmanuel fire. Sure, took a bit of money to provide full rides, but no other school in the area was thriving as much as we did, especially with our increased talent pool. But with a failing marriage and declining health, one can imagine I wanted to take precautions. Not to mention the nasty incident with Kim and the garden. That's what ultimately enacted my decision.
>
> So I set up the statue and pledge and caught it all on camera to establish to the surrounding schools that our student body and faculty had unwavering loyalty to the institution. This, of course, will bring up substantial funds in the future from alumni who took part. We could simply remind them of the pledge and video and urge them to reconsider donating.

Danny slammed his fist against the chair. "Son of a—"
Hannah snapped her fingers at him. "Not in front of the bird."

> Many were up for the challenge because we'd provided scholarships, full rides, or letters of recommendation to prospective colleges. Of course, we had a handful of dissidents ... I do regret causing the fire in Suanna.

"Not yet." Danny called Ned a name that wouldn't be allowed in his house.
"What do fatherless sons have to do with it?" Hannah asked.

> What those four didn't seem to understand is the importance of legacy. We all live to make one mark upon this earth before withering away into nothingness. Our only hope in life is that someone will pass our gravestone in a cemetery someday and not ask, "Who was that?" but instead, "How can I become someone like that?"
>
> I wanted King's Academy to be my gravestone, Ashley. Now, we're watching it die before we do.

Hannah clicked control P, and the printer rumbled to life. She'd beaten Danny to it. He didn't care how illegal, he had to protect his friends, like he'd failed to do before.

While it spewed out the legacy document, she cracked her neck and knuckles.

Now, it was time to protect July. "OK, let's see what Twitter has to say."

Chapter Thirteen

"WE APOLOGIZE FOR THE INTERRUPTION OF YOUR FIfth-period classes, students." The fabric announcement box garbled by the ticking clock in the government classroom. Today everything smelled of lemon fresh cleaner the period before sometimes used to wipe down the desks. "We forgot to mention something earlier in our morning messages just before we did the pledge to the American flag.

"Valentina Inanna has organized an Anti-Cyberbullying League, which meets after school at five, when most of the sports and after-school clubs have finished."

Of course she had.

"If you are interested in joining, she says the group would look good on a college application and they will be able to participate in some student council meetings as many of the school events involve social media." Beside Reuben, Valentina tousled her bob of fuchsia hair and sat a little straighter as the announcement continued.

"The group will have access to social media and will monitor any occurrences of cyberbullying that happen at King's."

Social media access, huh? Danny bet half the school would sign up by sixth period.

After all, he and Hannah could find almost nothing on Twitter. Whoever posted the insult toward Bel deleted it almost immediately after, as had been indicated before. But no retweets, no comments of any kind indicated who had affronted her. Instead, the students of King's Academy had filled Bel's page with sympathies and wishes for her to "recover soon." All posted before the social media ban. There were a lot of thoughts and positive vibes mentioned. Valentina posted a lot.

(1/3) Hey, girl, I'm so sorry that something like social media could cause you so much negativity. I was bullied back in seventh grade on here. People called me a slut and all sorts of nasty stuff. I started cutting until eighth grade.

(2/3) I'm sorry I didn't get to know you better. From what I've heard from @DeanLuvsVal you are very smart, talented, and beautiful. He said you really helped him get through a dark time in his life.

(3/3) Know that your life matters, and that you are a beautiful goddess. We at King's are all here for you <3

Much as Danny wanted to get mad at Valentina, he didn't know about her history of cyberbullying until now. As for Dean, Danny hadn't known about the "dark time." From hearing his phone calls with his family, he figured he had a difficult relationship with his dad and didn't talk much with his siblings. Guilt gnawed in his stomach for not trying to reach out more last year.

Even Dean posted a SpongeBob meme of the underwater yellow sponge holding a rainbow that stated, "FEEL BETTER."

July said nothing, posted nothing, liked nothing.

That didn't look good.

"Those interested in joining the Anti-Cyberbullying League can sign up at the administration building. Ask Ashley Penaz for a form. Thank you once again for the interruption."

A click ceased the garbling sound from the speaker. The sub at the front of the classroom, a woman in a pale-blue cardigan and navy skirt that slumped to her ankles, consulted a clipboard. "We have a Valentina Inanna in here, correct?"

Valentina's hand shot into the air, bangle bracelets sliding down her arm. "Present." Even from Danny's seat, he caught a whiff of her perfume, lime.

"Wonderful. When August sent me the lesson plan for the day, he wanted me to mention your club you just organized, young lady." A pile of white curly hair jerked at the announcement box. "Looks like the administration beat me to it." She glanced at Valentina over the rim of clear, thick glasses. "Still letting the class know that your name is Valentina, or do you have a question?"

"Question." She dropped the hand and folded it on her desk. "Why did Aug—Mr. Rezzen not come to class today? I saw him in the administration building when I handed Ashley a sign-up sheet."

Setting the clipboard on the desk, the substitute paced in black clunky heels. From Danny's seat, he caught a whiff of perfume that reminded him of what his grandmother liked to wear, a mix of potpourri and age.

"It seems they needed an extra hand in the blind interviews for the principal's position. None of the candidates so far have satisfied the criteria, so they enlisted his help as he was the son of the man who most recently held the position."

Ten to one said they'd hire him. Danny wondered if that would make August the youngest principal in America at twenty-three.

Her heel rapped against the tile, hands folded in front of her rotund belly. "But enough about August, we're well into September and need to walk you through the steps of creating a bill. Your teacher has assigned an activity today after we watch a video from several decades back."

She had Dean, the tallest member of the class, stand on his desk to click on the projector dangling from the ceiling. It hummed awake and flashed a blue light on the screen. For a moment, a weird image flashed across the board, like a skeletonic white hand.

What the—

Only for a moment.

Then the blue light danced around like a strobe for a few seconds before Dean pressed the on and off button twice.

As the blue dissolved into a YouTube video from *Schoolhouse Rock*, lights from phones hidden underneath the lids of desks illuminated the dark room after the sub killed the overhead bulbs. Danny crossed his arms over his chest and leaned back into his creaky desk, not too far. Not too close to Dean. He wondered what on earth they could be doing on their phones. Texting, just like last year, didn't seem to work.

Guessed August found a way to jam the Wi-Fi just as Ned had. Apple didn't fall far.

Bill, a cartoon rolled-up piece of paper, sat dejected and bent in half on the steps to Capitol Hill. The sub asked if any of the students excelled at fixing the audio. Valentina motioned to Danny.

Ah yes, first the email for Ned last year, which started the whole need for the pledge thing, now this.

Still, maybe the video could help him find a way to make a bill to ban King's Academy.

He toggled with the inputs until the gruff voice of the singer blasted from the speakers. Dialing the knob halfway, he returned to his seat and watched as the bill wailed about wanting to become a law someday.

When the YouTube video concluded with showers of confetti falling on the scroll that the president just signed as a law, the sub flicked on the light switch. Bursts of white brightness stung Danny's eyes.

She moved to the desk and reached for a packet of papers by the Hamilton bust. Perhaps the lesson plans?

"First we need an idea for a bill. Let's pretend this school is the United States. Anyone have an idea for a bill that should become a law? Remember from the video, it takes a very special one to pass all the hurdles."

Valentina's hand shot up like a rocket, but she answered before the sub had a chance to call. "How about expulsion for a case of severe cyberbullying?"

The sub flipped her name badge, which had spun backwards on her cardigan. "Any other suggestions?" Reuben's palm unfolded on his desk, a surefire sign it would rise from the dead any minute. Valentina caught his eye and shot a death glare. He crumpled it into a ball again.

One more of Valentina's bills to upvote.

"OK, so Miss Valentina gave us a bill. She puts it in the hopper in the House of Representatives." Goggling around her knees for some kind of box, she settled on the garbage bin and made it into the hopper. "The bill then goes to a committee."

She raised a raisin-textured finger and pointed at Dean, Reuben, and a girl with marcel-waved hair. Rayah had worn that curly hairdo once. "You three, go to the corner of the room"—gestured to the right corner with the American flag dangling over it—"as your committee 'discusses' the Valentina Bill."

Ugh, it sounded like a terrible Hallmark movie.

Desks screeched on the tile as the three lumbered to the side of the room, Reuben shrinking next to the gorilla-shaped Dean. The other girl's fingers twitched by her pocket. Probably one of the guilty parties who played on phones during the video, or sneaked a vape or two.

"They will research and revise the bill until they come to an agreement. Then they report it to the House of Representatives." She pretended to grab the "bill" from the committee and brought it to the center of the room. "It's up for debate now. Anyone wish to bring up a point about why the bill won't work?"

Come on, no one? He wished Hannah were in the room, or Michelle. They loved debates.

The clock ticked five times as Valentina glared at each member of the classroom. When she caught Danny's eye, he thrust his arm into the air.

"Yes, Mr. Danny?"

"It would have to be way more specific than that." Fire exploded in his cheeks as he spoke above the loud drumming of his heart. "What if people hacked someone's account or typed a tweet while not sober?"

"Then, they would have to be tried beforehand." Spit flew across Reuben's desk and hit Danny in the cheek—Valentina spit. That sounded like a horror movie. Hallmark would never pick it up. "And who said anything about tweets? It could have happened on Snapchat or somewhere else."

His skin cooled a little. "All right, what about someone stealing another person's phone and using their Snapchat? And also, what happens if some cases of cyberbullying are worse than others?"

Valentina rose a little in her desk, skin matching her hair. "Like what? Give an example."

Heart slowed to a thump a second. "Like what if one person insulted someone's clothing choice in one and another insulted someone's race. I think those would be two very different cases. Sure, expel the second one, but the first?"

The folds of the substitute's chin bobbed in agreement. "Good points, Mr. Danny." As she went to Reuben to tell him to "revise" the bill, Valentina sank into her seat and flipped off Danny.

Returning to the class, the teacher's voice quivered. "The reading clerk, Mr. Reuben, revised the bill. Now we're going to put it up for a vote. Stand if you approve of the bill."

In almost a rush, all but Danny hurled themselves onto their feet. Valentina smirked at him.

Not here, not for the King's pledge, and not for July.

"Bill has majority. We would send it to the Senate. Let's say the class down the hall. If they approve, it's off to the president."

August.

"If he signs it, it becomes a law."

Goodbye, July.

Outside the old principal's office, Danny paused before sitting on the hard wooden bench next to a woman in a long-sleeve plum dress with a plummeting V. Her long dark-brown hair turned silver in spots and unleashed down her slim back. She glanced up at Danny over a bright phone screen.

"It never gets any less nerve-wracking waiting outside the principal's office."

He chuckled. "Maybe it does when the school doesn't have a principal."

The woman allowed her purple-stained lips to charge up her dark cheeks. She extended a hand, nails freshly painted. "Name's Ari Kingsley."

Wow, no Mrs. or Miss, she went straight to the first name. They shook, firm grip, eye contact the whole time, a CEO in the making. "Danny Belte."

Ari slid the phone into her purse, which dangled off her right arm. "So what brings you here?"

"My school *accidentally* burned down, and I transferred."

"I meant to the bench outside Ned's old office. You tell off a teacher?" She raised an eyebrow. "Drown the classroom pet in the fish tank? Torch some poor girl's hair with a cigarette lighter?"

Yikes, what horrible school did this woman attend?

"August called me to help him with some computer difficulties. Already finished tomorrow's homework for the class he's making me miss."

"Oh, if that's what the students are called to the office for here, that'll make my job easier."

"Yeah?"

She pressed her lips together and gave a long mhmm. "Was a teacher for ten years at Mede Media. Those examples I just listed"—a short, sharp laugh—"those were the easier cases I had to deal with."

"You here for the principal interview, then?"

Ned's office door swung open. July emerged with her ashen face streaked with tears. She raised a hand and shook her head, indicating she didn't want to talk about it, before racing around the glass door into the office and out the heavy wooden entrance to the building.

That wasn't a good sign.

August poked his head out and his stern look, which resembled Ned's demeanor, vanished behind a smile, one a little too wide. He motioned Danny in.

Danny rose and reached for his bag, leaning over Ari. "August, don't you have an interview before me?"

Wagging a finger at him, he guffawed. "Mr. Rezzen to you, young man." He winked. "And, Ms. Kingsley will surely not mind waiting a few minutes for you to fix my computer bug. I'm in need of my laptop for the interview."

Ms. Kingsley nodded. "Not at all, Mr. Rezzen."

Following August, he stopped at the door when the bright light in the room stunned his eyes. He groped his way into a chair. Much of the incense had disappeared, replaced with a burnt trace, with a hint of lavender Febreze. Danny noticed many of the books had disappeared off the shelves, replaced by basketball trophies and a succulent cactus, which appeared to be withering.

"So Danny"—August fiddled with an origami crane on his desk, then wadded it and tossed it into the bin—"how have you liked taking care of the little guy at home?"

"He's easy. Stays in his cage, so don't have to worry about him running into anything."

"That is the beauty of cages, I suppose. That's why Dad didn't really like him leaving it much." He rolled a basketball off the middle of the bookshelf and rotated it in his palms. "Do you know if your friend Hannah lets him out at all?"

His blood iced for a moment. He kept his eyes from widening; palms still oozed sweat, though. "I'm never over when she's there, but I told her not to." His voice picked up the pace like the last leg of his cross-country races. "She pet-sat a lot over the summer, so she knows what she's doing."

After holding his gaze for a moment, August leaned forward and unscrewed the cap of his tin water bottle. The stuff inside didn't smell like H2O, not from Danny's position, anyway.

August screwed his eyes shut and shook his head, twisting the cap on again. "Did you two use the printer at all? I saw it was on when I got home the other day."

"Again, sir, you'd have to ask Hannah. I only watch the bird during the school day. I've never used the printer."

Protection Mode: Activated

Friend Needing Protecting: Danny

Sorry, Hannah. Didn't mean to throw her under the bus like that, but he hoped August would drink enough of his "water" to forget to ask her. Happened enough times last year with Dean to get him out of a bind with his roommate. Most of the time Danny found him asleep.

"You excited for the Homecoming dance in two weekends, little buddy?"

Irritation prickled all over his forearms like an army of ants. Little buddy? "Umm, yes. My girlfriend seemed to be happy when I asked her. Picked out a green dress, that's all her mom would tell me."

"Rayah, right? That's the one you're dating? The sweet girl with the bandanas in her hair?"

What was this? The kid's version of *Jeopardy!*?

Danny leaned forward in the chair, the cushion whimpering from his weight. "August, you said you needed me for some computer help. I love small talk and all, but there's an interviewee waiting."

"Yes, I want to ask you a series of questions, and if you don't mind, I'm going to record this on my phone. All technical questions, I promise."

His heart pounded so loud in his ears it practically roared. August had found out that he and Hannah sneaked onto his computer. Now he'd get him to admit it on a recording and release Ned's Legacy document that Hannah had printed. Could he deny it? Create an alibi? Surely August knew about cross-country practice getting canceled that day. Maybe if he said he'd studied for his Arabic quiz with Reuben, that could pass as a story. He'd have to get to Reuben before August did, though.

"First question." August slid the phone on the desk, a black app with a single red light blinking. Danny assumed that was the recording button. "When someone hacks a computer, what's the best way to track them down?"

Hacking, Dagon, he knew. He knew!

"Umm." He rubbed his clammy palms on the armrest of the chair. Why couldn't August shut the curtains over the windows? "Depends, did they hack you from afar or on your own computer?"

August shot him an odd look. "Afar."

Oh, whew, maybe August didn't know about the time Hannah hacked his computer at home.

"And you're trying to track them down?"

"Yes."

"I'd say you'd have to figure out their IP address. It's kind of your computer's fingerprint wherever it goes." He removed his hand and noticed how he left several fingerprints behind on the chair arm. He'd make a terrible criminal. "So if someone hacked your computer, they usually leave evidence."

"Interesting." August slid the phone closer until it leveled with the picture of him and Ned on their fishing trip. "What are some ways to obtain or track someone's IP address?"

"Lots of ways. There are lots of apps out there that can do it for you. If you just do a Google search, you'll find plenty. Actually, I think even Google has its own little tracker."

With a pen in hand, August scribbled furiously against a notepad at the corner of his desk, too far to the right for Danny to see anything.

Wait a minute. Was August a lefty? Bet that came in handy in basketball. No wonder he did well in college.

"Last question." He slid the phone until it almost edged off the desk. Just like all the objects Obi had pushed on the TV stand. "Favorite ice cream flavor?"

He winked and guffawed as he clicked the red button in the app, shutting off the recording.

"Umm, can't have a whole lot of dairy. Which made working at an ice cream shop hard. But I think mint chocolate chip is always a good way to go." Even if it took the strength of Thor to scoop it.

"Birthday cake kind of guy myself. Thanks for your help on the recording. Got what I needed."

Danny skidded back the chair and reached for his bag. "Which was what?"

"We just found who hacked the cyberbullying tweet through the methods you just described." He towered above Danny as he stood and opened the door. "And we just expelled her."

Chapter Fourteen

"*SO ALL YOU HAVE TO DO IS SET UP YOUR PROFILE PIC, and boom, you have a Twitter account.*"

"*Thanks, Zai. Mom doesn't really let us use the computer much, and says I can't have a smartphone till high school, so anything you can teach me helps.*"

"*No problem, Dan, but honestly, you're super savvy at this tech stuff. You catch on right away.*"

"*Eh, I learn from the best. Speaking of, where can I find your profile?*"

"*Just type my username in the search bar.*"

"*@Izaiah52, nice. Oh, bro, you post all the time.*"

"*Just verses and quotes I like, yeah. Only have, like, three hundred followers, but they say seeing the stuff on here helps. Some of them have gone through messed-up stuff.*"

"*Cool, I want to post stuff like that. My friend Hannah seems down a lot, maybe this could help her.*"

"*For sure, but be careful. I've heard words have the power of life and death. You might save a life on here or ...*"

"You forget what all happens when you get expelled from *the King's Academy.*"

July chewed on her lip as she nudged her red checker piece forward. Rayah's dark chip had an easy jump over it. She didn't make that move anyway.

Tilting his chin up, Danny drained the rest of his chai tea latte. His stomach rumbled, souring at the dairy. Probably didn't help to come straight from cross-country practice to the coffee shop. Amidst the shriek of a steaming milk machine, he spotted Judah and Faith tucked away in a corner booth, almost blinded by a sheath of sunlight from the window. His older brother reached forth and patted her belly, reassuring, despite the wrinkles boring into his forehead.

"I mean"—July slid another chip to the right corner, where Rayah kinged her—"it's bad enough to have on someone's permanent record that a prestigious school kicked them out."

"One medium iced mocha," a barista with a swoop of bright-blue hair called from his counter. A woman in burn-your-eyes-out orange leggings grabbed it and skedaddled outside on her matching running shoes.

Sighing as Rayah kinged her again, July drew something with her finger on the fabric checkers mat. "It's another thing to get kicked out of King's, which has all the connections anyone needs with colleges." Her teeth moved from her lips to her cuticles, making a mouse chewing on rope sort of noise. "People literally pledged themselves to Ned over their country to avoid getting expelled last year. That should say something."

It did.

"I mean, I even said it." Her eyelids glazed. "I did it because it seemed like my dad's health improved when he saw I went to a prestigious school and all, anything to keep the cancer from growing. But now ..."

She sighed and took another sip.

"I know my dad is trying to take this well, saying he knows I didn't do what they accused me of and that he's fine with homeschool, but with his chemo treatments, he can only handle so much. I hope my lack of getting into college doesn't kill him."

Then again it didn't. There was that legacy paper Hannah printed out. July's favorite quote still had a chance.

"King's is going down the tubes." Danny swirled around the remainder of the cinnamon film in his cup. "Give it a couple months, and a recommendation there will be no better than getting an endorsement from a fast-food restaurant."

The way July's eyebrows arched up, like a breaking bridge, indicated she didn't quite believe him.

Rayah tugged at her bandana. "Your parents say anything about taking it to court? You didn't send the tweet, after all."

July shook her head. "It came from my phone. August proved it through the IP voodoo or whatever." Her kinged piece jumped over Rayah's in the right-hand side of the board. "I tried saying maybe someone stole my phone during soccer practice, but August wouldn't buy it. He doesn't know how to operate the campus cameras, so he basically said it wasn't worth seeing if anyone grabbed it from my bag."

Plus there were places on campus where the cameras didn't reach. Danny never recalled seeing any cameras stationed in the locker rooms.

Besides, the story sounded too farfetched. Who would sneak into someone's soccer bag, log into a completely different person's account than the soccer player's, and post a mean tweet? The easiest explanations always won out.

The tune of "Cotton Eyed Joe" filled a momentary silence in the shop. Danny's phone rattled the wooden table before the milk machine screamed again. A number he didn't recognize flashed across the screen.

"Spam?" Rayah frowned at the phone as July stole her last checker.

"Maybe. Should I answer it in my Russian accent?"

His girlfriend pinched the bridge of her nose. "Those poor telemarketers. One of these days, it's going to be a Russian who will get so insulted he'll send Putin after you."

Laughter rippled throughout the group, even July.

Danny raised a fist in the air as he spoke from his throat. "For the homeland." Swiping the phone off the table, he answered in his best imitation of Gru from *Despicable Me.* "Vat do you vant?"

"Danny?" A hoarse voice prickled his ear as Rayah giggled into her palm. It sounded like thunder, weak, crackling, broken thunder.

The smile jabbing up his cheeks sheathed into a thin line. "How did you get this number?"

A high-pitched wheezing replied, "The Russians."

"Ned, I'm going to hang up in two seconds if you don't tell me who gave you my number."

"Ned?" Rayah's eyes went wide.

The other end of the phone died for a few seconds. Then the thunder resurrected. "Danny, will you visit me tomorrow?"

"At the ward? Don't you have a son?" Sons visited their fathers in those types of places, right? At least, that's what he'd seen on his crime show binges.

"Haven't had a visitor since I got here."

Guilt, icy cold, stabbed Danny in the chest. They were on the brink of October, and not even August spared a day for him?

People from church had at least cared to pay him a visit during his low points after his father's death and after the Zai incident. Some were almost strangers.

He goggled at Rayah and July for a moment and leaned back to stay out of earshot. The screaming milk machine didn't help. He rose and left outside into the dying warmth of the September sun.

"You still there?" Ned croaked into the phone. Probably didn't get many minutes. Danny tried to rack his brains for what he remembered from *One Flew Over the Cuckoo's Nest*.

In a softer tone, he replied, "Still here, Ned."

"Will you visit me tomorrow?"

A customer raced with a cardboard drink carrier in her hand, whipped cream spilling out of domed cups. She ducked into a lime-green bug car and sped off. "I don't have a vehicle. Hospital's way out of walking distance."

"Have Ashley take you. Right after school."

Excuse one: shot down. "Don't you guys have strict visiting hours or something? I can't skip class. Teachers have gone crazy with tests before Homecoming week."

"Hence the 'right after school.' You'll have plenty of time."

Excuse two: gone like Donkey Kong.

He could pull out the wild card, the ace of spades of all reasons to get out of events: he didn't want to.

Groaning through his nostrils, he leaned over a metal railing that led down steps to the parking lot. He let the hot metal dig into his palms, bite his skin, like he had the ring around Ned's tree. "Does four thirty tomorrow work?"

"See you then." Three beeps later, the call died.

Ashley's Lexus smelled like a mixture between fast-food French fries and wet garbage. She had to toss a handful of plastic water bottles and a breakfast sandwich wrapper in the back before Danny could slide into shotgun. Could explain the clatter of K-cups on her desk. At least she ironed her clothes.

"I apologize for the mess."

The seat belt made a zipping noise as he plugged it. "You should see my mom's car. Can't even stick your feet on the ground." As he turned to tighten the harness, he saw much of the back floor had a layer of banana peels, La Croix cans, and coupon magazines.

"You like to listen to music?" She dug up an aux cord, sending a paper coffee cup tumbling toward the back. No liquid.

"I have a feeling we won't like the same stuff."

She dug the key into the ignition. "Fair. I'm listening to an audiobook if you don't mind."

"That's fine." He pulled his book bag to his stomach and brushed off a candy wrapper that stuck to it. "Got plenty of homework to do on the ride there."

Ashley pressed the ancient CD button. The speakers muffled to life about a girl finding some man from the Greek Dark Ages in a British museum. At least, what Danny read from the back-cover blurb provided on the back of the CD case.

"Ned didn't ever ask you to come visit?" They seemed close in that picture on the mantel.

The car jerked a little as she swerved to turn left. "Mr. Rezzen had asked, but I was advised to keep my meetings with him to a minimum." Her left hand resumed its spot on the nine position on the clock of the steering wheel. At least, that's what his mother had counseled during Danny's driving lessons. The ring finger was empty.

"By August?"

"If you don't mind, I'd just like to listen to my book, please. I don't get to read often."

Silence got them through a handful of chapters about bloody bathtubs (not in the British sense) and past the scenery of the Pennsylvania countryside. Of trees bleeding orange and red and hills of browning grass tumbling into one another like the rolling creeks they passed. They approached the hospital by chapter three. A squat brick building greeted them after meandering through a path guarded by trees.

"This is the hospital?" Danny squinted at the glare of sunlight shining on the barbed wire looping around a wire fence.

"A mental health and recovery building. The hospital's down the road about ten minutes when you hit a city." She rolled down the window and spoke with a guard stationed at the entrance. After she gave the lady Danny's name, the guard mumbled something into a walkie-talkie on her shoulder. A yellow Security patch was situated right beneath it on the pale-blue uniform.

Ashley's tires rumbled over the loose stone pavement as they rolled to the back of the building to park. No windows or doors led to the rear of the center. Only one door and a handful of glass panes at the front. Smart.

They walked to the entrance and met a woman with a name badge placed on the lapel of her soft pink cardigan.

"Danny Belte to see Mr. Ned Rezzen?"

He stared at the *Psychiatric Services* in metal letters on the front of the building. "That's me." Then to the scraggly bushes planted out front. No flowers, except for a dandelion sprout or two. Maybe this was the place Hannah stayed years ago.

The woman punched a series of numbers at the door. The doors snapped to indicate the locks had disconnected. She swung open a door and had them sign in with a frumpy man with a frown to match. As Danny scribbled his name in red ink, he thought someone would have to pull at the man's face like taffy to get it to sag that way.

They turned to the left where the lady pressed another set of numbers into a keypad. Through the windows, the white on the walls just about blinded Danny. No pictures, no hint of eggshell or even an off-white, just pure, silent snow white enveloped everything.

When the double doors clicked, she led him past the patient check-in desk to the right toward a set of small lockers on the wall. Ashley didn't follow. She wasn't invited.

In the pale light, the acne on the worker's chin and sallow cheeks protruded more than it had at the front desk or outside.

Giving him a combination for locker 45, a tiny locker like the one he had for mail at school, his guide warned him to put all phones, and anything else in his pocket, in the locker in case a flight-risk patient tried to steal an item from him.

What was this? Airport security? Perhaps they'd fly all the way over a cuckoo's nest, or to Babylon.

He banged the metal door shut, recollecting the tiny lockers back at Tagged. Still, a security guard lurking in the corner patted him down after he asked if he was bringing Ned any gifts during visitation time. Gifts? Whoops.

Clean of all potential valuables, he followed his guide into an elevator that went up three floors.

Arrived.

Everything smelled sterile and mechanical, like the nurse's building back at campus. But at least at King's the main nurse seemed nice. All the workers here, bustling in taupe-hued scrubs, seemed as though they had ten years sucked from their lives since they started working. They all had purplish eye bags, sagging chins, glazed lids.

Reaching a room with blue trim—all of the doors had been removed—he read the label painted at the top, Day Room.

They entered. The pastel-green backdrop wall drew Danny's attention right away. A TV hanging in the corner played some rerun of *General Hospital*. A patient or two watched on brown couches underneath the hum of a bright light.

It surprised Danny for some reason that they weren't wearing hospital gowns of some sort. Perhaps measures had changed since *Cuckoo's Nest*.

Three patients, huddled around a small round table, pieced together a puzzle. On the box, a picture of a kitten stared at Danny with cuddle-me eyes. And, at the end of the room, sunken into a bright-green chair, sat a withering Ned. He appeared far more skeletonic than ever before, just like the hand that had flashed on his classroom screen when they watched the video about the bill. Ned had lessened from his football player size to almost that of a cross-country runner, still enough bulk for an in-between.

He perked up when he spotted Danny across the room. His face brightened as his lips forced their way up a scraggly chin. Knotted, the beard had grown quite long since two months prior.

Maybe they didn't let the patients use razors, smart.

A lady they passed, doing the puzzle, muttered something to herself. Something like "fallen, fallen" but too slurred to tell.

"We've brought you a visitor." Lady in the pink cardigan's voice shot up a few octaves. She even pressed her hands onto her knees as if commanding a dog to come to her. "Shall we take him to your room so you have a chance to talk with him?"

Ned's room? Was that normal protocol? He guessed so.

Ned didn't take his eyes off Danny as he nodded. His foot tapped to some indistinct rhythm. The song must've sounded nice to him because he smiled.

As Danny glanced at the brown pattering shoes, he noticed the ward had removed the shoelaces.

Escorted to a room down the hall, once again no door, no one said anything. An occasional cry or moan rang out in the hallway from some far-off door, but the workers appeared to pay no mind.

And he thought working in an ice cream shop was bad enough.

"You'll notice Ned got a room to himself." The lady waved an arm inside, beaming. Voice still skyscraper high. "He's awfully lucky. Most of our patients have roommates, but we kept this one special for him."

Peering in, an elevated bed with the gray sheets tucked firmly into the mattress received his gaze. For some reason, Danny expected to see some sort of restraints strapped onto the bed; once again, no dice, no *Cuckoo*. Whoever built the room positioned a camera in the corner of the yellow wallpapered walls and a chair in the other end of the room. Everything fit tight into the room, just in view of the door. Security guards patrolled the hallways, making another passage by Ned's room as they entered.

Situating himself at the edge of the bed, Ned began tapping his feet again, shoes sliding off his socks because of the lack of laces.

"I'll be back in when your visitation time is up." The woman folded her hands, smile withering into a thin line. Too tired for holding it so long, he bet. Danny shot her a help-me-don't-leave-me-alone-with-him sort of look. She paused and eyed the door as a guard faded in and out of view. "You'll be fine. Just talk, and if you need any entertainment"—a nod over her shoulder—"head to the Day Room to play cards or watch TV."

Her graying bun disappeared behind the blue doorpost to the sound of a moan and Ned's tapping.

"So"—Danny inched toward the door, calmed by the sound of the heel clicks of the guards—"you wanted me to visit you, Ned?"

Ned's glazed eyes met his. "Danny, have you ever had a son before?"

"Not that I can recall, sir."

"Ever held a child in your hands?"

"I've had to wrangle a few toddlers when I helped with the Sunday school classes."

He rubbed his chin, fingers catching in the beard briars. "They're a lot heavier than you would think. When you hold your kid, it feels like you're holding glass. That's what a legacy feels like, glass."

Cupping his palms, he held them out as if grasping at something. "Danny, you ever had a son not visit you in a mental institute?"

Swallowing, the saliva got caught in his cotton throat. "No, sir."

"Feels like what I imagine glass feels like when you knock it off a mantel." He looked up at Danny, jaundice rimming his eyes. "Mead5124."

Flakes of dandruff cascaded from Danny's eyebrows as they furrowed. "I'm sorry, what?"

"Mead5124. Uppercase *M*. Rest lowercase. Use it well."

Without another word, Ned sank back into his bed as he drifted off to sleep.

Chapter Fifteen

"HANNAH, IF YOU'RE GOING TO LET THE BIRD OUT, AT least close the door to the computer room. There's less glass in there."

Danny ducked under Obi's well-aimed swoop as the little blue beast landed on a wooden table by the front door. In a rapid motion, he shut the door before the creature had a chance to escape outside. His eyes took seconds to adjust to the low lighting, but when they did, he puffed a sigh of relief when seeing Obi remained put amongst the forest of glass trees.

"Keep your voice down." Her fingers did a tap dance on a computer nearby. "Remember he can feed off of emotional states."

Well, they probably didn't want him to be severely depressed either, so there, Hannah.

Obi bounced up and down to a silent beat, kind of like Ned had hummed something to himself. Danny kicked off his shoes, peeled off the socks, and let the cool floor embrace the balls of his feet.

Shuffle, ball change went the bird. The keyboard did another number. Step-heel, ball change. He needed to stop watching YouTube videos of *Dancing with the Stars*.

Hannah released a sigh. "Good thing you're not Rayah. She had another panic attack the other day. Think about what it would do to Obi."

His heartbeat thudded. Rayah hadn't mentioned it. Then again, last year he didn't tell her all the times he threw up.

"Glad we never let Michelle over here either." Hannah's eyes glowed a slight red from bloodshot. When did this girl ever sleep? "She's dying for whatever information we have on Ned's computer. Next thing you know, Obi'll work for the *Daily Planet* and hunt down pictures of Spiderman."

"Well, she is a journalist in the making."

"Her parents play the news 24/7 in her house. It just runs constantly and chews up the electricity. No wonder she wants to save the earth."

"What did Michelle say about the document you printed? The legacy thing?" He slid his finger onto the hardwood table and commanded Obi up. The bird tilted his head to the side and bobbled up and down.

"Not good enough. Guess it's not incriminating or can easily be turned over by some lawyer." She huffed above the sound of a whirling ceiling fan. "'Sides, something tells me we have bigger sea creatures to fry."

At last, the bird crawled onto his finger, but not before nudging a scraggly skeletonic elm paper weight to its almost demise. He carried him back to the computer room, book bag tugging at his back.

"What do you mean?" As he stooped to unlock the cage, Obi took flight again, chirping a taunting song. Yeah, yeah.

Hannah faced the computer screen as she scrolled some website with a horrible neon-blue page. "With Bel's attempted suicide and Valentina's witch hunt for July, got a feeling we have to focus on other things than suing Ned."

"Like what?"

"Like the fact that Ned's legacy is shattering." She scraped a rainbow-kaleidoscope paper weight and cradled it in her palm. "When that happens, the whole school shatters with it."

"Put down the glass ball, Han."

"And when that happens, people are going down with him, down in the chaos. That's how the game works."

"OK, agreed, now be nice with the expensive rainbow thing."

"How to win that game is to make sure you don't let them take you down."

She tossed the orb and caught it as if trying out for a great American sport, then set it down and continued to scroll.

His backpack slumped to the floor as he approached the computer.

"Digging up more stuff on Ned?"

"Nah, looking for speech pieces. Season starts in less than a month, and Coach wants me to find something to perform."

With a knuckle, she rubbed at a bleary eye, smudging mascara on her cheek. Danny scanned the room for a seat, legs feeling gelatinous from his quick cross-country sprint. Locating a stool by the bookshelf, he slid it next to Hannah's chair and watched as the neon screen burned his vision. "Going for another one of those sad pieces of death? Or you plan to ruin children's books like you did last year?"

Who could forget about how *Goodnight Moon* turned a bunny suicidal in Hannah's version?

"Actually, I'm going for the humor category. I could use some laughs for a change. That's how you've gotten through all the traumatic stuff that's happened, anyway."

Danny remembered how he left one of the dramatic interpretation rounds quivering after hearing a piece on sexual assault. "This a movie script or something? Hard to tell because you're scrolling so fast."

"Yeah, *Get Smart*. It's a spy movie."

"Seen it. It's pretty funny."

Hannah smudged her cheek, mascara all the way down past her cheekbones. "Since we're snooping on Ned's computer and all, I decided it was a good fit—spies, I mean."

He swallowed, esophagus burning from a lack of water at tryouts.

"You have to boil the whole movie into a ten-minute speech, so gotta be selective about what you perform. Wanted to do James Bond, but it didn't fit into any of the categories. Thought I could do a drunk version of him. Maybe they'd let that slide for humor."

"James Bond?" Bolting out of his stool, he raced to the kitchen for a glass of water. Not H2O. His whole throat felt just like it had been scratched by a shattered paperweight.

"Yeah, the dude drinks all the time. I'm surprised they didn't do a segment on liver poisoning in the last movie."

Opening a sawdust-scented cabinet, he pulled out a glass and clacked it in the sink, turning on the spicket. "Well, they gotta keep the guy alive for another fifty movies at least."

"Then he needs to chill and go for froufrou stuff like *Mike's Hard*."

"You can't perform James Bond for a humor piece, so I don't know why we're having this argument." He swigged the glass, letting the lukewarm water quench his throat. The taste had a hint of metal. "And how do *you* know so much about alcohol?"

Long pause.

"Hannah?"

"I mean, I don't know as much as *some* people, cough, cough, August."

He drained the rest of the glass and went to refill it, finding his voice no longer crackled. "You caught a whiff of the stuff he brings in that water bottle to class?"

Something clapped against the kitchen window that caused him to jump and spill water on the floor. A bird? He reached for a paper towel to wipe up the puddle.

"No." Hannah's fingers tapped against the keyboard again. "Just take a peek inside the cabinets. He's got anything from wines to mead to really dark beers in sketchy bottles."

"Mead?" Something clicked inside his head like a light bulb.

Buzzing wings flashed by his ear before something landed on his head. He hoped Obi liked salty nests from all the cross-country sweat.

"You know, it's like fermented honey or something. Mom says it tastes like sweet wine that's hard to swallow, whatever that means."

Placing his water glass on the counter, he returned to the computer room, a light flashing in his head. "Hannah, when I visited Ned he said something about mead. Like, mead with a bunch of numbers following it."

Eyelids tacked shut, he concentrated.

They flew open. "Fifty-one, twenty-four. I figured he was listing his age and the age of August. At least, that's roughly where they'd be?"

Hannah tugged her hair behind her ear. "Um, what?"

"Mead5124. *M* is capitalized, the rest in lowercase."

"That a password or something?" She logged out of Ned's account and clicked on the icon that read *August* beneath a vector of a beer glass trimmed with foam. "Think it's for August's account?"

The bird shifted on his head, making a chewing noise. He liked to peck at his feathers, weird.

"Ned did talk about his son before telling me it. It's worth a shot. I mean, if not, it'll just think we mistyped or something."

Cracking her knuckles, Hannah flew her black-tinted nails across the keyboard and numbered keypad on the side. A 5124 later, the blue spinning wheel dissolved into a background picture of August with his arm tucked around Bel. This time, they were on a beach, Bel in a red halter bikini, August in Corona-labeled swim trunks with an overcast sky behind him. A blurry seagull flew into the right-hand side of the screen.

Hannah hummed the *Mission Impossible* tune to herself. Stopped after a dun-dun, dun-dun, dun-dun, "Wanna hack all of his accounts and see how he likes it?" dun-dun, dun-dun, dun-dun, dun-dun, dun-dun. Buh-duh-duh. Buh-duh-duh.

As always with Hannah, she got way into her speech pieces.

He slumped onto the stool again, balancing the bird on his head. The gnawing sounds had grown louder. "Maybe don't post as him. That would sort of give away who did it since no one else bird sits for him."

And since he knew about IP tracking and all now ...

Ignoring him, Hannah nudged the mouse onto the Internet browser and pulled up Twitter. "Let's at least see if he's been DMing anyone. That's a start. We'll work our way through all his accounts."

The arrow pressed the envelope icon as she searched through the names starting with *B*. When she reached Bel, she whistled low. Obi paused to try and imitate the din.

"This is extensive."

"He has his arm wrapped around her in skimpy clothes on his computer screen, of course it's extensive."

"Let's scroll to the most recent convo. Looks like they last talked the first day of school. The day she ... you know. Ring any bells?"

They read from the start of the conversation at 8:09 a.m.

> @thebelsthebelsthebels: Augs, why won't you answer your phone? Been trying to get ahold of you.

> @meadmiser:

Danny paused. "Meadmiser? What the heck?"

Hannah shrugged, shoulders scrunching the fabric in her rolling chair. "Maybe it's his favorite kind of drink. It's hard to get an original username on Twitter, you know."

He did. Apparently @dannyintheden was already taken. Had to add some numbers to keep it original, @dannyintheden456.

He squinted at August's username again. "I don't think Rezzen is that common of a last name."

"OK, he just got out of college. 'Course he's gonna be obsessed with alcohol. Keep reading."

He did so above the loud racket of Obi chewing on his feathers. Got a little bit of Danny's hair, too, as he tugged.

> @meadmiser: The cell service is crap at this school. You know that.

> @thebelsthebelsthebels: For a week straight? Come on, Augs. Talk to me.

> @meadmiser: About what? Sorry I couldn't make it to the ultrasound yesterday. Things have been busy, and Dad's not handling the divorce well at all.

> @thebelsthebelsthebels: Or the ultrasound before that. Or the one before that?

> @meadmiser: Sure. Didn't see Dean at any of them either.

> @thebelsthebelsthebels: You know he's not the father.

Guilt twanged in Danny's gut. How did Michelle do this on a regular basis? Sneak around to find information? Heck, how did Bond or any other spy manage it? Heat surged to his cheeks as he leaned back, forgetting the stool had no support for his spine.

"Hannah, maybe we should stop reading. This feels wrong."

"You would think removing a pillow tag is a capital crime. Keep going."

@meadmiser: Last time I checked, you guys slept together close to the due date.

@thebelsthebelsthebels: Two months removed, unless I was having a preemie. Since we're about to hit month eight, I think not.

@meadmiser: Does Dean know?

"Should we? Where do we draw the line?" Perhaps Reuben had been right. King's Academy absorbed them. Any further, and could they call themselves Emmanuel students anymore?

Hannah growled. "Never been a fan of those things, lines. People have no problem crossing mine, so why stop now?"

Smacking noises from the bird filled the room along with the hum of the computer.

"Think about Bel, Han."

"Yes, think about her and about July. We can't help them unless we read."

So they did.

@thebelsthebelsthebels: I think he thinks he's the dad. Never been great at math. Poor guy's dad thrashed him when he failed his Pre-Calc class.

@meadmiser: And?

@thebelsthebelsthebels: He told me to avoid him. Didn't want to spoil anything he had going with Julia, or whoever he's placing socks on doors for now.

@thebelsthebelsthebels: Augs, what are we gonna do? I have class with you later. Is this going to be weird?

@thebelsthebelsthebels: Augs?

@meadmiser: Sigh. Bel, I think it's best if you avoid me too. With the whole Enlil thing, it's going to look really bad if a teacher slept with a student, even if I wasn't a teacher at the time. It's the last thing my dad needs. He's already suicidal.

@thebelsthebelsthebels: Come on.

@meadmiser: Listen, you don't know how stressful it is to get a job after college. I'm lucky my dad runs a school, but I've had friends submit as many as 200 job applications. I don't want to be barred from every school at 24.

@thebelsthebelsthebels: It's your freaking baby. You're just going to act like I'm a student you've never met in your class?

@meadmiser: It's not my baby.

Hannah exited out of the chat and typed in Bel's profile. "Blocked her, typical."

Something wet oozed onto Danny's temple. He swiped at it and his fingers glistened with scarlet. "Am I bleeding?"

Hannah squinted at him. "Obi is."

Jabbing her finger into his hair, she waited for the bird to climb on it. The rev of its wings flapping sent spatters of blood across the room, hitting the printer and computer screen. Danny's heart thundered in his ears.

"I heard flour helps stem the flow." Hannah's face darkened as she stroked Obi with her free hand. "Think we should try that?"

"Something tells me he doesn't have a lot of blood to give. I'm going to call August." Instructions he left on the fridge mentioned something about a blood feather.

Pulling his phone out of his athletic shorts, he wiped the screen of sweat and dialed. Two rings later, a deep voice answered. "Yello?"

"Bad news, August, Obi's bleeding everywhere. I think he must've bitten a vein in his wing."

Breathing sounded on the other end. "Did you let him out of his cage?"

Ice filled his chest. "Just now to hold him and make sure he didn't injure himself. He likes to bang against the bars." He rose to slam each of the doors to the room shut. "Don't worry. We quarantined ourselves in. He won't fly into any other place in the house."

"On my way. Be over in five. We gotta get him to the vet. Have Hannah grab flour and try to clot the bleeding."

"Got it." The hang-up tone beeped before he got through the last word. He swung open a door and dashed for the kitchen. Veering into the pantry, he groped past several glass bottles full of dark-brown liquid to locate a small flour bag buried in the back. Everything smelled of alcohol.

By habit, he checked the expiration date on the bag. The average age of a food item at his house was two months past due. Shaking his head to clear his thoughts, he reached in and grabbed a handful of flour. As he rushed to the computer room, it trailed behind him like snow.

Red streaks ran down Hannah's pale hand. She knelt as he brought the powder and tried to press it into the wing/armpit area, the source of the bleeding, best he could. Didn't help that the little guy squirmed around, causing more scarlet to drip down the blue body. Flour flakes littered the carpet, coating his knees and half the bird.

"Think it did anything, Han?"

"Keep pressing. We're not letting an animal die on our watch."

He bit back a comment about how they were one flour coating away from being able to fry little Obi up and serve him in a bucket.

Minutes passed. At last, the front door banged open as the clunk of August's shoes deadened on the carpet. His knees cracked as he knelt to inspect the patient covered in a white film. As Hannah passed it off to him like a baton, heat flushed in Danny's cheeks from the ring of powder left in the kitchen and carpet. He retrieved a Swiffer and swabbed the floor with one swerve of the arm. Returning to the room with the vacuum, he saw August had already retrieved Obi's cage with his free hand.

"I'm taking him to the vet, but I think the flour clotted the bleeding for now." He panted, sweat glistening on his large forehead and in his red beard. "I'll have to ask you two to leave. We don't feel safe with anyone in the house other than for cleaning and pet-sitting purposes."

Danny glanced at the vacuum and then to the coat of flour on the floor. "I'll just take a minute or two."

"No, please, let me do it when I get back home. I must insist you leave."

Feeling useless, he shielded his back with his bag and shoved his hands into his pockets and followed Hannah out the door, August not far behind. The jangling of keys jolted his heart a little. Perhaps it was habit for him to lock and unlock the doors in the late evening and early morning. All he knew was that he came to an unlocked house every morning.

No sooner had they reached a sidewalk that led to the King's entrance than they heard the purr of an engine and shriek of wheels spinning off a driveway. The car zoomed with impressive speed, much faster than the allotted fifteen mph for the school zone.

They traversed in silence as the weak September sun died in orange on the horizon. Give it a couple of months, and by five, a dark shroud would have covered campus. Air smelled nice, though, like wet leaves and dwindling warmth. He inhaled it deeply and hoped the bird would turn out all right at the vet's office.

Sounds returned as they did to campus. A scoreboard blared in the direction of the football field and the smell of donuts wafted nearby from some school club fundraiser. If only he had ten dollars to spare.

Upon reaching Suanna, Hannah dug around her tattered bag for her keycard. Already lost the thing twice that semester. Lipstick cartridges and pens rummaged against each other as her hand bulged from one end to the other.

She stopped and chewed on her lip so hard Danny thought she would bleed like Obi.

"What's the matter? You need Michelle to key you into the building again?"

Her large orange hair tussled in the glow of the faded sun. "It's not that."

"What?"

"Dan, we left the computer on in August's house, logged into his account."

Chapter Sixteen

ZAI: Thanks for sticking up for me today, man.

DANNY: There's lots of trolls out there. I'm sorry for what they said about your mom.

ZAI: Me too, but there's no way they could know. I think one of them lives in China, not exactly Washington County.

DANNY: I think I know what you mean about words being able to give people life or destroy it.

ZAI: Yeah, I'm sorry to hear your dad isn't doing well.

DANNY: Me too. That's why I've been posting so many encouraging things. I don't want anyone else to feel this way or the way you felt earlier today.

ZAI: I appreciate it.

ZAI: I just wish I could say the words to help your dad feel alive again.

DANNY: You know, I think we all wish that. But you keep posting, man. Something tells me you've already saved lives.

"What did you put down for number ten?"

Danny slid his Arabic test on the table at the front of the room. Mr. Parsin licked his thumb as he turned the page of a book with a yellow fabric binding. Returning to his seat, Danny clicked a pen on the rough wooden surface, carved by knives with initials of previous classmates' crushes.

"Couldn't have asked me until I sat down, Reuben? We're not supposed to talk about the test."

Reuben rolled his eyes. "There's only two of us in this class." For a brief moment, he observed a desk with the bottom silver legs rusting, July's preferred place. "I'm sure Mr. Parsin doesn't mind if we ask questions *after* we took it. Now, number ten?"

Sighing, he rubbed the bridge of his nose as a headache loomed at the front of his brain. Anxiety meds were beginning to weaken. "That the one with the plural versus dual verbs?"

Reuben nodded.

"Always get that one mixed up. I went for dual."

Nostril flare. "Really? I put down plural."

"Guess we have a fifty-fifty chance then."

A giggle erupted from the hallway behind them. Why did Mr. Parsin always leave the door open? The desk groaned as he lifted himself from it to shut the door. Approaching the hallway, he paused as the Homecoming banner seemed to wave at him as it dangled halfway off the wall. It let out a half-hearted flutter as the vents in the hallway blew on it.

The bang from the door shutting boomed in his ears. Returning, he dug through his bag to find some extra homework to complete. Had that test in AP Language, might as well go over the study guide for *One Flew Over*.

His hand met a bent packet of papers he always forgot to stuff into the purple English folder. Unraveling it and ignoring the scent of crushed-up granola bars from his book bag, he scanned through the papers.

ONE FLEW OVER STUDY GUIDE (It's *crazy* important that you remember these items)

Ah, at least his English teacher this time around had a sense of humor.

I. Names to Know and Describe—Briefly explain each of the characters listed below. Give examples from the book about their importance. Specific page numbers will earn bonus points.

    a. Chief Bromden

    b. Nurse Ratched

    c. McMurphy

Ah, he knew these; better skip to the symbolism section.

II. Explain the following symbols (short answer)

    a. Fog

    b. Rabbits versus the wolves (the patients versus the doctors)

Eh, who was he kidding? He could point at a symbol while asleep. There was, of course, that one time with the computer image of Ned. Oh, Ned. Ned in a psych ward like *Cuckoos*. Not fantastic to think about that. Or poor Bel for that matter. Essays, how about those?

III. Essays—Answer two of the following three.

    a. Nurse Ratched is by far the least likeable character of this novel. She manipulates, tortures, and even leaves some of her patients brain-dead. Explain to me her redeemable features/aspects? After all, no villain is entirely all-bad. And no hero all-good.

Tricky; still, how could he see the good in someone who only brought about bad situations?

Then again, some Emmanuel students had elements of King's ones. Reuben not standing up for July when Valentina convinced August to oust her, Danny and Hannah sneaking onto August's computer.

And King's students had pinches of Emmanuel. Duke with late-night talks where they'd split Zebra Cakes. Valentina with her enthusiasm at the soup kitchen—never saw someone so excited to get up at 6:00 a.m. to serve cream of mushroom to the homeless.

Heck, even Dean, last year, giving Duke a ginger ale to hand to him during one of Danny's many sicknesses. Turned out to be real ale, and made him throw up even more, but perhaps in some sick way, Dean meant well.

With parents like his, apples never fell far. With the bruises and shouting matches Dean would bring back to the room with him like battle scars, Danny often wondered if perhaps Dean's apple tasted sweeter than the rest of his family.

And of course, there was Ned, the embodiment of King's, now jaundiced and withering away like Emmanuel.

Perhaps people didn't fit into King's and Emmanuel. Perhaps people were just meant to be people.

He skipped down to the next two essays. The first, a boring analysis of the plot progression from beginning to end. That would take far more effort than number one, and he had to answer two of three.

No, he'd have to do the first one. Something clawed at his abdomen, like a lion threatening to tear him inside out if he didn't answer the Ratched essay.

Again, the image of Ned collapsing on his bed, withering on the spot, polluted his mind. Why couldn't he burn it out of his brain?

It had been easy to see the bad in him before, but at the hospital, he had thought his looks finally caught up to the rest of his inside.

Three nice things about Ned. If he could do this, he could imagine some good in the hyper-organized nurse Ratched who liked to send lightning bolts into the brains of her patients.

1. Ned was organized

A stupid reason, he knew. But after living in a dorm that stank of beer and weed the past year, tripping over crumples of paper towels to get to his bed, he'd take it.

2. Ned cared about his kid

Which made the lack of visitation from August all the harder. A lump formed in his throat as he thought about the number of times he'd visited his mother his freshman year. Even at home, he clamored to escape the house. If they sent her to a hospital, would he have dropped in?

3. Ned gave him the clue about Bel

The real reason she attempted suicide, not some stupid Twitter post, but because August refused to claim his baby as his. Did August do that with all his family members? Knock them over like glass fixtures on the mantel?

A fist nudged his arm. He jolted as Reuben motioned to the clock. "We have two minutes before the bell rings."

"Thanks." Danny stooped over the side of his desk to stuff his packet into his bag. Two bright-pink Converse tapped in the hallway. Valentina had a free period and liked to walk Reuben from his Arabic class. "Uh, Reuben."

"Uh, Danny?" He imitated Danny's whisper. "Why are you talking in a quiet voice?"

"Listen, I need to talk to you about July before ... I know your girlfriend likes to bring it up when you walk from this class."

He exhaled through his nostrils. "Rayah already talked to me about what you found at Ned's house. Look, I believe you, but have you ever tried to tell your girlfriend she was wrong? Might as well strap a target to your chest now."

Fair.

"A student got wrongly expelled. Your *friend,* who you've known since kindergarten at Emmanuel, got wrongly expelled. Doesn't that mean anything to you?"

He swung a gray strap onto one shoulder. "What do you want me to do?"

"I—I don't know. Tell her to call off the witch hunt? She's digging into other social media accounts, you know. In fact, she confronted Michelle the other day about a post that was too homophobic."

"So?"

"It was an article about a Chick-fil-A sale."

"Valentina doesn't like that company."

He leaned in, spit flying off his lips. "How long until she reports you to the principal? Or me? Or anyone with a hint of different ideas than her? I know how much you post, bro. She's bound to disagree sometime."

Reuben clenched his jaw and glanced down at the Emmanuel logo on Danny's T-shirt. "See you at the football game, OK?"

A bell gonged as Reuben raced out the door, fingers lacing with Valentina's ready hand.

Halftime.

Mede Media's, the rival school, marching band played to the theme of Kingdoms. Danny didn't recognize most of the tunes, so Hannah had to list them off as the Mede color guard waved red, white, and green flags.

"So, they just played something from *Game of Thrones*, and what's this one?" She leaned forward in her hard metal seat as a passerby spilled popcorn on the dark steps. "Ah, *Prince of Persia*. Mazda, that's obscure."

The song concluded on a drumroll and a toss of the flags. One of the girls missed and had to drop to her knees to catch it. October fourth, she still had plenty of time to perfect the routine.

"You won't miss Homecoming tomorrow for a speech tournament?" Danny shuffled in his seat, the cold metal biting into his backside.

She shivered, leaning into Michelle for warmth. "Not until November. Duke was worried about that too. I promised him I'd wear that cute little red dress on our next date if I couldn't make the dance."

"The one with the sparkles and stuff? Didn't you already wear it to class?" Then again, she once wore a moose onesie to class. Hannah was never one to shy away from weird.

All decked out in glittering gold and scarlet, the King's Academy marching band flounced to the center field. Feathery plumes on their helmets rustled in the swift night wind.

Hannah blew into her fingerless-gloved hands. "Laundry day is rough in Suanna. Half the washers have collected enough mold to start a cheese business. Smells like it too."

A trumpet blared the start to the *Mission Impossible* theme. He and Hannah shared a wary look before they turned their attention back to the field. Instead of carrying flags, the color guard waved prop rifles in slit dresses.

Not one of the girls could tip a scale at 120 pounds.

Rayah, on his left side, burrowed herself into him. Tearing off his hoodie, he handed it to her as a freezing breeze chilled through his long-sleeve shirt. October knew its entrance. At least it had Halloween for good ol' Hannah.

During a pause in the music, Danny's stomach imitated the sound of a whale mating call. He clutched at his burning abdomen and shivered once more. "Hey, Ray, want me to grab you something at concessions?"

She buried herself deeper into him, turtling herself into the hoodie. "No. Sooo warm."

"You can walk with me if you want, get that blood pumping."

Agreeing, they rose as the music transitioned to the *Pink Panther* theme. The color guard grabbed pink twirlers and formed spiral-shaped patterns in the air. Danny and Rayah found a snaking line around a small shack near the restrooms. Pretzel and nacho cheese scents intoxicated him for a moment. Everything went all fuzzy in his vision and balance. When was the last time he ate?

"Too bad all meal options have meat." Rayah motioned to a menu behind one of the student workers. Half the red letters had faded to a dark brown or were missing.

"You eat meat."

"But you're a vegetarian."

A trombone behind him blurped to the *Get Smart* theme. Something tugged at his shoulder. He whipped around to find a sheepish Reuben buried deep into a hoodie himself, a red one instead of Rayah's blue.

"Can we talk?" His low voice barely rumbled above the *buh-buh-dum-bah!* of the trumpet.

"Last time I checked, our vocal cords are still working."

The whites of Reuben's eyes showed for a moment. "I talked to Valentina today, about the July thing." He nudged his knee forward along with the line. "She was talking about reporting a student for sharing a pro-life article, so I brought up what you found at Ned's house."

"You want a pretzel, Dan?" Rayah squeezed his hand.

"Wha-yeah, sure." Back to Reuben. "How'd she take it?"

They scooted to the side as his girlfriend ordered a pretzel for each of them. He slipped a five into her fingertips before Reuben whispered his answer.

"Said to drop it or she'd drop me, from Homecoming, dating her, everything."

He whistled low as the band blasted a loud note, color guard switching to grab fedoras and trench coats. "That escalated fast."

Reuben rubbed the back of his neck. "This wasn't actually the first time for me to bring it up. I've known July since kindergarten, as you know. I mean, all of us who went to Emmanuel knew everyone." He sighed as a guitar strummed the James Bond theme in a sloppy chord progression, Mede and Mead indeed. "This was the first time I brought up the stuff you found on August's account, though."

"So, you dropped it right after she threatened you? Thanks, Ray." He bit into the pretzel, finding that without the salt, it would taste remarkably like wood. But he was hungry.

Cringing, Reuben shook his head.

"You didn't?"

His eyelids crinkled so much they got lost in the darkness. "You know me, Dan. I like to debate, like your friend Michelle. But yeah, she said she had a backup date for Homecoming, so that's that, I guess."

They approached the fence as the band formed the shape of a pistol, "blasting" out a tuba player who finished with a low, somber note. It sounded almost odd and out of place, like a sudden death of tune. As Danny recalled his cross-country runs, the band usually played another number: *Kingsman.*

As the band and flag corps dispersed, August approached the center of the field with a microphone in hand. His pinstriped suit formed illusions of waves in the field lights.

"Thank you once again to the bands and flag corps of both teams. Let's give them a hand, folks."

Half-hearted applause declared from the stands. Meanwhile, a group of students trailed behind August in two lines, one girls, the other boys. Roses adorned the lapels of suits and the arms of the girls in sparkling dresses.

"I am pleased to announce the Homecoming Court for King's Academy. We ask that the parents and spectators hold all applause until the very end."

Several photographers grappled the fence, shoving aside Danny and his friends enough for him to get a view of the scoreboard. They were losing by five touchdowns to Mede Media.

"Thought we weren't supposed to lose the Homecoming game." He nudged Rayah, who had cheese sauce spilling out of the left part of her lip.

"We aren't. They often will choose the weakest team for us to face for this game."

"For our Homecoming Court, I will read the following names and grade of the winners of this year's voting. Freshmen Isaiah Abeno and Deborah Reynolds—"

A cowbell sounded from the stands. Well, it *wasn't* applause. Isaiah marched to the front where Ashley hung a sash over his shoulder. Deborah, a bald student in a sequin silver dress, bowed as she received hers.

"Sophomores Timothy Cape, Josie Panthera, Ben Transvaal ..."

Danny nudged into Reuben when Rayah bumped into him. She muttered an apology and jerked her head at the photographer who needed more space to the left. The three backed up into a patch of large rocks on a grassy island between the concessions stand and the field.

"You know, Reuben"—Danny's knees cracked as he perched on the rock—"you could always just come to Homecoming with us since you paid for the ticket and all. We know plenty of girls who are going alone."

He settled on the slope that led to the fence, now swarming with photographers and cheering parents. "I know. Actually, bought off a ticket from one of those girls to take someone last minute, since ticket sales ended a week ago and whatnot."

"Oh, really? Who are you taking?"

"Juniors Remington Musk, Annabelle Ruger, and Seniors Travis Savage, Skyler Weatherby. That concludes our Homecoming Court. Now for the duke and duchess, from the sophomore class."

A shadow hovered over Danny as Hannah peeked out from her cloak she'd bought at a Renaissance faire over the summer and thrust out a fingerless-gloved hand. "You got any cash left over from concessions?"

"Umm, yes? Also, how were you cold in the stands with that big thing on you?"

The microphone shrieked from the feedback as the scoreboard blinked on and off, King's score switching from 14, to 7, to 6, to zero. Then something that looked like a fist with thumbs up. Somewhat resembling a skeletonic hand, as much as it could with the limited lighting in the scoreboard. Then back to fourteen as the lights stopped flickering on the field.

Just like the projector flashing strange images in his government class. Wasn't there a hand on that screen as well?

"Technical difficulties, we apologize, folks. As I was saying, for duchess of the sophomore class, Tula Mossberg."

Hannah pulled her cloak tight against her skin, showing off her ruler-shaped figure. "Look at me. I got no body fat. That's how I'm freezing in this. Now will you give me any cash to try to build up my lipid count?"

He agreed and dug out a wad of two ones from his pocket. "Go get yourself a nice bag of popcorn, kid."

The cloak flew as Hannah sped toward the thinning line at concessions. His stomach rumbled once more, abdomen burning, and he wondered if he should hop up there with her to grab another pretzel. Only had so much cash, though, since August paid them in checks for bird sitting.

But by fall break, oh boy, he and Rayah would take on the town with laser tag dates. That is, if she didn't get a panic attack every other day. At least she liked ice cream all right.

"For the junior class prince and princess." Only one boy approached with a gap in the line between the duchess and soon-to-be queen. "Prince goes to Gabe Adams!"

Danny whooped and pumped a fist. "Didn't tell me he was running. Couldn't even tell who he was from back here and with those bright lights." But now as he squinted, he saw the flash of white hair as it stooped to receive a sash.

"For junior class princess." August swallowed, the noise picking up in the microphone. "July Jackson."

"Someone call my name?"

The girl with a large Afro pinned back by a headband wavered by Reuben's side. She parked beside him.

Danny's lips quirked into a smile. "Yeah, they voted you princess, I guess."

August cleared his throat, white teeth a blur in the stadium lights. "However, Miss July has been disqualified from her position as she no longer attends King's. Of course, voting closed long before that, so we will announce a runner-up tomorrow when Ashley Penaz has a chance to retally the votes. For Homecoming king, Dean Chahal."

The beefy ex-roommate sauntered to the sideline to receive his sash. His cheeks appeared more pink than usual.

"Nice to see you, July." Danny nodded at her from the rock as Rayah gave her a hug.

"You'll actually be able to see me tomorrow when we have lights and stuff." Her hand waved wildly in the darkness, perhaps to swat at the moths and mosquitoes that swarmed.

"Tomorrow?"

Reuben twisted around, hand inching behind July, like Ned's had in the picture with Ashley. "Danny, meet my Homecoming date for tomorrow."

"For Homecoming queen: Valentina Inanna."

A pink bob hovered above a pale-blue dress that shimmered in the lights and clung a bit too tight to Valentina's skin. As she approached Ashley, she didn't bend or dip her head. Good thing she was short.

White sash emblazoned across her chest, she turned in Danny's direction to pitch a glare he could spy even from that far back. Not at him, down a ways, at Reuben. Through the grit-tooth smile and orange-thick foundation, everything about the narrowed eyebrows and squinched eyelids read: You're next, kid.

What the next was, Danny didn't know, which scared him all the more.

Chapter Seventeen

"I DON'T KNOW IF I WANT TO GO TO THIS."

Reuben straightened his pink bow tie in the clouded mirror situated by the door. The room sounded empty with the box fan no longer running, stuffed somewhere into Duke's closet. Occasional toilet flushes from the hallway filled the silence of the room along with the noises of zippers flying up pants and silky ties looping around fingertips.

"Why not?" Danny fiddled with the buttons on his oxford. He'd started from the bottom wrong. "Rayah said July already got here. They're getting ready in Suanna now."

"Had a really creepy dream last night."

"Me, too. You think it was a full moon? That's when I get the strangest ones."

Duke bumped into the closet as he forced a worn dress shoe onto his left foot. He backed up into the wall where a window should've been if the builders had made the place proper. Reuben released his bow tie, and it slanted at an angle again like a pink knife sticking out of his neck. "Saw the moon at the football game last night, not even close to full."

"Walk me through your dream, then. Was it at Homecoming?"

Not quite. As Reuben set the scene, he transported them to the gymnasium vacated just after the dance. A single light blinked while the rest deadened in the darkness. Tiptoeing toward the center of the floor, he spotted a tree sprouting just under the light, like the olive by the ex-garden. Much of its skin had paled, leaving behind white skeletonic branches that flaked onto the smooth floor.

In the strobing of the light, something felt off about the sign that read *WELCOME TO THE DEN* in the fan section of the wall. It oozed with blood.

A foul stench filled his nose. Formaldehyde from frog dissections? It was coming from the tree that now also bled, liquid pooling at his feet. It felt warm and sticky. He wasn't wearing shoes.

Hot, now, the liquid snaked up his legs. Doing so, it traced his veins. He tried to move, failed. Stuck on the spot, he gasped as the lava-hot fluid reached his neck, choking him, liquefying the tree until it disintegrated into a heap of smoke and ash at his feet.

The letters on the wall transformed from *WELCOME TO THE DEN* to *WELCOME TO DEATH*. Once, twice, the lights flickered to the sound of a bang, like a cross-country pistol.

And then darkness, the dream had ended.

Dagon, Danny's nails bit into his hands. How in the world did they have the same dream?

Unclenching his fists, he swallowed. Not entirely impossible—Jeremy had done dream research for one of his books and mentioned people could share dreams, especially close friends who shared an emotional bond.

He dug his teeth into his bottom lip. But Reuben was not a close friend, not yet.

Duke was combing out his hair with gel. "I mean, it sounds creepy. But we've all had our fair share of nightmares. You aren't seriously avoiding the dance because of a dream?"

"You don't get how real everything looked, felt. I could even smell stuff and feel heat. That's not normal in dreams." Reuben tore off the pink bow tie and tossed it in the direction of Danny, who just placed the last button. "How about you? What was your dream about?"

Avoiding eye contact, he fiddled with the spaghetti laces on his shoes. "Hannah was chasing me around with scissors screaming, '*Do try this at home!*'"

Laughter crackled in Duke's throat as he shrugged off the jacket. Still too hot in the dorm for that, even in October. "That's my girl. You sure it didn't happen in real life?"

"I'm sure it did."

Reuben raised his wristwatch to eye level. "Any word from the girls?"

Danny shot them a text and waited as Duke described the list of items Hannah had chased him with, which included a plastic lightsaber, a Nerf gun, a toy battle ax from her brothers, and a stuffed dinosaur with fuzzy horns jutting out of its head.

"Last one sounds out of place." Reuben flipped open his laptop and straightened a book that tilted on the shelf above him.

"Yeah, and to add insult, the pachycephalosaurus ate plants. A vegetarian! She made me do several loops around Phrat River thinking it was some carnivore."

A *bing* alerted Danny to his phone.

"Michelle says to give them, like, ten more minutes. So, we gonna show up in half an hour?"

"Sounds about right." Reuben's fingers raced against his keyboard. "To kill some time, shall we see if I got any more hate mail from Twitter today?"

Danny slumped onto his bed and inhaled his pine-scented cologne to avoid the mattress stench. Even without the heat stroke from summer and the litter from Dean last year, the room wouldn't be featured on a Febreze commercial.

"Five new messages."

Sighing, and wrinkling his nose from a perfume headache, Danny stumbled out of bed to shut the laptop. "OK, don't do that today, Reuben, not on Homecoming."

"@catlover40404 says, 'Way to be a misogynistic ...' name I won't pronounce since I went to Emmanuel. 'Hope you burn.'"

Danny's fingers grasped the lid. Reuben jerked his arm forward and clamped his hand around his wrist. "@lioness4lifffe says, 'Wow. You seriously think you can understand what a depressed pregnant girl was going through? Look at the tweets, the facts. I hope King's expels you like it did that ...' another name I won't pronounce."

"I just thought of something." Duke peered at the top bunk boards, carving into the wood with his fingernail. "August and Bel had been dating when I got a scholarship to attend here. They'd been going strong since my freshman year. You don't think Ned gave a job to my dad and to me because they were dating."

In that moment, Danny decided thinking was the most dangerous of sports.

"Tell you what I think." He released his grip from Reuben's laptop and straightened his green tie in the mirror. "I think we should go to Suanna early, meet up with Michelle's boyfriend, bring a deck of cards to avoid his discussions about his books, and save the thinking for tomorrow."

They all thought it was a grand idea.

"What is with you and games that have to do with luck?" Jeremy slumped into a seat, goggling at a water stain in the ceiling in the shape of a *K*. "For once let's play euchre and get some strategy going."

"A) Euchre requires maximum of four players." Danny nodded at Hannah, who cuddled with Duke on a couch nearby, red dress leaking sparkles all over his suit and the carpet. "And B) what's wrong with Suicide King? Hannah loves this game."

Jeremy snapped in half and raised his eyebrows, as if to indicate that the second reason gave enough grounds to quit something right away. "Let's start with the name."

"Fine, let's go for something more politically correct, Sleeping King."

Hannah growled and shuffled her position, hooking her head into Duke's neck. "That makes no sense. They call the game Suicide King because whoever gets the king of hearts loses. They commit suicide."

She grabbed the deck and pilfered through the cards. When she found the king of hearts, she flashed it at the group. The king's right arm cradled white fuzz on his robe while the left drove a sword into his temple. "Does it look like he's tickling his head with that sword?"

Slumping his arms over his pale-blue suit jacket, Jeremy hmphed. "Fine, I'll teach Duke and Reuben how to play three-man euchre. They look eager to change the game, especially Reuben."

Couldn't blame him. He'd drawn the suicide king twice in three rounds. With that dream and all, WELCOME TO DEATH, Danny could see them wanting to play something happier and less morbid than

Suicide King or Exploding Kittens, which Jeremy had brought. Twitter DMs didn't help.

"Fine." Hannah rose and showered Duke with sparkles. "Danny and I will take our party over here."

In ruby-red slippers, like the ones in *Wizard of Oz*, except more daggerlike, she strutted to the other side of the Suanna lobby. Overwhelming perfumes, all citrusy and acrid, stunned Danny as he stumbled into a seat underneath a hanging TV. Concrete stairwells echoed with the sound of ringing laughter and the swoosh of dresses. His brain bobbled in a watery skull for a moment, in that odd thin line that divides dreams and reality.

"Forget to take your anxiety meds today?" Hannah sent red snow onto a green chair. Christmas two months early. "You look pale."

"Hannah, have you ever had the same dream as someone else?"

She leaned back, translucent petal sleeves sliding down her thin shoulders. "Can't say that I have. Fascinated by dreams, though. I make sure to write down all my nightmares."

"Because I think Reuben and I had the same dream last night."

With a few removed details.

For instance, instead of a tree at the center of the gym floor, Danny found a bird. Somewhat like Obi with the blue and black feathers, but with reddish eyes. It, too, exploded into powdery ash when the hot blood drowned it. And Danny also felt the fiery touch of the snaking liquid. But instead of *WELCOME TO DEATH*, the oozing letters read *WELCOME TO THE END*.

He observed Hannah's reaction as he explained the dream. To his lack of shock, not much about her features changed. Her cheeks did blanch a little, but he attributed this to her pale complexion.

At last, she folded her hands in her lap, covering them in scarlet sparkles. "Dreams are dangerous things."

"You think it means something?"

"I think"—she drew in a long breath as laughter sang in the stairwell again—"you should stick to reality. We already have enough to deal with there, let alone focusing on things that happen while we sleep."

A loud clump filled the concrete walls near the lobby entrance, followed by a "Whoops!" from Michelle. "Didn't mean to bump into you, Ray. This long fabric makes me trip."

Michelle emerged in a long silvery dress that clung to all her curves. Unlike most of the Homecoming styles, she stuck to something floor-length and with no jewels crusted around the breast area.

Rayah and July followed seconds later. July scanned the lobby, and when she located her date, her golden dress and jeweled headband flounced with her. With no time to coordinate with the last-minute ticket change, she and her date wouldn't match, but no one seemed to care.

Bolting from his seat, all the strange confabulations of Danny's brain withered into an ecstasy he could only describe as a bright light in his head and chest. The deep-green dress, the color of all gardens, and trees, and good things in the world, blossomed at her hips like an upside-down flower. As always, it had a modest cut, perhaps from her mother's insistence. But Rayah, on many occasions, asserted she'd fit better in a timeframe fifty or sixty years prior. "Without all the blatant, horrible racism, of course."

He reached for her hand and noticed she'd even tipped the fingernails in an emerald-green polish. "How do you manage to outdo yourself every time?"

She twirled, letting the skirt puff out. "Just happy that no one is trying to murder me at this dance."

Saliva caught in his throat, chest tight, as he moved back to his seat to grab the plastic case with the corsage his mother sent in the mail. Even sticking it in the mini fridge in their room failed to prevent brown from reaching the ends of the pale-yellow roses. He slipped it onto her wrist and pretended to be pained as she jabbed the pin for the boutonniere into his lapel.

"Oh stop that." She gave a playful tap to the other side of his chest. "You know I'm scared of hurting anyone."

A giggle burbled in her throat. Then her smile disappeared. She clutched at her chest and fell to her knees, ragged breaths trailing from her purple-stained lips.

"Rayah?" Danny lunged onto the ground beside her. "Can you breathe?"

The bodice of the dress did cling tightly to her skin. Red sparkles tumbled over Rayah's back as Hannah reached for the zipper and pulled it down halfway. Rayah's gasps came in and out more drawn, but the breathing never slowed.

"Another panic attack?"

She nodded, a tear muddied by mascara trailing down her cheek. Hannah stepped back to give her some air as Danny palmed her back, making sure he was still touching fabric. He lowered his voice, just as he had done to Obi.

"Everything's going to be OK. Is it about the dance last year?"

Sweat dribbled from her face as she nodded. He reached for her hand, which had grown clammy and cold. Reassurances raced through his mind, but those didn't help last year. He had told her Ned wouldn't hurt her.

"He's locked up in a psych ward." He rubbed his thumb against her back. His father used to do that when he was a kid to comfort him. "Can't get out. Doors are locked and—" No windows, just like Suanna. Best not to remind her of the fire. "And he retired. No way Ned can get to you here."

"So, so many." Rayah choked on her words as more tears spilled down her red-blushed cheeks. Danny didn't watch as the red rivers touched down toward the carpet.

"So many what, Ray?" He cringed as she sobbed again. "Take your time."

Wheezing, breath catching, she swallowed. "So many Neds."

For the next thirty seconds, Hannah reminded Rayah how to breathe and observed how large her pupils had grown.

By luck, the Suicide King kind, Rayah's lungs filled with air once more and she craned her neck to the ceiling, mouth gaping as the rasping breaths died. Clamping her eyes shut, her lips traced the word *Ned* over and over again.

"Do you mean August?" Danny waited to ask her this until several minutes had passed. By now, the group surrounded her, giving enough space for breathing room. "Do you mean August when you say too many Neds? Since he's Ned's son?"

Rayah nodded and then shook her head. "I don't know." She turned to Hannah. "Help me with my zipper again, please."

Dress secured, she raced up the stairs and returned minutes later with her makeup redone. Her eyes still looked puffy, but Michelle assured her they could erase most of it through a filter when they took pictures.

A chill met them outside as they stood in a line of people waiting to snap photos with their dates. Hannah clutched her tattered bag and growled, "For once, I'd love to see it be trendy to take pictures in front of a graveyard."

Ah, yes, Hannah's dream proposal spot. She'd mentioned it at least on one occasion to Duke.

Danny tugged Rayah to his side as she quivered like the leaves that had begun their descent across campus. "You sure you want to go tonight? I'm fine if we just stay here."

She set her jaw and leaned into him. "I'm going. Even if Ned sets the gym on fire, I'm going."

He noticed, as they posed for their picture, how much Rayah straightened her spine, almost to Reuben-length. The other, on the other hand, slouched and grimaced for his shot. Squeezing Rayah's fingers, Danny muttered about returning to the dorm as he pulled his roommate aside.

"Look, Reuben, I know you're nervous about the dream and all, but look at July." He gestured to her as she beamed at a sparrow hopping from one sidewalk block to the next. "Focus on how beautiful she is tonight. You'll forget everything else. That's how I dealt with last year."

Reuben shoved his hands into his pockets. Lucky guy, the seamstress hadn't sewn them shut. "With all your anxiety stuff?"

"Felt like I was going to throw up until I saw Rayah."

He bobbed his chin once and threw another glance at his date as she bent to pick up the bird with her finger. It flew off. After all, it had no cage.

"Just remember July's favorite quote."

"What is it?"

"The Lord is a refuge for the oppressed, a stronghold in times of trouble."

Reuben returned to Danny and clapped him on the shoulder. "You're not half so bad, even if you run at the pace of the government."

"Back at you, man, even if you know facts that would only be useful on game shows."

They traversed campus toward the gym, which throbbed with a basslike rhythm. A bob of pink hair with a Homecoming crown trailed down to a skin-tight dress, cut off very high up the legs. Valentina looped her arm around a tall figure with reddish hair several feet ahead.

"That's not—" Danny squinted in the dimming light. "Is that August?"

Reuben, a step ahead with his arm around July, shrugged. "She did say she had a backup date."

"Is that even allowed? Isn't he twenty-three or twenty-four?"

July rolled her neck to half face Danny. "He's been acting as a kind of principal until they find a new one. Why else was he allowed to expel me?"

They approached the glass doors, Judah at the front next to a lady who was collecting tickets. Rayah reached into her purse and handed over two red-tinted slips. Without looking at them, the frumpy woman dropped them into a bin.

"Why are you making the lady carry the tickets?" Judah winked at Danny as he held up a breathalyzer for Reuben.

Danny patted his pants. "Pockets are sewn shut. Can't even bring my phone."

"My poor little brother. How will you and your generation survive without these?" He dug into his pocket and flashed a smartphone. By habit, he looked at it and his face fell. He swore just above the pumping music inside.

"What's wrong?"

"Shouldn't have put it on Do Not Disturb." Judah shoved the breathalyzer into the woman's hand and muttered something about a substitute.

"Judah, what's wrong?"

"It's Faith." He shoved the phone into his pocket. "She's having her baby."

A month early.

Chapter Eighteen

"*D*ANIEL MICAH BELTE, DID YOU KNOW THAT ZAI WAS *planning to ride his bike down Devil's Backbone?*"

"*Yes, Dad, but—*"

"*And you didn't think to tell his mom, who lives two doors down? You know that road is too narrow for two cars side by side, let alone a bike.*"

"*He wanted me to film it. I-I didn't. I said I couldn't watch.*"

"*You might as well have. You knew he needed protection from himself, and you stood back.*"

"*How is he?*"

"*He found someone else to film it, anyway, and went live. All his followers watched him fly over a pothole into an oncoming car.*"

"*I know, I-I saw it. Dad, I'm sorry. P-please tell me if you know how he's doing.*"

"I should go with him."

"Maybe not." Rayah clutched his hand as the bass dropped inside the pounding brick walls. Still outside, he stared as Judah fled down the sidewalk. The woman collecting tickets motioned for students to drop them in her bin as she took hold of the breathalyzer.

His feet itched. He hobbled from one to the other. "But, like, he just dropped a bombshell. Shouldn't I go to be with him or something?"

What if their baby didn't make it, like the last one?

As Rayah jerked her head, her hairspray intoxicated him for a moment. "Labor can sometimes last a day. And I have a feeling, with a preemie, they'll be at the hospital longer. Just keep in touch with him."

He patted his non-existent pockets. "How? Can't keep my cell phone with me."

She tugged at his arm, toward the glass doors that emitted bursts of sounds whenever couples passed through them. "Enjoy tonight. Save thinking for later." Another yank, it came gentle still. "If I can do it, so can you."

How could he say no to those beautiful brown eyes and short braided hair? The cute little emerald dress certainly helped. He let her pull him along through the barrier of sound that assaulted his ears with drums, and eyes with strobe lights.

Right beside the gym, in the lobby where they sold concessions, was a photography station. They waited in line and grabbed various props to pose with: Danny a large pair of sunglasses, Rayah a pink feather boa scarf. The cameraman made Danny hold a sign, "Homecoming 2019: Tech-no? Tech-yes Party." The flash blinded them when he snapped the photo.

"Photo's ten dollars if you order it online." He slipped Danny a yellow sheet with an online code. Danny noticed that several yellow slips littered the trashcan by the gym doors.

Per usual, the gym stank of sweat when they entered.

Projection screens lined the sidelines of the court. This shortened the spacing of the dance floor by a significant amount. They found a pocket of air toward the edge and watched as images danced on the screens. These ranged from geometric shapes to lion vectors, in case members forgot which school they were attending.

Ned lived on.

Lasers assaulted them left and right in dizzying arrays of green, blue, and red. He blinked away spots from his eyes, losing Rayah for a moment in the haze.

Something odd in the middle of the floor caught his eye. A dead tree, much like the one by the ex-garden, stood resolute on the center floor. Someone on the Homecoming committee had wrapped the ashen bark with Christmas lights and glow sticks to make it appear relevant and pretty. Looked like when they put makeup on a corpse, Danny thought. Just like they'd made his father's face appear all waxy in the casket.

A group of girls without dates screamed when the DJ, who was buried between two projection screens, switched the number to "Bohemian Rhapsody." All movement ceased as just about every student pretended to grab a microphone to lip-sync to real life versus fantasies. Danny slumped to kneel to "seeeeeeeeee" before singing about his woes as a poor boy. Before he could mime the lyrics, the fan section wall caught his eye.

For a moment, just a moment, the *DEN* in *WELCOME TO THE DEN* read as *END*.

Heart throbbing so much it hurt his rib cage, he rose and knuckled his eyes. Stupid lasers and strobe lights, it blurred back to *Den* again.

Arms swayed back and forth with phone flashlights as the singer droned about killing a man. Nearby, Reuben and July slow danced, ignoring the mosh pit forming around them, despite the slow, somber lyrics. Rayah and Danny followed suit, dancing their way toward the two friends.

"Wonder where everyone else went!" Even shouting, he had to repeat himself above the chorus of ooooohs.

"Maybe to get a drink." Rayah released her hand from his suit to fan herself. "It's hot in here."

"You wanna get water already?"

They were into only the first song, but his neck felt clammy against his suit collar. Not a terrible idea, and he bet Rayah didn't get much hydration during her hours of preparation. Not with a bunch of girls crowding the bathroom and hallway drinking fountain.

Breaking through the encircling mosh pit, they raced for the red doors that led to a hallway with a drinking fountain. In spite of the early hours into the dance, a line coiled from the fountain all the way to the corner. He heard the doors burst behind him, and Dean shoved past them to near the edge of the line. Reuben followed, stopping to talk with them, not without panting.

"J-July goes h-hard."

"You guys were slow dancing."

"Until we got to the part of 'Mamma Mia.' Goodness, she can bounce."

Danny smirked as they rounded the corner, almost bumping into girls who were reapplying lipstick. "Says the guy who has the top cross-country time on the team."

"Well, I don't run in three-piece suits."

In an alcove by the men's basketball locker room, August and Valentina waited in line. Reuben swung to the far left and ducked under Danny's shadow as they passed them. Rayah stopped as Reuben continued to the end of the queue where Dean stood.

"You know, I'm not *that* thirsty."

"We could always try for another building."

She frowned in the dim lighting of the hallway. Felt like the perfect atmosphere for a horror flick. "The lady took our tickets though. What if she doesn't remember us?"

"I hear they stamp your hand when you leave so you can come back later. At least, Dean had mentioned something about that last year. Trust me, he left with his dates from a lot of dances to take some breaks."

Rayah swerved on her soft green heels as they clip-clopped back down the hallway. A couple ladies in feathery dresses followed as they overheard them, but most of the line stayed. Passing by the alcove again, he felt a shove in the shoulder.

He rounded on August, who cracked a grin. "Enjoying the dance, Danny?"

"Sure." You creepy twenty-something-year-old man who is taking an underage girl to a dance.

August nudged Valentina. "This little lady worked her little tail off on all the decorations. Did you see the hanging CDs and the glow-stick patterns on the walls?"

Not having the heart to tell him he couldn't observe anything in the dark room with the blinding laser lights, he opted for, "Yeah, everything looks great." He coughed, throat dry. "So you chaperoning this year, August, like the rest of the teachers?"

Rayah pulled at his arm before he could receive an answer. But based on the darkening of August's features, he didn't want to know.

Shoving themselves into the doors, they ran into a dark room full of screaming. The lights must've just flickered off, because the shrieking died down as soon as they'd tottered two steps in. Now Danny could see the glow sticks Valentina set up. The starlike patterns didn't catch his eye until now. Rather, the spattering of pink glow fluid appeared like drops of blood on the wall.

A single projection screen, by the farthest basketball hoop, flickered. Fading from black to white, a single image of a skeletonic hand displayed over and over again. Kind of like it had on his government class screen, and at the football stadium. Small words in another language followed.

Was that Arabic? It blinked too fast to tell.

White lights flashed on the horror-stricken faces of the students. Phones glowed from pockets as people recorded the strange phenomenon best they could in the low lighting. After several moments of silence, Michelle's voice broke into the echoing arena.

"Danny, where are you?"

A handful of gazes darted his way, but most at each other, confused as to which Danny she meant.

"Here!"

He parted through a sea of students and found Michelle at the accused projector and screen. A student beside her, perhaps Jeremy, shined a phone flashlight on her face. "Think you can fix this projector thing?"

"I can try." He tripped over a red cup a student must've dropped from the punch table. Students whipped out phones and lit his path toward the small box on wheels. "Don't you think we should turn on the power first?"

Somewhere in the crowd, a student voiced agreement.

"One battle at a time. We can all agree this screen is freaking us out. Like, how the heck is it running and everything else is shut off?"

Assent rippled throughout the sea of students to his left.

Danny stumbled over a thick wire when he reached the table. "Still think you should get a tech guy to check out the lights."

"Calling campus tech support now," a voice, female, announced somewhere behind him. Her phone dialed as someone's flashlight illuminated the projector. He pressed the circular power button on the top as the girl growled at her phone. "'Course there's no service in here."

The projector shut down with a hum, a flash of blue light, and then nothing. Another scream erupted followed by shushing and cursing. Groping the device, he pushed the button again, and a pale loading screen displayed to the sound of the machine purring. *Click, click, beep*, and the skeletonic hand disappeared. But it left behind a single Arabic word, red on a black screen. It flickered from red to black nothingness and back to red:

موت

Where had he seen that word before? He blanked as he thought through his previous lesson plans in Arabic class.

"Anyone pull that thing up on Google Translate?"

The tree at the center of the floor flickered to life. Although the glow sticks had outlined it in the darkness, everyone gasped in reaction.

"Looks like tech support got something to work." This announcement from the crowd was followed by laughter. "But seriously, any luck with Google Translate, anyone?"

Another person piped up, male, gruff. "Yeah, got one of those apps that can translate a word from a picture. But it keeps flickering too fast. Can't get a clear shot."

Someone in the crowd muttered something about foreign exchange students. King's didn't have anyone from the Middle East.

"Anyone taking Arabic class?"

Danny raised his hand, noticing how his fingers turned red as they reached in front of the screen. "I do. I'm trying to remember where I saw that word."

He'd seen it on an early vocab sheet, one that he and Reuben studied back and forth in their room. Used to sometimes meet up with July to go over those sheets until she got expelled.

A light groaned as it flickered on, just a single light, right above the fan section. *WELCOME TO THE DEN* blinked in and out of view as the bulb flashed on and off. As it guttered, something connected in his mind. As if his whole brain had been made of plywood and someone just tossed a torch at him.

His stomach seared like never before. Suddenly he'd retreated to his sophomore year, and the taste of vomit, of burning and reeking, filled the back of his mouth. He swallowed and gasped for a breath, face and skin growing hot.

And then he remembered the word. Always had a tricky time with it. Now he saw why.

موت, *almawt*, pronounced el-mon-too, was the word for death.

Reaching forward, he snagged Michelle's arm. "We need to get everyone out of here now."

"What?" Spit flew into his face along with something cherry-scented. "Why? What does the word mean?"

"Death, Mitch. I have a really bad feeling about this."

Even in the darkness, he could see her pale complexion. She sucked in a deep breath and faced the crowd, both parts of the sea now one. "OK, so here's an idea. Let's wait outside until they get the lights back on." It amazed him how calm she kept her voice. "Since the AC kicked off, we're going to burn up in here anyway."

Even though various members of the crowd voiced agreement, no one moved. So Michelle did. Phone flashlight torch lighting the way, she maneuvered through the students to the doors, Danny and Jeremy trailing behind. The crowd, pulled out of a stupor, followed, and Danny felt the heat of several hundred bodies encroaching from behind.

Michelle reached for the handle.

Right as she did, a gunshot echoed.

It sounded like a BB gun pop, not as loud as Danny expected. But right when it went off, the crowd surged for the door, screaming and shouting. Michelle yelped as she pried open the right door, pressed against the left from the sheer force of the crowd. Danny elbowed them back. But as the light from the concessions foyer spilled in, they lifted him off his feet as they tumbled forward.

They carried him all the way to the glass doors. When he regained his footing, he launched out the entrance and sprinted all the way to the parking lot. He watched the crowd dart en masse toward him, goggling the faces for Rayah.

They met eyes as she dashed toward him with one shoe off. She must've lost it in the scuffle. He flung open his arms and caged her in. She sobbed into his chest, and they crumpled to the asphalt.

Students fled every which way, most back to their dorms. Everyone and their brother had hopped onto a cell phone, dialing home, 9-1-1, and anyone who'd pick up the receiver.

He hovered over Rayah to shield her from students sprinting away from the building. With one hand she clutched at her chest, and the other fumbled with the zipper. She let it down a ways and gulped in large breaths.

Her lips quivered, stumbling over various words. "S-sounded so f-far away."

"Don't think about it, just breathe."

But it did sound distant. He'd wondered why it hadn't deafened his ears. After all, Olympic shooters often wore noise-canceling head-phones to block out the clamor.

"M-maybe someone p-pulled a prank." Snot dribbled from her nose as she released herself from his chest. "O-or the e-electrical box b-blew a fuse."

"You're right. Maybe that's what happened. Keep breathing."

He instructed her to place her hands on her head and face the sky open-mouthed. At least, that's what Coach suggested whenever anyone hyperventilated after races or tough practices.

"Danny." July's sharp voice cut into his instructions.

He tossed his hands off his head and faced her. "Give us a minute."

"Reuben." Her chin jabbed at the direction of the doors. By now, the crowd had escaped the building. "I didn't see him come out."

Rayah choked on a breath and began to hyperventilate again. "So many Neds." She muttered this over and over between gasps.

"I can't leave her like this."

"Fine." July balled her fists. "I'll go look for him myself."

"Leave her, Danny," Michelle barked, thrusting her bag into Jeremy's arms and crouching by the poor girlfriend. "Don't let July go into the building by herself. Emmanuel students stick together." She palmed Rayah's back and the fabric made a swishing noise as she rubbed up and down. "She'll be fine with us. Now go."

"Shouldn't we wait for the police?"

July was determined. "I'm not waiting on any cops to tell me what happened to my date. Can't trust the ones in this town. They don't do squat with all the crap King's pulls."

Fair, they honestly let people at King's get away with ...

"Danny, you coming with me or not?"

Spit caught in his esophagus. He stared at Michelle a moment, nodded, then turned to July. "All right, let's go."

They charged back into the glass doors. Their shoes scuffled through deflated balloons, beer cans, and photography card slips. July swung open the doors to the gym and a heat wave of body odor overtook them. Danny staggered back before sliding off his suit jacket. Should've done that before. He tossed it onto a pile of others, hoping he'd remember to pick it up.

July's nose wrinkled as she passed the boozy punch table, heels crunching on chips from a spilled snack bowl. She squinted into the darkness, into the flickering lights of the tree and the bulb above the fan section. "Not here."

"Where did you see him last?"

She clenched her jaw, swallowed hard. "He left to go grab a drink during 'Bohemian Rhapsody.'"

"That long ago?" He remembered now Reuben at the end of the line as he and Rayah left to scavenge another building. They should've invited him.

"The power went out after that, so I didn't see much of anybody."

Danny's temples pounded as his abdomen burned. Vomit relaunched into his throat as he choked it down. He had told Reuben not to think about danger, just as he had told Rayah at prom.

They burst into the back hallway, finding the drinking fountain empty. Walls were filled with the scent of wet and rust. "You think he got out in the crowd, but you didn't see him?"

July marched ahead. "Let's keep looking."

A step ahead of him, her silvery heels glimmered as they clacked in the echoing hallway. They especially glinted in the red glow of an exit sign next to a door. Danny bet most of the members of the drinking fountain line used that door to escape the sound of the gunshot.

She raced around the corner, darting ahead of Danny. The sound of the shoes stopped. A moment of silence.

And then a scream bellowed, a low, hoarse one that could break a throat. It didn't belong to a human; it shouldn't have.

Rounding the corner, he stopped short of a pool of blood. Following it, he finished the path at the slack-jawed face of Reuben. Lifeless eyes staring at him, arm slumped over his body, holding a gun.

Chapter Nineteen

"I APPRECIATE YOU COMING TO GATHER HERE AFTER your extended fall break. As the new principal of King's Academy, I figured the students deserved to stay in the loop as much as possible."

Ari Kingsley took a pace onto the track, approaching the students huddled and shivering in the stands. Michelle elbowed Danny in the ribs. "Ever heard of this chick?"

"Yeah, I met her right before her interview." He nestled his chin into his hoodie. The October chill chewed at his nose and fingertips stuffed into his pockets. Luckily, they had only two weeks left of cross-country season. Not that it mattered much with the fastest runner being dead and all.

A V of birds soared over Ari as the microphone picked up the swishing of her purple skirt. "I'm sure many of you read the email sent out to the school about the passing of Reuben Benjamin."

Yeah, something along the lines of: "Campus mourns the loss of a beloved student. No details. Oh, and by the way, don't sue us. Not that you were planning to, but even if you tried, we'll zap all your funds and make your child's future miserable. Oh, the tragedy! Also, we have an art session/therapy available on campus to help students cope. No, we will not hire any more counselors."

At least, that's how Danny had read it. It probably sounded a tad more professional.

"I will not dive into the causes or force any of you to relive any of the events that took place October fourth."

Danny and Rayah tucked into each other, forming a yin-yang of warmth, not that it helped with the chill.

"However"—a bright-pink tongue glazed Ari's dark lips; they matched the skirt—"we have cause to believe online forums provoked action on the part of Reuben Benjamin."

Great, and now they'd take away social media again. A bright blinking light sidled out of Michelle's jean pocket as she tried to pry her phone out of her pants. "Might as well get a last-minute post in."

His fingers inched toward his to post another verse on his @danny-intheden456 account. Perhaps July's favorite verse would do at a time like this. Then again, it didn't seem to help Reuben that much.

Ari approached the fence and linked her fingers around the chain links. "I know previously August Rezzen attempted to ban all online communications to prevent another occurrence, since another suicide attempt arose earlier this semester."

Served them right. After all, Valentina's gang had sent all those death threats and private messages the day of Homecoming.

Michelle clattered her fingers against her glowing keyboard with all her might. It appeared at least ten students in his row alone had similar ideas.

He shuffled in his seat, cold metal stinging his thin jean fabric.

"However, that is not how I run my school." With each word, she banged her palm against the clinking fence. "You would find another way to torment a classmate without social media. We're all human, after all."

Danny raised his head a little. At least, as far as it could go when restrained by a hood.

"Since you are near adulthood, some already there, I believe I should treat my students as such. *Individuals* in the adult world face punishments for actions, not entire corporations."

Her eyes sparkled in Danny's direction for a moment. Even in the frigid air, they warmed him. Reminded him of Rayah's.

"Students, let me tell you a story. I went to a school with a strict dress code, mind you, twenty years ago. Before boarding schools like this decided to forgo uniforms. The skirts girls could wear had to extend two inches past the knee." Her fingers dipped down and touched the spot as if they needed a demonstration. Danny noticed her skirt rose at least two inches above the kneecap.

"Does she have a point to this?" Hannah bled red onto a drawing of a grim reaper planting poppies.

Even if not, Danny enjoyed stories, unless they were written about him.

"And they were these honest-to-God-awful khaki, those skirts." She made an indistinct movement. "I *hated* them. So take a first guess at the thing I wore the day after graduation."

"A miniskirt." Someone shouted this from the bottom of the stands. Uncomfortable laughter, light and breathy, filled the student body.

"A purple one." She placed her fingers two inches below the thigh, shorter than a Homecoming dress. "Believe me, most of my friends hiked theirs much higher."

The petal of a poppy smudged over the line as Hannah nodded at the lady, rare smile crawling up her cheeks. Was that approval?

"Not to say I have a problem with short purple skirts." Ari motioned to hers and did half a twirl. A sign for an advertisement for computer repairs clapped in the wind against the fence, as if applauding. "In my years of working in schools, recently Mede Media, I've learned that the tighter you enforce a rule, the more students will want to rebel. Again, we're human."

Orange and red trees dipped in the wind to nod.

"I will not force the whole school to give up social media."

Claps and cheers erupted from the stands. One male gave a loud whoop. Ari raised a finger and waited for the crowd to die down.

"However, if a student chooses to keep his or her head in their behind in a public forum, whether online or in person, I will not tolerate it. And believe me, I do an excellent job at making examples out of those who do not listen."

Dead silence choked the students.

Then a groan from the bleachers as everyone leaned forward to cling to the rest of her words. But she had none. She dismissed them by rows and that was that.

An office assistant burst into Danny's AP Euro room during a test. Quivering and looking no older than an eighth grader with his cherub cheeks and short stature, he consulted a pile of yellow slips that usually indicated office appointments or package receipts.

"M-Mr. Judah Belte?" he stammered, eyeing the teacher. He licked his lips and narrowed his eyelids, almost as if trying to determine why a Mr. Judah Belte suddenly transformed into a wrinkled woman with brown-dyed hair.

"They're in the middle of a test." She tempered her usual piercing voice. "Show me the slip and I'll give it to the right student."

He almost tossed the paper at her, arms shaking.

An "eep" escaped the plump lips of the kid before he dashed out the door, colliding with the Colosseum model made of marshmallows and toothpicks stationed on a side table.

Danny shook his head at an Egyptian sarcophagus made of cardboard by his desk and returned to question eleven.

They'd already gotten to the Black Plague.

A yellow slip fluttered onto his desk.

It read, *Danny Belte, report to Ms. Kingsley's office.*

He eyed the substitute and flashed his test. "Still have thirty questions to go."

"Go to the office after you finish."

She threw a dismissive wave and settled in her chair by the bracket Judah had going for who was the worst pope in history. He planned to do another one for European leaders once the class decided between Stephen VI and John XII.

He rushed through the remainder of the questions and slapped the finished product on the teacher's desk. This scuffled Judah's pile of character cards for all the important figures of the Crusades.

Chilly October breeze had reasoned to a goosebump-rippling temperature when he reached outside. He hunched into himself all the way to the large brick administration building. The golden lions at the top appeared dimmer in the pale autumn light.

Swinging open the heavy doors with a grunt, he burst inside and sighed as the heat filled his cheeks and unfroze his hands. He stood in the entrance for a few moments, kicking off any dirt on the carpet and breathing in the burning heater smell.

Slip in hand, he marched through the glass barrier that separated the entrance from the offices. But to his surprise, when he went to give Ashley the paper at the counter, he found Ari on the wooden bench.

She scooted to the far side and patted the other end.

"Are we not going to meet in your office?" He crumpled the yellow slip into a ball.

"I have requested that any employee, when meeting one-on-one with a student, needs another party in the room." She gestured at Ashley. "After allegations, we don't want to take chances."

He recalled August saying the same thing. "You talking about the Mr. Enlil thing?"

She pinched her nose and sighed. "August Rezzen was accused of making advances at a student at Homecoming." Ah, Valentina. Maybe he tried something at Homecoming. "An email was sent out right before they hired me."

Once again, the email had read something like:

August Rezzen retired. He did some inappropriate things. We won't specify because that could land us in legal trouble. Or that would bring down our donor dollars. So we'll just say he's "unfit" for his position and let the students speculate all the heck they want. Also, allegation is a scary word, so we'll say "complaint." We got a complaint from someone. But don't worry, kids who had him in class. We did extensive background checks on the new teacher in his place. Why hadn't we done those before? Umm, let's put in a statement from our school code of ethics. Yeah, we like things like trust and the safety of our students. Those are good things. Truth is cool too. We kind of like justice, so let's toss that in there with maybe a pinch of vigilance. On the students' end, not ours. Oh, speaking of students, did you see what his date to Homecoming was wearing? Girls ought to be more careful about those things.

Of course, they worded it a little more professionally than that.

"I'd prefer to stand. Been sitting all day."

"If you like."

He noticed a pattern on her skirt he wasn't able to spot from far away at the football field, a bunch of black bears woven into the silky fabric.

"I'm sure you want to talk about my roommate." His Adam's apple bobbed. "Everyone does." Now he knew how July felt after everything that happened with Bel.

"Bet that fall break didn't last long enough, even with the extra two days."

His feet shuffled together. "No, ma'am."

"I didn't call you in here to discuss Reuben, not exactly, I should say."

They met eyes. He now realized how different they were from Rayah's, a little harder, smaller, and not quite as warm. "What then?"

"I've been going through the academic records of high-achieving students to form a new student council. Some of its previous members"—she flashed a smirk—"let's just say I want to run things a little differently."

Ashley's receiver rang once before she picked it up.

"Danny, I want to offer you a position on the student council."

Didn't seem like much of an offer. He'd served last year. She raised an eyebrow.

"And my protection."

"Protection, ma'am?" The weight of that word burned his ears like hot metal. How much had he failed with it in the past, and now a near-stranger offered it to him.

"If you work at a school like Mede long enough, you can tell the difference between a death and a suicide. Even if the police in this area seem content with the easiest explanation."

Student died with a gun in hand, wound in temple. There were no fingerprints on the weapon except his.

Bears ruffled on her skirt as she crossed her ankles. "The students will know who is a council member and will know not to lay a finger on them."

A soft chuckle scratched the back of his mouth. "Why not put everyone on it then?"

"Anyone ever tell you your eyes look like they're full of dreams? So blue. Almost like a blind man's eyes?" She lifted herself from the seat and handed him a packet titled "Student Council Information." "I'm not a hero, kid, but I'll protect who I can. Believe me, a student at my last school had a lot of enemies. But he survived because of my system. He graduated last year, Harvard bound."

"Good for him."

"You going to take the position or not?"

How could he refuse?

He decided Rayah looked great in every color ... except red. And, of course, the King's soccer uniforms came in a grape-tomato-fresh-off-the-vine red.

Still, she did look great as a defender during the second overtime of the game. The JV second string brought a teeming crowd of about five onlookers, three from the other team and Danny and Michelle.

"How'd the match go?" Danny's ankles itched from the dirt mound they were sitting on. School couldn't afford benches for the less kept fields. In the first overtime, a girl in a green uniform tripped over an aluminum can buried by the far-left corner of the field.

Michelle shrugged as she chewed on a granola bar. "Other team forgot to show up. Just got out of practice?"

"Yeah. Did your coach work you hard? We did hill sprints today." No one ran as fast as Reuben, after all. But Coach could definitely make them try for it.

"Yeah, I can smell you from here." She sat four feet away. "And, no, tonight, the parents brought food for the team. Every team gets a mandatory parent-sponsored dinner. Didn't they already do it for cross-country?"

"Uh-huh, it's nothing like what the football players get. Dean, last year, said they stuffed them full of pasta, grilled steaks, and cake. I think the parents ordered us *maybe* three pizzas for the whole team. There's like fifty of us, mind you."

She waved the granola bar and brushed off oat crumbles that landed on her tennis skirt. "Look what they brought us."

"That's it?"

"Welcome to girls' sports."

Rayah charged across the line as the other team formed a blockade around the goal. Perhaps a foul had been committed. He faintly remembered a whistle.

The scoreboard still read 0-0 in a dull orange.

A girl kicked the red soccer ball at the goal. Without a hint of surprise, it bounced off the wall from the other team. Rayah raced back to the other side. A wrapper with half a granola bar flashed in front of Danny's nose.

"You want it?"

"I'm not going to eat your dinner."

"Don't be ridiculous. We'll all go to the dining commons after this, and after Hannah gets out of her speech practice. You want it? I hate raisins."

"Then why did you take it?"

"Thought it was chocolate chip. Found out a bite in."

Grabbing it from her, he picked off some of the top bits. Then he drove the rest of the thing into his mouth and let his saliva drown the cinnamon and raisin treat. He wadded the wrapper into his athletic shorts pockets and watched as an opposing player grabbed Rayah's shirt as she kicked the ball toward midfield. "Did Ari call anyone from your classes into her office?"

A whistle trilled on the field, foul on Rayah. "Valentina, Annabelle Ruger, and Travis Savage. All previous student council people if I remember right."

"And those on the Homecoming Court." He squinched his eyes and envisioned the group cradling roses in lapels and arms. "Not you?"

"Nope. Why?"

He explained about his encounter with Ari outside her office and about her offer to protect him on student council. To his surprise, and even hint of dismay, Michelle's silvery eyes did not bulge the way they often did when confronted with a conspiracy.

"Valentina mentioned something about that. I think the principal's drawing from a smaller pool, like an oligarchy."

"I still think you guys should be on it. Rather have protection for Rayah than for myself."

An image of laser tag beams hitting her glowing suit flashed through his mind, the way he'd shielded her as she collapsed into a panic attack.

Michelle's sharp fingertips made patterns in the dust. They tapped this way and that, as per the normal habits of her footwear. "Can you really blame Ari, though? The previous system didn't work, led to Bel's near-death and Reuben's actual one."

Why had it become so normal to talk about this already?

On the sidelines, Rayah tossed the ball to one of her teammates. They missed, and a player in emerald green nudged the ball across the white line again.

"Speaking of, Ari said something weird about Reuben's suicide when I met with her today. Said she could tell the difference between murder and when someone takes their own life. She thinks Reuben didn't kill himself."

"Again, makes sense." Her fingers traced a curvy line in the sand. "Long line for the drinking fountain, right? Bet one of Valentina's fans had a prime chance to off him back there."

A video camera stationed on top of an electrical box caught his attention. "Ned filmed the whole place."

"Not inside locker rooms and in tight corners. It's very, very possible to get away with murder here."

Ice spread across his chest as he thought back to the hallway. There were plenty of suspects.

"Valentina said something today." Michelle's finger stopped tracing. She rubbed it on her skirt. "About Twitter and Reuben."

"Did she distance herself from any of the friends who sent him a DM?"

Rayah raced back to form the wall of people blocking her goal.

"No, she said someone had posted a tweet about how he should die after fooling around with Valentina. Something about how he probably slept with her and was going to hell."

"Yikes."

"Yeah, apparently had plenty of room to fit in a bunch of verses in 280 characters, just like whoever tweeted at Bel."

"Have you pulled it up?"

A whistle trilled on the field.

"No, it got deleted. But Danny—"

The other team kicked it. The ball skidded past Rayah's foot and into the goal.

"—Valentina says July posted it."

Chapter Twenty

"HOW'S LITTLE TAYLOR DOING?"

The pixelated image of Judah on the phone broke into a staccato. "F-fine. We'll be ou-out of NICU in ab-about a week i-if things ke-keep improving."

Danny shifted on the couch and held up his phone so his brother could see into his nostrils. The video stopped glitching. Judah's shoes paced the round sidewalk at the entrance of the hospital. A burst of wind cut off whatever he said, something about terrible cafeteria food.

"How's Faith doing?"

"Happy but sad that she's spending a good chunk of her maternity leave in the hospital. I am too. King's wants me back on Monday."

"In our defense the substitute teacher doesn't even divide us into feudal castes like you did with your fun interactive lessons. Treats us all like peasants with her boring lectures." He puffed his chest. "Doesn't she know I'm a noble?"

Judah laughed through his teeth and began to pace the other way, near a scraggly brown bush that reached toward his leg. "How are things holding up at King's?"

Gabe laughed as he flicked a page in his textbook on a nearby chair. Danny's fault for taking the call into the lounge outside his room. But Bel called Duke around the same time. As always with sibling talks, that one trumped any.

"That Gabe I hear?" Judah squinted into sunlight.

"Catch him before he's gone." Danny flipped the screen to face the friend who turtled into an oversize hoodie.

"Why? Because he's a fast runner?"

Somewhere down the hall, someone bounced a tennis ball against a door.

"No, because he kept disappearing last year. Lucky jerk got out of doing Ned's pledge."

Gabe glared at him over *Understanding Psychology*. The textbook featured a face on the cover crafted out of geometric shapes.

"There was a family crisis, you know. I left right before Ned shut campus down."

"Sorry about that, bro. Death in the family?"

"Death of sorts."

Scratching his neck and frowning, Danny spun around the screen to face himself again. Judah had pixelated himself again.

"T-tell you wh-wh-what, Danny. I gotta g-go. D-Dinnertime w-with Faith."

"OK, have fun. Say hi to little Taylor when you see him. Text me when you can bring him to campus. I'll try to clean out my room beforehand."

Darkness fell over the screen before he could hear Judah's reply. As he slid his phone into his pocket, something small and hard stung his forehead. Rubbing it, he watched as a tennis ball bounced from his chair and rolled toward Dean.

"Hi-ya, Princess."

"Dean." A curt nod and a wince. Had almost forgotten about him. At least, tried to purge all images of him and Frenchie on the Homecoming court in the center of the floor, umm, dancing.

"My girlfriend says you posted a meme the other day that was homophobic. Care to explain?"

"Girlfriend as in Fren-Julia?"

"As in Valentina. Started dating after we hooked up after Homecoming."

Oh, guess that was a thing now. As for the homophobic meme, he had posted a picture of SpongeBob holding a rainbow that, in bold letters above his head, declared "Subjectivism."

The ball thwacked against his chair, missing the crotch area, a very close miss. "Princess, I asked you a question."

"Thanks for clarifying, Dean."

"Listen, I'm letting you off easy. In my family, questions get asked once. If you don't answer them on time—"

"I'd put that away if I were you." Gabe flipped a page in his psychology book, eyes on Dean.

"Stay out of it, red eyes."

"Your girlfriend informed you, I'm sure, that Danny here is on the new principal's student council. Valentina's on it, I'm sure you know, and that means immunity from any harm. You touch a hair on his head and you seal your fate, got it?"

Gabe's sallow cheeks flushed pink. He'd risen from his seat, elbows angled back like wings as if they were ready to launch a punch. Now, it seemed as if he'd filled out the whole hoodie, looking twice as large as before.

Dean let the ball drop with a thud. It rolled underneath a green chair and disappeared. He jabbed a finger at Danny, shoulders hunched to his ears. "Watch yourself, Princess. Would be a shame if you lost the principal's protection."

He huffed as he stormed down the hallway and down the stairwell. Each footfall echoed on the concrete steps.

"Thanks." Danny leaned over and groped underneath the green chair until he found the ball. A layer of dirt and dust covered it now. His phone binged. "Ah, gotta meet the girls in the dining commons for dinner. Wanna come?"

Gabe jerked his head.

"OK, well, see you around then."

At last, he smirked. "We'll see. Family crises happen often."

"All right, which one of you had the bright idea to come to the dining commons at six?" Hannah slammed her plate onto the chipped corner table they managed to snag at the back. "When everyone and their mother decided to come at this time?"

"Because we like to eat at normal people times." Michelle bit into a forkful of liquidy lasagna. Danny praised the good Lord they made the thing out of meat so he didn't have to try it.

Then again, facing his plate crusted with food of dinners past, he plugged his nose at the stench of the overcooked asparagus, the only vegetable or fruit option from tonight. Smelled like just about everything his mother made, expired and sour. He hoped Faith could cook, because Judah learned nothing from their kitchen.

He sighed and leaned his head over his chair seat to gaze at the faded painted lion on the wall above their table. It held a whisk in its paw.

Snapping forward again, he pushed his plate out of the way. Just in time to watch Hannah spit a mouthful of chewed potatoes into a brown paper napkin.

"So what happened to the changes we made in the cafeteria last year?" Hannah picked at a glob stuck in her molars.

"Ned made those changes." Michelle motioned to the hanging plant over their table. It had browned and wilted. "By the time Ari gets through this school, there won't be any of his legacy left."

Ketchup from a pump container in a condiment station nearby squirted. A freshman girl positioned at it pressed the lever as hard and fast as she could, yielding an inch of spattered red sauce.

"We could've gone at an earlier time," Hannah grumbled. A boy inched past her chair, bumping into her and the seat behind her. They'd pressed the tables so close some lay only a handful of inches apart. "You guys usually finish practice by five, and I had nothing after school besides doing my speech for my coach, which takes all of half an hour."

Michelle grimaced at another bite of the gooey lasagna. Swallowed. "Danny had to call Judah."

"How's Faith?" Rayah chugged a glass of murky water to wash down her so-called burrito.

"Faith? As in faith in this school? In this cafeteria's food? Not biding very well, I must say."

Frowns all around for good ol' Danny boy. Rolling his eyes, he explained what Judah had talked about on the phone call. Rayah and Michelle pressed hands to their hearts to let out awws while Hannah's lip curled in a sneer.

"Hate babies." No one but Danny heard her.

Michelle slid her lasagna away from her. It hit the napkin dispenser and wobbled. "Do you know how Bel's baby is doing? Did she have it yet?"

He inhaled and regretted it, too close to his asparagus plate. "Will have to ask Duke. He was still on the call when I left. You don't think they'll make her give birth at the psych ward, do you?"

Hannah snorted into her waxy pasta salad. She squinched her eyelids and shook her head, face pinking from withheld laughter.

His stomach gurgled. Not good to have the anxiety meds without food. He squeezed Rayah's hand as she grimaced at her plate. "You want to make another round? Sometimes they put out new stuff when they run out of leftovers."

She nodded.

Screeching their chairs back against holey carpet, they sucked in breaths to cram between tables blocking the tile path that wound around the food stations. They reached the grimy floors and took their plates to the conveyor belt by the stairs. They tossed their forks down a silver chute and placed their dishes on the wet winding belt.

Dodging past snaking lines, they examined each station like tourists who traveled to the wrong destination.

Rayah peered around a student reaching for a plate to read the label. "Oh, that's the lasagna. Someone must've taken all the cheese on top."

"No way I'm doing that salad station, babe." Valentina released Dean's hand to grab an orange plate by the lasagna and stone-hard breadsticks. "That asparagus smells awful."

Danny yanked Rayah to the back of the lasagna line, not a long one. A student in front of him stuck his hand in a cup of silverware. He huffed. "Why do they never have spoons?"

Rayah massaged her wrist when Danny let go. He cringed. "Sorry."

"You're fine."

"Dean, you sure you didn't see anything else?" Valentina poked at the gloppy mass with the metal serving spoon. "Thing looks like a bunch of fetuses. Didn't help we were talking about the birthing process in health class today."

Ugh, a sour sensation filled Danny's abdomen. Heat flushed his skin. His throat grew tight and suddenly he didn't feel much like eating anymore.

"Think Bel had her baby yet?" The spoonful of so-called lasagna splattered onto Valentina's plate.

"Don't know or care. It's not mine, you know."

She nodded. "I'm just happy we actually got the new principal's attention on July. August did nothing with the Bel thing. Look what happened. She targeted my ex."

Dean grabbed the spoon as she slid a breadstick onto her plate. "August expelled her."

"Yeah, but didn't press any legal charges." She sighed, turning her nose up at the asparagus dish. "Couldn't even convince him at Homecoming, waste of a night."

"Hey, don't say that. You stopped by my room after."

"True."

They disappeared around the path after Dean nabbed three breadsticks.

Rayah linked her arm in Danny's. "I'm not hungry anymore."

"Me neither."

Swerving around a mass of tables and a group of guys having a chocolate milk chugging contest, they returned to their friends with news of Valentina.

Michelle gripped the table. "We need to do something about this. Reuben doesn't seem like the kind of guy to end everything after a simple tweet. He was levelheaded."

"Describe how you found him." Hannah's eyes went wide.

Danny winced but obliged. His stomach boiled inside him as he described it.

Hannah twisted her fingers in a hair tangle. "I think it was murder."

Michelle sighed. "You always think it's murder."

"Come on. There are better chances at getting killed at King's than finding edible food. Just look at the school's track record."

The sounds of a boy sputtering from too much chocolate milk filled the friends' silence. Moments later, he vomited all over the carpet.

Michelle clicked the top of her phone and slid it back into her purse. "Even though we have no solid facts"—she eyed Hannah when saying facts—"I also don't believe July would post something to his wall mean enough to send him over the edge. From how Danny described him, he seemed to have a good head on his shoulders."

"What? People who are depressed can't be levelheaded?" Hannah growled.

"We need a different explanation than the one given by the school, that's all I'm saying. No matter where the *facts* lead, they didn't give us enough to make an informed decision."

Forming three fingers into an *M*, Hannah mouthed the word *murder* over and over. Rayah excused herself to go get dessert. She left in a hurry.

Michelle glared at Hannah. "Why can't you accept that it was suicide? You didn't have any trouble with Bel attempting anything a couple months ago."

"One seems realistic. Two in two months is just asking for an investigation. Three if you include all of Ned's pills."

"Fine." Michelle plucked a dead brown leaf that hung in front of her face. "Since you're convinced, give me a suspect."

A flash of red hair whipped off her shoulders as she stared at Danny. He clutched his stomach and scowled.

"I didn't do it!"

"No, but you have a photographic memory. Did anyone in the hallway by the drinking fountain have something against him?"

His eyelids shut upon the warm glow of the dining commons light. "Hard to tell; there were a lot of people I don't know back there."

"Start with who you do know."

He followed the hallways, blinking in the light of the red exit sign, followed the faces obscured by darkness.

"Any guesses?"

Prying open his eyelids, he squinted at the glowy haze of the room. For some reason, it now seemed brighter. "Yes, three."

"All right, let's have them."

"Let's start with the obvious, Valentina."

Michelle reached into her bag and tore something out of a notebook. She shoved a piece of paper, side frillies intact, and tossed him a pen. "Write down all the reasons why she would murder Reuben."

So he wrote.

Suspect One: Valentina

Relation to Reuben: Ex-girlfriend

1. She dumped him right before Homecoming because he sided with July in the Twitter wars. Exes are usually the first people investigators go to, if I remember my crime shows right. Don't fail me now, Sherlock and Bones.

2. He went to Homecoming with July. For some reason Valentina hates July. So that would work as reason two, I guess. Maybe she didn't like July because she went to Emmanuel. She never did like that school. People from there rarely upvoted her bills.

3. She could easily blame the whole death on suicide over a Twitter post. Because Bel almost died over similar causes, they would be less likely to launch an investigation.

4. I just don't like her.

Michelle took the list from him when she finished. She nodded as her eyes darted back and forth across the paper. "Good except for the last one, Sherlock." She tore off another piece of paper. "Suspect two."

Suspect Two: August

Relation to Reuben: Teacher and Girlfriend Stealer

1. He wanted to get to know Valentina in an Adam and Eve type way during Homecoming. What better way to do so than to off the one person who your date hates? Girls are very impressed by murder, as we all know.

2. I remember him now acting all weird in government class the first day. When he talked about government as a mountain lion, he stared at Reuben when he said that if they weren't careful government would destroy them. Yeah, I know teachers stare at

students, but he held the gaze for longer than comfortable. And August kind of was *the* government until we got a new principal. So why not act out your lesson plans as a form of murder? Education in practice, yay!

3. I just don't like him.

Reading the second sheet, Michelle pursed her lips. "Not as strong as the last one. I could *maybe* see the first argument. The others not so much."

When the third paper reached him, he stared at it for a long time.

Suspect Three: Dean

Relation to Reuben: He used to be my roommate instead of Reuben? Maybe Valentina mentioned him to Dean when they weren't dating? Classmates in government

1. I really just don't like him.

Michelle smirked at the paper as he finished his first and last point. "You could've at least used the same argument that he wanted to impress Valentina by offing her ex."

"You still thought that argument was weak."

"It is." She pressed her cup to her lips and drained a light reddish liquid. "I say we go with the simplest explanation. Last time, with the whole fire thing, it had been Ned. Should've seen it a mile away."

"So Valentina then?"

"Or no one and it was suicide."

Rayah returned with a bowl of ice cream. She glanced at her shoes, having caught the last bit of conversation. "I can go get some more if you guys want to keep discussing."

"Nothing newsworthy. Sit."

So she did.

Chapter Twenty-One

Obituaries

IZAIAH (ZAI) NAPHLI, 13, WENT TO BE WITH OUR LORD July 2, 2016, after puncturing a lung in a bicycle accident. Izaiah recently finished his seventh-grade year at Emmanuel Middle School, with high marks in all his classes, and was known to be a delight and pure joy to everyone who knew him.

Preceded in death by mother Naomi (Rahab) Naphli. Izaiah is survived by his father Zachary Naphli. Memorial will be held July 6, at the Darius-Mandane Funeral Home.

David Belte, 46, went to be with our Lord July 16, 2016, after having battled an aggressive form of melanoma for four years. David worked for twenty years as a music teacher at Emmanuel High School. Preceded in death by mother Esther (Dunagan) Belte and father Jonah Belte, survived by wife Ruth (Amos) Belte and son Danny Belte. Memorial will be held July 20, 2016, at the Darius-Mandane Funeral Home.

"I swear, Lion Tamer, if you got me a birthday present, I'll burn it with my lighter right now."

Danny shoved the Zebra Cakes wrapped in a campus newspaper into his desk drawer.

"Doing anything crazy for your big day?" Danny clung to the top bunk and pulled himself atop it. Without a replacement roommate, might as well use the spare bed that smelled of sticky beer instead of urine. "Seeing a rated-R movie?"

"Dude, I watched the *Saw* movies when I was ten."

"Ah, well I guess that's all you can do at seventeen." He scrolled through his email on his phone to double-check the meeting time. He still had thirty minutes.

Staring across the room, he watched a crumpled soda can land on the pile of trash developing on his old bed. A Styrofoam cup fell onto the carpet amongst the litter.

Duke's head popped out from the lower bunk as he grabbed his laptop off the floor. His knuckles nudged a paper plate painted in some orangish tint. He paused. "You think he ever saw anything rated R?"

"The plate? Doubtful."

Duke rotated his head to glare at Danny. "Come on, you know who I mean."

Danny twisted to face the ceiling. He traced the brownish stains with his eyes, like he used to do when finding shapes in clouds as a child. That one looked like an inkblot from some weird psychological test, and that one, a tree, like Ned's tree.

"I didn't know enough about him. I think his mom banned Teletubbies as a kid, so maybe not."

"She banned Teletubbies? Then again, that sun looked like the product of a drug trip."

"Yeah, conservative parents will sometimes prevent their kids from watching certain shows. Mom banned all of Cartoon Network."

The third stain resembled a tongue of fire, licking the off-white ceiling.

Duke's laughter rattled the bed. "My parents banned TV too, you know. Bel and I would have sleepovers at the neighbor's apartment constantly just so we could catch up on episodes of *Phineas and Ferb*."

"Isn't that a mild show?"

Hey, that blot could pass for a lion or a bear.

"They were fine with the actual show. But Bel wanted a platypus as a pet. She even snuck a raccoon into the house to get something more 'creative' than the stuff at the pet stores."

Once again, the bed wobbled. Laughter died on Duke's lips with a wheeze as he inhaled, exhaled, sighed. "Lion Tamer, you don't think he—you believe someone else did it, right? Took his life and all?"

Twisting again, Danny found himself facing the pile of soda cans on the stripped mattress. He dug his fingernails into an itchy comforter. "He never seemed down, so it makes no sense."

"Not everyone who is down looks like it." Rustling of sheets sounded from below. "But, I really don't want it to be suicide."

"Oh yeah, murder is a way more fun option." He buried his nose into the comforter.

"Not like that. My family's Catholic. A lot of them kind of view suicide as a barrier to getting to heaven."

Peering through the slats of the wooden fence on the top bunk, he caught a glint of light from a beer bottle near the head of the unused bed. That made sense why Bel's attempt shocked Duke. Not only could he lose his sister here, but for all of eternity.

Danny drew in a breath and shoved his blanket off his nose. "And what do you believe?"

"With luck, not much."

A fist slammed against the door. It swung open with a squeak as Dean lumbered into the room, face red. He shoved a phone in front of Danny's eyes, burning his retinas temporarily. "Look what my girlfriend discovered, Princess."

"That technology's been around for a while. Make sure she has a patent." He blinked away purple spots. With any imagination, they could've passed for bears or lions too.

Dean gripped the siding of the bed with his fist. "Principal Ari wants to see you in her office." He suppressed a giddiness in his voice. It came out more tenor instead of the normal bass bellows. For some reason, the higher registers sent goosebumps rippling up Danny's arms. Perhaps because it sounded more like a scream.

Purple cleared from his eyes. He slid down the side of the bed, making sure to choose the end where Dean wasn't standing. Sliding his feet into untied tennis shoes, he shambled toward the door.

"One more thing, Lion Tamer."

Danny turned as Dean plowed past him into the hallway. "Yeah, Duke?"

"Mind staying out of the room until late tonight? My family's coming up for my birthday. *All* of my family."

"No Protestants are allowed, got it."

Duke sighed. "That's not what I meant."

When he reached the office, he noticed Ari had replaced the hard wooden bench with two green fabric chairs and a side table. A number of posters decorated the wall behind it. One, which Ari's head wasn't covering, contained a black border with bold white letters reading *TRUST*. Above it featured a picture of a silhouette collapsing into the arms of a group of people.

Ashley rolled her eyes at her screen. "You're here early. We don't leave to see Ned for a couple more minutes."

"I have a meeting with the principal."

Ari set a green mug onto a coaster. Some sort of tea, herbal and strong, wisped from it. "Sit." She crossed her legs in a lilac pantsuit. It aged her about ten years.

He sat. Settling into the soft cushion, he watched the smirk disappear with Dean outside the office doors. It was a pleasure not talking to him all the way there.

The principal pressed the mug against her lips and sipped. "I've never been much for small talk, so let's get to the point. Valentina raised to my attention that you wished Reuben's family prayers on Twitter."

To the point indeed, throwing himself, Valentina, and polite conversation under the yellow school bus at once.

"Yes, Reuben's brother had talked about struggling with the loss. I thought I would offer a bit of comfort."

Wrinkles tugged at her eyes and lips as she exhaled. Did she own any other lipstick than purple? "While we appreciate your attempts to help, do you recall the tweet which Miss July Jackson posted the night of Homecoming?"

Her plum-taloned fingers scrolled through photos until she pulled up a screenshot. She handed him the phone.

> @christmasinjuly67 2 Tim 2:22 Flee the evil desires of youth and pursue righteousness, faith, love and peace, along with those who call on the Lord out of a pure heart. Going to HC with a dude who clearly didn't read this verse. Praying for him. He's gonna need it.

Oh Dagon, his stomach burbled with fire.

She grabbed the phone from his fingertips. "We advise you to tread carefully with your posts on online forums. This isn't the first time Miss Valentina brought to our attention your history on Twitter."

Saliva caught in his throat. It tasted like blood. He choked it down.

Ari's features softened. She looked five years younger as a smile swam up her cheeks. "Breathe. We're not planning to discipline you. You had good intentions with your post about Reuben's family."

He relaxed and found his shoulders and back had grown stiff from how much he tightened them.

"However"—she sipped from the mug again—"I still want to caution you. I will not tolerate stupidity on my student council. Bigoted posts will result in serious consequences."

Doo-doo-woo sounded from Ashley's computer as the bright light died. She swung a black bag on her shoulder and knocked two K-cups into the trash. She missed a number of them hiding behind the computer. "If you don't mind, Ari, I need to take him to a meeting."

"Not at all." Ari leaned forward and reached a hand toward his shoulder. She stopped and folded it into a ball. "Promise me you will throttle back the posts, for your sake, not mine."

No kidding, he could risk losing that precious protection.

Chewbacca noises gurgled from his abdomen. He clutched his stomach, winced, and nodded.

"Good kid."

Always was, he hated it.

Ashley's radio blared something about a young girl visiting a mansion. A new audiobook. From what he could tell, the house with its stained-glass windows, large garden hedges, and gaslit rooms had Arthurian legend buried inside it.

He screwed his face as he listened harder. The driver seemed to catch his eye for a moment. "My niece gave it to me. I don't usually listen to books like this."

She reached forward and dialed the volume knob a little louder. As a dog in the book dashed forward to chase a squirrel in the hedged maze, he watched a chipmunk dart up a tree with bark so gray it could be stuck in a nursing home of old age. A fresh Febreze scent disguised the stench of moldy fries from the various fast-food bags by his feet.

His phone buzzed, and he answered it far faster than he expected. No time to do so in the psych ward. Not with it buried in a small locker.

> DUKE: Lion Tamer, can you do me a favor and get back
> to the room fast?

> DANNY: I'm seeing Ned. He apparently improves when-
> ever he gets visitors.

He shifted in his seat and pulled out a stack of napkins buried underneath him. Toss in a few ketchup packets, and Ashley could start her own food truck business.

> DUKE: Can you make the appointment quick? My family
> just got here and … it's awkward.

> DANNY: Well I'm awkward, so I don't think I'll help
> much.

> DUKE: I mean can you, like, come in and act like we have
> to do a group project. I tried to get Hannah to come, but
> she's busy practicing something for a speech tourna-
> ment.

Cotton candy clouds covered a November sky. Already five, and the sun had begun to sink in the horizon. They'd have limited visiting hours anyway.

> DANNY: I can try, but he's kind of clingy. No one really comes to see him.

> DANNY: What's wrong? Did your mom just ban you from watching My Little Pony?

> DUKE: (Expletive Danny refused to read) you Lion Tamer. It was the one time. Hannah told me we were watching Teen Titans. She tricked me.

> DANNY: Friendship is magic.

They rolled into the parking lot. The building appeared even more dreary in the slate background with the black silhouettes of trees bordering the area. All had sheared off their leaves, leaving behind skeletonic branches.

> DUKE: It's not that. It's Bel. She came to visit. Apparently was just released from the ward.

> DANNY: Oh, is she doing all right?

"You might want to put that away." Ashley nodded to the phone as she yanked out her keys from the ignition.
"Just waiting on a reply."

> DUKE: She lost the baby.

Ned stared at the column, bloodshot eyes perusing one block and then the next and the next. His fingers twitched, moving toward one and retreating. As he bent in closer, Danny noticed he smelled like someone who needed a shower that week ... and sterile.
He centered on a target.

His finger poked a wooden block that landed with a dull thud on the table. He pinched it and placed it atop the shaky Jenga tower. Folding his arms, he leaned back in his plastic chair and grinned. Today he wore a Steelers shirt and gray sweatpants to match and gray socks, no shoes. He looked human.

Danny frowned at the Jenga tower. "Checkmate, Ned. No way I can move another piece without making it fall."

He flicked up a silvery eyebrow. "Try anyway."

Resting his hand on his fist, careful not to place his elbows on the table, Danny observed each of the small blocks. He poked one with a shaky thumb. The tower didn't collapse. He inched it out more and more until, at last, that row shook on a single slat. Placing the brick on top, he exhaled as the top-heavy tower remained put.

"Checkmate indeed." Ned rested his folded hands on his stomach and tilted back his head. "This is why I wanted you in charge of my school when I was gone. You wouldn't let it collapse."

"Maybe you should've waited a couple years to have a breakdown. They don't let minors principal schools."

Ned chuckled, burying his chin into folds of skin. His watery eyes and taffy-pulled skin resembled those of Danny's grandfather.

"Any chance your mother wants to put you up for adoption?"

"I don't know how she feels about parents who try to set their kid's friends on fire."

At this, both of them snorted. Danny almost bumped into the table, a disaster for anyone working at Jenga Corporation. The chuckle caught on the back of his tongue and tickled his throat. What in the world was he doing? Months ago, he wanted to sue Ned over arson. Now? Well, now, everything about the situation filled his diaphragm with a light, bright sensation.

Perhaps he needed to check himself into the ward.

A flickering TV in the Day Room filled the room with light and the image of a couple in *General Hospital* kissing. Nearby, a couple of patients flipped a pile of cards on a small table.

"Ned, do you see a lot of suicidal patients around here?" He leaned forward, to the right of the tower, keeping his voice down.

Ned's thumbs chased each other in a circle. "I suppose it would be like me asking if you saw a lot of tired high school students at King's."

"Fair. What are common symptoms you see in them?"

Breathing through his nostrils, he stared at a bookcase that flashed bubble-letter titles from children's books and soft-touch self-help books for the adults. "It depends. Some withdraw from activities." A man in a 76ers tee curled up in a corner, staring at the wall. Moans from the hallway penetrated the noise of the *General Hospital credits theme*. "Others forget to shower or eat. 'Course, the workers here make sure to"—he cleared his throat—"encourage patients to maintain personal health."

Danny winced at Ned's oily hair that clumped into feathers. Perhaps the employees, even if forcing him to bathe, didn't check for thorough work.

"Why do you ask?"

"Did anyone fill you in about Reuben?"

"We have ways of finding out about the outside world." His eyes flicked up to the smoke detector on the ceiling. "Even if they try to prevent it. Guess I got a taste of my own medicine, huh?"

"I'm asking because Reuben didn't seem depressed. He gave no warning signs. I have a"—he leaned forward more; the Jenga tower wobbled—"I have a feeling someone took him out."

Ned's features darkened. Still smiling, he glanced at the table. "Not on a date, I imagine." He met Danny with an icy stare. "Why do you ask?"

All the memories of last year came flooding back. He knew that tone, a tone you don't want to mess with, even in the strict confines of a ward. A voice that said, "I've taken lives before, I'll do it again."

"No reason, Ned. Now how about we stack this Jenga tower again?"

Chapter Twenty-Two

A CADEMY HERALD NEWS
Why the jailbird sings: Two previous King's employees indicted

Michelle Gad

Last month, during the Homecoming dance, senior Valentina Inanna accused her date, August Rezzen, of attempted sexual assault. August, a former government teacher and alumnus of King's, offered to take Inanna to Homecoming after her previous date supposedly bailed. Although the regulations for school dances state a date must not exceed the age of twenty-two, Inanna said she didn't mind bending rules.

"He'd turned twenty-three not too long ago," Inanna said. "And this isn't the first time someone's brought someone outside the age restrictions. Dean (Chahal) brought a college student with him (Julia Mesh, 19)."

She also noted that King's, in a school-wide email, made a big deal about her breaking the rules and about her style of dress.

"Even if I was wearing a nun's outfit, they would've made a big deal. It's classic victim blaming."

After the two took a break in line for the drinking fountain during the dance, August suggested they head outside to catch some cool air. This was shortly before Reuben Benjamin committed suicide in the very same hallway.

"We were both hot," Inanna said. "It seemed like an innocent suggestion. So much heat builds up in those hallways and in the gym."

When they went outside, Rezzen suggested they go on a walk around the loop of campus. Inanna agreed. But as they made their way around buildings, she noticed he avoided pathways that contained people, such as couples who were running late to the dance.

A half mile into the walk, Rezzen started acting strange, according to Inanna.

"He kept brushing hands with me and leaning uncomfortably close. I kept stepping away, but then he'd take a step closer, almost bumping me off the sidewalk."

Inanna suggested they return to the dance. As she did so, Rezzen grabbed her wrist and shoved her against the brick wall of the mathematics building. He tried to kiss her as she pushed him away repeatedly telling him "No."

A scream heard from the gymnasium — later revealed to have surfaced from the incident of Benjamin committing suicide — caused Rezzen to release his grip. Inanna broke loose and bolted for her dormitory. She says Rezzen didn't follow behind.

A number of eyewitnesses claimed they saw and heard the end of the occurrence. Junior Annabelle Ruger says she shouted at Rezzen to release Inanna but was too far away for him to hear. Junior Remington Musk, Ruger's date, also described what he'd seen.

"When I saw Rezzen push her against the building, I was about ready to deck him in the face," Remington said. "Luckily by the time I ran over there, she'd escaped. Annabelle and I met her back at the dorm, but by then, she'd already called the cops."

A number of sources who wished to remain anonymous also reported Rezzen for attempts of assault. Several had noted cases of Rezzen brushing hands with them in his office and kissing them on the cheek before they left meetings with him. Many of these sources reported these incidents to the police after Inanna had.

Prior to his arrest and arraignment, Rezzen commented that Inanna had fabricated much of the story.

"We were close by when everything with Reuben went down. I think she was so traumatized by that that she mixed up details. I don't even remember seeing either Annabelle or Remington."

At Rezzen's arraignment he declared not guilty, as did the former employee Roger Enlil. Those who had accused him of sexual misconduct refused to comment and asked to remain anonymous.

Danny folded the newspaper and tucked it away into his bag. A gavel rapped on a podium at the front. He crunched his knees on the chair in front of him to hide his phone as he texted.

DANNY: Great job on the article. I'm sure all ten students who read it will be very informed.

MICHELLE: Ha. Hilarious.

DANNY: So I guess that rules out murder for Reuben, huh? Since two of our suspects were supposedly walking around campus during it.

MICHELLE: There's still Dean.

DANNY: Ha. Hilarious.

MICHELLE: And a bunch of randos who were in that back hallway.

DANNY: Reuben didn't know a whole lot of people besides us and our suspects. So that sort of rules out motive. Let's cross our fingers for Dean and get him expelled.

MICHELLE: I'm trying to decide who hates the other

more, you or him.

DANNY: I don't hate anyone. But if he's the murderer ...

Valentina called order, even though the room had silenced by then. She glanced over her shoulder at Ari for a nod. Approval sealed, Valentina returned to the classroom.

"All right, student council, we have a number of things to cover today. We're down on numbers for the food drive on the eleventh, a week from now. It's at five o'clock in the evening, so most of you should be free. I've checked schedules. So far, it's myself and my boyfriend—who is not a member of this council, by the way. Any takers?"

Oh boy, a day third-wheeling with his two favorite people? Dean and Valentina?

"Come on, guys. We're all required to do ten hours a semester. The only one who's already got his done is—" She aimed wrinkled nostrils at Danny. "We need at least three people to sort through the cans."

Students shuffled in their desks, heads bowed. Ari nodded at Danny from across the room. Why him?

Danny's cheeks flushed as he raised his hand. "What time on Monday?"

Valentina glared at him, then her list on the podium. "As I said before, five."

"Cross-country's done by then. I can volunteer." Might as well remain on Ari's good side. He didn't want to lose that protection with Dean and Valentina down his throat.

Pinching her eyelids into slits, she rotated a glower at all the other heads in the room. She sighed and clicked a pen. As she signed, she wobbled the podium more than usual. "Guess that settles that."

Heat died in his face as he stole a glance at the principal, who beamed at him. Her face returned to stone. Hopefully this would make up for the so-called mistake of wishing Reuben's family prayers on Twitter.

"OK, next order of business. We need to start using the boys' gymnasium again. The men's basketball team can't keep doing practices at seven in the girls' place. And let's not even get started on the number of complaints we've gotten about PE classes running up and down hall-ways of academic buildings to avoid class time in there."

The only person who hadn't complained was Martin. Academic buildings were far more sanitary. Far less Purell to use in those, but his hands still bled most days.

A hand shot up next to Danny followed by a whimper. A girl in all dark mascara and lipstick shrunk into a leather jacket twice her size. "Can we wait until at least next semester?"

Valentina's lips pursed. "No."

"B-but, it's on-only been a month."

"We have at least ten basketball games from now until December. Stuffing that many parents and athletes into the girls' gym is a fire hazard."

Oooh, those were fighting words.

"If you want to forgo safety of students"—she licked her lips—"that's fine. But I move that we open up usage of the boys' gym. Especially because we're using it for the food drive next Monday. Any opposed?"

Shoe shuffles and the ticking of a clock with math symbols such as pi and $\sqrt{49}$ filled the room. Valentina banged the gavel against the podium.

"All right, now to the nitty-gritty. Since the school is considering pressing charges against the student who cyberbullied Bel and Reuben, I move that we implement stricter measures on social media usage."

Danny crunched his knees again.

> DANNY: News lady, do you know if the school is pressing charges against July?

> MICHELLE: Not sure. Valentina keeps talking about it like it's headline material. Something tells me Ari's got a better head on her shoulders.

Ari's icy voice across the room caused him to snap his legs forward and shove his phone into his pocket. He missed. It clattered onto the floor.

"I appreciate your enthusiasm, Miss Valentina, but as I stated in the October assembly, I don't want to restrict freedom of speech. Any student who chooses to post something unwise will reap the consequences."

In the glow of a projector light, Valentina's face still managed a rosy hue. "But how do we *measure* that? Sure, we can pick out slurs and stuff. But what about gray areas?"

"Tell you what." Pulling out a notepad, she flashed it once in front of the blue projector light before sliding it into Valentina's fingers. "Create a list of objective things for me to find. If I approve, we'll go from there."

Valentina set the notebook on the podium and reached for the pen she'd dropped on the desk. "What does 'go from there' look like?"

"We'll have students register all social media accounts for us to monitor. Any infractions will result in discipline."

"Discipline? Like expulsion?"

Ari thrust her fists on her hips, and her dress expanded and contracted in a deep breath. She settled on the teacher's desk, skirt bumping into various photographs and pencil containers. "Whoever ran this school before acted like the worst thing that can happen to a student is to be banished from a place."

Students in the rows in front of Danny shifted in their groaning chairs, all leaning in. A gust from the side wall heaters ruffled some orange sheets dangling on a corkboard.

Scooping a picture frame into her hand from the desk, Ari stared at it a long while.

"The worst thing in the world isn't being banished from somewhere you loved."

She set it down and sighed.

"It's when you're forced to live, to survive in somewhere you hate."

Obi's chirps met him before he swung open the heavy door.

"I'm coming, little guy." He kicked off his shoes at the front Persian carpet.

In the computer room, he found a bowl of diced apples and a blue bird bopping up and down in his wiry cage. Danny stooped and grabbed an apple slice. He poked it through a hole. Obi nibbled it for a few moments and went back to a plastic ball with a bead inside it. For some reason, the noise fascinated Obi.

"Found the toy in a buried box upstairs," a familiar voice called from another room. "He had one in there shaped like a bird, but ... well, you better come see her."

Dropping his book bag on the carpet of the computer room, he meandered past a maze of walls that blocked the family room entrance. He sniffed and noticed a distinct lack of incense or Lysol. He discovered Rayah on a family room couch. With one hand, she traced pictures of flowers on the soft brown upholstery. Her other clutched a chewed-up plastic bird. She slid it into his palm. He ran his fingers over the grooved bite marks that ran up and down the green wings.

"His first date with her didn't go so well." Rayah "erased" her picture of the flower by smudging it with the side of her hand.

"He's not the only one." He slumped next to her and draped an arm over her shoulder. "Have your episodes gotten any worse?"

She shrugged and stared at a blank television. "It comes and goes in waves."

Craning over her, he snagged a remote. "So Ashley recruited you for this too, huh? She mentioned there was no way she could watch the bird."

Rayah nodded. He pressed the on switch.

"Your student council meeting got out early."

"Ari doesn't let Valentina talk for an eternity. Kind of nice to have the principal in those meetings. That way we can't make everything about school dances." He navigated his thumb to the Hulu button.

"I didn't know you'd get back so early, so I asked someone to take over after I left."

With a flash of light, the screen silenced. He set the remote on the side table. "Oh, I didn't know you needed to leave."

She chewed on her lip. "Group project, sorry."

He swung his arm over and returned to nursing the plastic toy back to health. Rubbing his thumb up and down it, the fluted texture bit into his skin.

"You wanna try to do something over Thanksgiving break? I know we haven't had much of a chance to go on any dates at King's. Figured the dining commons is the equivalent of taking you out to eat at a gas station."

Thin, her smile dashed up and back down into a straight line. "I think they'll be arriving any minute."

"Who?"

"My replacement."

A knock at the door was followed by the sound of Obi rattling and revving his wings against his cage. In an instant, Rayah bolted out of her seat and scrambled toward the TV where she'd set down her bag. Right above her, glass objects shimmered on the mantel. Danny's fists itched to knock one of them onto the hard floor.

"So, about Thanksgiving break?"

Rayah winced as she tugged her bag over her shoulder. "I'm sorry, Danny. I don't know if that's the best idea."

"Christmas break? Or Kwanzaa-Christmas-Hanukkah-Omiso-ka-Yule-Guadalupe break?"

"I promise it's not you."

His heart throbbed in his temples, so loud that he heard thunder. "I don't understand. Are you saying it's not me it's you I want to break up with you sort of thing?"

"No." She sighed and shied back as he reached his hand for hers. "It's not you, or me, I don't know. I need time."

Right as the front door swung open, Rayah hurried down the hall and out of sight. July replaced her moments later as she fixed her headband, which had tilted the red bow too close to her ear. With her hair in two buns atop her head, she looked like Minnie Mouse.

She jerked her chin into a single nod. "Rayah said she needed someone to grab third shift?"

He retreated to the couch and sank into it. "She didn't know I was coming."

July swung keys around her ring finger and dropped them into a macramé bowl. "Drove all this way, I might as well check in on the bird."

Her neon tank and shorts disappeared with her around the corner. In a stupor, Danny stared at the mantel, fixated on a single glass tree at the center. The leafless branches glinted in the light of the ceiling fan like empty veins of a once vibrant heart. Why didn't trees bleed, he wondered? With so many veins and so many branches to snap, why didn't they scream as their bark flew up in a haze of smoke and fire?

Returning, July tossed the plastic ball from the cage to herself and rolled it on the ground. "If I had to hear that thing jingle one more time."

Danny set the plastic bird on a side table. He'd almost forgotten he was still holding it. "Let the poor thing have its fun."

She kicked off her tennies and selected a chair by the fireplace.

"July, does Rayah hate me?"

"Danny, is King's a good school?" She sneered at him and threw her head back over the top of the chair. "Oh goodness, Dan, I was kidding. Why would you ask such a stupid question?"

Locking his gaze with the glass tree, he recounted Rayah dashing out of the room.

With an eye roll, she pinched the bow on her bandana again. "You'd want space too if you had an episode every other day. The Reuben thing didn't help, you know."

"Yeah but—"

"You weren't dating anybody last year, but tell me, with all the vomiting flareups you had, did that make you want to get up and go to a buffet with some girl?"

"Who'd take a girl on a date to a buffet?"

"What I'm saying is, some people need space, even from those they love the most." She crossed her ankles over the armrest and leaned back sideways. "Some birds need to stay in a cage before they feel free to fly again."

Chirps to a somber song sounded from Obi's cage. Danny lumbered out of the squashy couch and retrieved the plastic ball. He dodged around the walls and into the computer room. Obi bobbed so much when he saw the ball, he looked like a pump on the syrup containers in the ice cream store.

"I'm blaming you if I go insane with how much he moves that thing."

"Insanity is worse than most things." Danny checked himself. He was going to add "even dying." He hovered over his seat on the couch for a moment and straightened himself again. "July, I have to ask. Did you—"

"No. I didn't post anything to his page. Yes, it was linked to my username. Yes, they said I'd also posted for Bel. I know it looks bad." She returned to an upright position and deadlocked him in a serious gaze. "You *have* to believe me."

"I trust you." He slumped into the couch. "But Valentina's talking about pressing charges. I think you should present your case to Ari before things get out of hand."

She had to before Valentina created a criteria for what tweets could result in discipline.

"Besides, the principal who kicked you out is in jail now," he added.

She relaxed, letting the fabric consume her shoulders. "I could schedule something Wednesday. That's the day our homeschool co-op doesn't do anything. But it might be late notice."

"Got the secretary's cell." He dug his phone out of his pocket and rattled a quick text to Ashley. "Even if she says no, I'll ask Ari myself. Something tells me she likes me … as a student." He felt it was important to add.

"Every principal likes you." July chuckled to herself. Then she bolted upright. "Be careful, Danny."

"Why?"

"Take a look at any teacher's pet in history. The more the adults love you, the more the others will figure out a way to make your life hell."

Chapter Twenty-Three

JULY: Hey, Danny, left my government textbook at Ned's house. It's the one titled We the People. You didn't grab it by chance?

JULY: I have a test on a chapter in it on Thursday. The lady in my homeschool co-op is strict. She looks like Frida Kahlo but meaner and without a cute monkey on her shoulder.

DANNY: That the one you left under the chair? Found it. When you coming up to King's?

JULY: This afternoon, I should finish right around the time your PE class does. I remember Reuben said he had it at the same time as you.

DANNY: Dagon, that's a hard commute. Any chance you could stop by the boys' gym to pick it up? I have to sort of rush to my next class (the gym is far away from literally everything).

JULY: No problem, see you there after PE.

Ari set a plate of Danish on a side table as the group of four huddled in the main office area. Behind her hung a curtain and photos of her children.

Danny reached for a Danish and bit into it. Flakes showered his jeans like the light snowflake frost outside. Cream cheese stuck to the roof of his mouth as he swallowed.

"I appreciate you three meeting with me prior to your morning classes."

Ashley hid a yawn behind a fist, noise blocked out by the coughing heater stationed somewhere far off. Her typing continued after the brief break.

"For the food drive this Monday, as you know, we've placed bins in every academic building for each grade to drop off food. We'll send out an announcement today to remind each grade what to donate. Freshmen: peanut butter; sophomores: canned meats; juniors: canned fruits; and seniors: granola bars."

He bit into the Danish again. Eyeing the raspberry ones on the plate, he wondered if those would taste less like refrigerated paper. Dean grabbed the two remaining scarlet pastries and handed one to his girlfriend. Danny scooted his chair two inches to the right, nudging it as close to the principal on the bench as possible for a male student.

Out of the corner of his eye, he saw Valentina fiddle with her fuchsia skirt and salmon leggings to mismatch.

"Of course, we'll also announce that the grade with the largest amount of donations will receive a pizza party at a set date. I realize this may sway more in the favor of upperclassmen because they have access to cars, and therefore, more access to items for the food drive."

An orange parking registration sign dangled above Ari's head. To think half a year before, Ned didn't let students venture off campus for any reason. Now, students vanished during free periods for Taco Bell runs and to load up on 64-ounce frozen sodas at faraway gas stations.

"I also ask that you enlist other student council members to watch the bins for any case of thievery. They don't have to stand guard, but if they spy someone grabbing an item, to warn them to put it back. We've had some items go missing these past few days."

By habit, his eyes flicked up to the ceiling. Two holes remained where Ari had dismantled the office camera. The smoke detectors had been removed from the dorms as well.

"So far we've had no one else sign up to help with the drive on Monday." Ari pressed a clipboard against her knees. Her lilac leggings clashed with a deeper shade of purple on her skirt. "And every time I give a student an option for detention or helping with the drive, he or she chooses detention. Go figure."

The deep-purple skirt melted on the wooden bench as she sat. "Any questions?"

When Valentina's hand flew up, crumbs fell by her ankles. "Did you get my email about the criteria for hate speech and social media posts? I sent it last night."

"I meant questions about the food drive."

"One of the students on the speech and debate team, a debater, looked over the points. He says I have a solid argument. He might even use it at his next tournament if his team is given that topic."

Ari aimed a glance at Dean, then at Danny. Danny's abdomen burned as he half raised a hand.

"I know a number of students with other perishables that don't fit into a category. Had a friend look it up last night, and food drives need those things too—oil, vegetables, spices. Can we find some way to incorporate those?"

Pressing a pen cap to her chin, Ari nodded, lips quirking upward. "Will students donate those even in the absence of a competition by grade?"

"I was thinking maybe we could have a school-wide reward. Since some grades are having a harder time than others for items. I hear peanut butter's the most expensive."

"What kind of reward?"

"If we reach a certain number of items, they could give each student a number of bonus points in a class or a day off of school next semester."

"Choose one."

Fire flushed his cheeks. He glanced at Dean and Valentina, who offered nothing but glares. "What would you guys prefer?"

Exchanging a troubled glance, the couple shared shrugs. At last, Valentina sighed and pursed her lips slathered in some sort of pinkish glitter. "I could use bonus points in Spanish, to be honest."

Ari scribbled something on a notepad and tore out the paper. She rose and handed it to Ashley. "Add this to the morning announcements."

Yawning again, the secretary slapped the paper next to a stack of others on her desk.

Returning, the principal jabbed a pen at Danny, almost poking him in the nose. "My student council doesn't have a president ... yet. But when it does, consider running."

His gaze shifted to the floor to avoid Valentina's burning glare. He did manage to watch her hand fly up.

"I'd still like to talk about the criteria for social media."

The principal lifted her watch. "According to this, you have about ten minutes before class. I'm sure you'd not like a second detention for punctuality, Miss Valentina."

"I can meet up later in the day during my free period. What are you doing around fifth-period range?"

"A meeting."

Valentina's cowboy boots bounced up and down. "Can you bump it?"

"Considering Miss July Jackson will be driving a long way to discuss the reasons against her expulsion, I would say no. From what she's emailed me so far, she has a compelling case."

Maybe a debater from the speech team had looked over it as well.

"She can wait until sixth period." By now, Dean had clamped his hands onto Valentina's shoulders to stop her from shaking.

"I have another meeting with a faculty member then. My afternoon is booked."

"Can she try for another day? Isn't she homeschooled or something? That means she has a more flexible schedule."

"If I have to argue with you one more time, Miss Valentina, I will guarantee a detention with you. She emailed me first; she gets first pick on a meeting time. Understood?"

Valentina fixed her shoes with a dead clunk. She must've nodded because a soft "good" escaped Ari's violet lips. Collecting her clipboard and the plate, she retreated into her office. Danny grabbed his swivel chair and veered it into the office of an advisor who wouldn't arrive until the afternoon. He went to grab his bag but stopped short when a heavy black boot stepped on the front pouch. It led up to Dean towering over him.

"Can I help you, Dean?"

Out of his side poked Valentina's head. "You have July's number, right?"

He chewed on his cheek to avoid any clever remarks such as "Thirty-one, that's the number of days in July" and "Why? You want to apologize?"

Instead: "Yeah, why?"

"We were wondering if you could possibly text her to ask if she could move her meeting to another day." Valentina elbowed Dean. He eased his foot off the backpack. "Ari's awful at checking her email, unlike Ned. And since it's early morning, I figure July can have time to plan ahead."

In a rapid movement, he swung his bag onto his shoulders before Dean had a chance to rethink.

"I don't know if I can. She mentioned something about needing to pick up a book after the meeting. I was going to give it to her in the gym after PE."

"Can she pick that up and still move her meeting to another day?"

Coughing sounded from a heater's blast of warmth. "It's a lot of gas to drive from her home to here. And I think she needs the book for a test on Thursday. I'm going to say no for now." He goggled the clock to avoid Dean's shadow as it loomed over him. "Sorry, but I need to go to class. Can't risk a first detention."

He ducked on his way out in case Dean swooped his arm to grab him, but neither Dean nor his girlfriend moved to stop him.

"What do you mean we're doing PE outside?" Martin shoved his glasses up his nose and tucked his fingers underneath his armpits as if bracing himself for the burst of cool outdoors. "It's, like, negative ten out there."

"Positive thirty-three." The teacher looped a whistle string around her finger. "And we've had a number of parents complain about having class in there since the Homecoming incident."

Danny's legs itched as he twisted toward the door that led to the entrance. Why did his last class have to get out so early? And why did he choose today, of all days, to stuff his belongings in a locker room?

"What about doing laps around the academic buildings?"

"Also complaints, Martin." A chink sounded from the whistle as it collapsed onto the teacher's chest. She wore a Pittsburgh Steelers shirt, just like the one Danny'd seen on Ned at the ward. "I emailed you all this morning to remind you to bring leggings and sweatpants."

Exposed skin from the shorts and tees appeared purplish in the dim lighting of the concessions stand area.

Martin inched a hand in the air; it looked red from fresh blood. "Most of us don't check email during the day. We're too busy shivering on our way to classes."

The teacher pinched her nose. "Go back to your dormitories, grab warmer clothes, and jog at least a mile outside. I expect you to run in pairs to keep you honest. Get a running partner and go."

Before Danny could dash toward the locker room, he felt an arm loop with his.

"Partners?" Martin gripped his bicep with fierce clawlike hands.

Umm, he was taken? "Don't you usually pair up with a kid named Reggie? Short stocky guy? Does role-playing games on the weekend?"

"Out for the day, bronchitis. Don't you usually pair up with Reuben?"

Touché.

Still, Danny lifted Martin's pinky to unhinge his grip from his arm. They hunched into themselves as soft snowflakes pelted their faces on the way to their dormitories. Martin lived in Kading, so they visited that first. Danny waited in the lobby while Martin trudged his way up three flights of stairs. Perusing the photos of Kading Hall doing their annual Attack of the Zombies, Yule Ball, and Renaissance Faire events, his legs itched again, compelling him toward the door. Perhaps he could sprint back to the locker room to text July about the change of location. He could stop by Ari's office and pop into their meeting to let her know.

But again, *We the People* was stuffed into a locker. Didn't make much sense to reroute.

Not to mention Martin seemed like the kid who liked to ask the teacher for more homework and to tattle if Danny didn't run a full mile during PE.

Martin returned marshmallowed into a stuffed winter coat and burnt-orange sweatpants to match. He'd wrapped a scarf over his nose and face to eliminate the pinkish glow they'd received from the cold.

"Phrat River next?" His voice came out muffled through the fabric.

"I'm fine with running in shorts. We do it in cross-country all the time."

After all, their final meet, last weekend, a shower of sleet and hail followed them down muddy hills and across creaky wooden bridges. Best believe that all the runners wore shorts cut off unfortunately close to the backside.

Martin let out a miserable moan as they entered into the frozen what he called "tundra." Flakes spotted brown grass.

Two minutes in, Martin stopped by a building to clap his hand against the brick and heave asthmatic breaths. Danny jogged in place. He stopped when he remembered Reuben liked to do the same.

"You do realize, Marty, that a *running* buddy requires you to run."

They puffed breaths fogged with a November chill. Even Danny's nostrils had frozen and his purpling skin stung with the cold. Perhaps he should've gone to Phrat to grab a hoodie.

"It's Mar*tin*." This came with a whimper. "And I'm not used to running out in the cold."

"Come on, you've had to be outside in the cold at least once. The school makes you do a sport."

"Yeah, I did golf, in the spring." He added this with a dignified sniff, which caused him to sneeze into his large coat.

"Well, a mile isn't that far, so let's keep going."

He groaned into his scarf. "Fine, but go slower. You run too fast."

Why choose him as a partner, then? Danny's legs hurt from pacing so slow. Each rock he stepped on sent shooting pains up his calves. But he continued, knowing the mile would elapse soon and he could text July.

"So, Mar-tin. You got any plans for Thanksgiving break?"

Martin stopped to retie his shoelaces. "Family gets together to eat way too much of Grandma's applesauce. Everyone's required to bring a dish. Dad can't cook for beans. Literally. He. Can't. Cook. Beans."

Oh Dagon, what had he unleashed?

He unbent himself and began a slow jog, almost as if Danny had plunked him underwater. "There was this one year he tried to tackle the turkey. We told him to take something simpler. Like the cranberry sauce, or the gelatin stuff straight-up from the can, but no sir, he *had to* make the turkey."

They ambled past a cardboard turkey stuck into the ground of the football field.

"So he decided to deep-fry it." His breath trailed with wheezes. He stopped to walk, placing his hands on a pompom winter cap. "Mind you, he can't deep-fry cheese, but he tried for a whole turkey. Long story short, it backfired, and he got horrible burns and ended up in the hospital. Some Thanksgiving, huh?"

"Uh-huh." Danny angled toward the direction of the gym. Perhaps they'd make a mile by the time they reached it.

"So can your dad cook?"

Heat surged in his neck veins. "I imagine the angels taught him a trick or two on the grill."

"Huh?"

"He died, Marty. But he did make a mean corn casserole. We have the recipe if you want."

Martin didn't. He also apparently didn't feel much like talking for the rest of the jog.

Danny dropped Martin off at his next building, the LLC. Then he sprinted to the gym, catching his breath at the door. Rawness from the cold seared his throat. He let his lungs adjust for a few breaths and dots in his vision blur away before entering.

Heat warmed his fingers and nose as he veered left toward the locker rooms. He had to grope the wall to find the doors to the back hallway. Gym teacher must've shut off the lights.

He entered the one for the men's golf and the smell of feet fragranced his entry. Locker 616. Spinning the lock, he eyed the other ones dangling off the handles of the lockers. He bet the most complicated one, one with three dials for numbers and a fingerprint lock, or something in a spy movie, belonged to Martin.

A rusty *click* and open went the locker. He pulled out his cell phone and rattled a quick text to July.

> DANNY: Gym got out early by ten minutes. Let me know if you get out of your meeting before the original planned time. It could actually help me arrive to my next class without me having to sprint there.

No read receipt flashed across the screen. Odd, she usually replied in an instant. Then again, she probably was still in the throng of her meeting with Ari. He pulled out a plastic bag of his day clothes and tossed a quick prayer that the principal would hear her case. See her innocence.

After slipping on jeans and a hoodie, he crumpled the bag into a trash bin and exited the room, inhaling the fresh air of the hallway. He clutched July's government book in his hand, wondering why the homeschool co-op didn't just use eBooks. Didn't they do most classes online?

Right as he creaked open the door to the locker room, he heard a loud popping noise. The same one from Homecoming.

His heart thundered in his ears. He raced down the hallway and thrust open the doors. Blinking into the shafts of light from the hallway, he saw nothing at first.

He groped the wall for a light switch and found one by the foam padding underneath a basketball hoop.

The lights hummed alive, a single one blinking above the *WELCOME TO THE DEN* sign. Underneath it, at the bottom of the bleachers, lay a figure in a pool of scarlet blood. Her head tilted toward him with a familiar headband and a bow out of place, shot off by the gun that dangled in her hand off a bleacher step.

July.

Chapter Twenty-Four

"IT HAS TO BE MURDER. WHY HAVEN'T THE POLICE investigated further?"

Michelle blotted green paint on her canvas. Pale, the watercolor bled a sickly khaki onto a blob that Danny supposed resembled a treetop. She dipped her brush into the palette again. Much of the color and paint had dissolved from overuse that afternoon. "I mean, they arrested August as soon as Valentina and other victims reported him. I feel like murder is something they should take even more seriously."

Danny sighed. "She had some friends who claimed to be eyewitnesses. No one saw Reuben or July when they died."

"Can't they trace the guns back to their owners and find out who did this?"

"Not if they change a lot of hands, like from dealers and stuff. At least Hannah said something or other about it." His head felt a million miles away when she had explained it.

"They've got to be investigating this as we speak. No way three or four so-called suicides can happen without something suspicious."

Oh, but they could. Not with varied methods. Bel and Ned: pills; July and Reuben: guns. If they counted the teacher over the summer, Mr. Peterson, they would have to throw illegal drugs into the mix. No clear link between the deaths and attempted ones except they all happened in the gym, aside from Ned. Besides, Hannah had found a single school district with six suicides in six months. No way Washington County would spend a dime without clear-cut evidence.

"Can we please talk about something else?" Danny tapped the hairs of his brush over and over again in the red paint dispenser. It was the least-used one.

He sought distraction by watching the other inhabitants of the performance center atrium. He'd never been here before; they used it for events such as orchestra concerts when the time conflicted with a theater production. Light spilled from large windows and high ceilings, almost celestial. Rays drifted in soft shafts on curtained walls and large banners with photographs of past performances. One featured Michelle in a skin-tight toga dress from *Julius Caesar*.

Beware the Ides of March—every month felt like mid-March at this school.

All the way down, the lights landed on potted plants in cases large enough to fit a human body, if said person crumpled into a fetal position. He'd once watched a video that talked about human ashes fertilizing plants.

A person at a table across from him asked to borrow a paper towel from their table. He'd spilled the cup full of brown paint water all over his table. Danny handed his towel and Rayah's, since she left her canvas and expression blank at the table. She also decided to put Hannah between herself and her boyfriend.

Much as he appreciated the fiery redhead, she'd decided to mock up a graveyard on her canvas, full of ghosts and broken headstones. "July showed no warning signs of depression or suicidal thoughts." Michelle plunked her brush into a cup of milky gray water. "Bel, I could see, and some upperclassmen said Mr. Peterson seemed off in class some days. Reuben, not so much. But July? Never seen her shed a tear once. And we watched *The Boy in the Striped Pajamas* in one of our classes."

Hannah traced the *P* in a RIP on the main headstone. "You know, sometimes the strongest ones are the ones who hurt the most." She dipped her brush into the yellow, tainting it with black paint. Spikes erupted from her brush to form the head of a dandelion.

"It doesn't make any sense. She had a meeting with Ari to plead her case. Danny said Ari thought it was convincing. She could've cleared her name and gone back to King's. There was no reason for her to pull the trigger."

"Maybe it didn't go so well." Danny dropped his art tools and let the clots of red paint spatter the white tablecloth. "Again, let's stop talking about it."

He shoved himself out of his seat and marched toward a winding staircase that led upstairs. Pulling out his phone, he checked the time. He was ten minutes early.

Upon reaching the top, he peered over the banister at the inhabitants below. Students exchanged smiles and laughter that stung his ears. Cookie and cinnamon roll scents drifted all the way up to the top level from tables set up along the edges of the walls below, as if the taste of baked goods could lull any trauma from the day before. If he replaced the tile floors with dirt roads and the columns with booths, they might as well be participating in a painting activity at a county fair.

Before shoving his fingers into his pockets, he glanced at his hands, covered in scarlet paint. He strode past offices clustered on the top level toward the men's restroom. He wrinkled his nose at the scent of urine that blocked out any chocolate chip baked good stuck in his nostrils.

He pumped foam soap into his hands and scrubbed until his pinkish skin felt raw. Even as he pulled his hands away and thrust them under a roaring dryer, he still saw red. Maybe that's why Martin always used hand sanitizer.

Moisture clung to his hands. Who invented hand dryers and why did they think they worked? He rubbed his palms on his pants and exited the restroom. Now a snickerdoodle smell wafted up the stairs. Crumpling his nostrils, he ducked in an all-glass office door that read *Counseling Center* and dodged around students slumped into fabric chairs.

A heavy-set woman at the front desk beamed at him with bright-orange lipstick and hair to match. She grabbed a tissue box and passed it to a student near the counter who was sniveling.

"Do you have a scheduled appointment?"

"Signed up this morning, Danny Belte."

She slit her eyelids as she peered at a list on her computer. "Found you, Danny. And I see you already did the online form, so you don't have to fill out any paperwork here."

"Yes, ma'am."

"Have a seat. You'll be speaking with Vera. We apologize in advance if she's late. We've had a backlog of walk-ins today."

"Not a problem."

He spaced himself an extra seat, nearest to a larger student with a buzz cut and splotched birthmark on his face. All the kids in the room sat at least a seat apart from each other.

Distracting himself, he scanned titles on a bookshelf. *Self-Help for When You Can't Help Yourself, Worrying about Worrying, Why Doesn't Mommy Get Out of Bed in the Morning?*

He missed the *Code of Hammurabi* at Ned's place.

In the warm glow of the salt lamps in the waiting room, he spied a Rubik's Cube on a side table, atop a pile of health magazines. He grappled it and spun it with his fingers while observing the rest of the room. By now, the distinct smell of lavender from an essential oils diffuser caught the attention of his nose. Photographs of beaches and majestic forests lined the walls. From the mountains to the prairies, to the ocean shots that were situated above stacks of pamphlets on another side table. Far away from them, Danny could barely make out the bolded title of one in neon pink: *How to Cope with Racial Tension at School.*

"Daniel Belte?"

"Danny, yeah."

He set down the Rubik's Cube and approached a woman with bunned brown hair in a heathered cardigan and yoga pants. Her name tag read *Vera* in bright-blue letters. They shook hands. The corners of her lips stretched across her face as she motioned for him to follow.

They ambled into a low-lit office with a plush couch on one side and a leather chair on the other. A teddy bear was situated in the middle of the couch, and a coloring book and crayons awaited some artsy student on a side table. Danny sidled next to the bear and placed it at the other end of the couch.

Vera settled herself in the chair, organizing sheets of paper and compiling them onto a clipboard. She beamed at him for a moment. They wavered in silence. Danny cleared his throat. Was he supposed to say something? Didn't therapists ask a lot of questions?

"How are you feeling today?" Vera crinkled her eyes and wrinkled her forehead as if in a motion of pity.

"I don't know." It was an honest answer. He didn't plan on starting the session saying, "I kind of am half hoping it was a suicide, because if it was murder, I probably gave the murderers July's location." His mind trailed back to the principal's office. He'd told Valentina and Dean about July coming to collect her government book in the gym. With August in jail and out of the running, that left two suspects, that Danny knew of.

Then again, he half hoped it wasn't suicide, because, well, suicide.

"It's difficult to articulate how to feel about the situation, I imagine." Vera prompted this after ten seconds of silence. Danny nodded and avoided wincing at the burning sensation in his abdomen. Why had he come here?

A cat clock by a box of tissues ticked away a handful of seconds.

"Were you close with the student?" Vera flinched and shifted in her chair. She looked uncomfortable asking so many questions. Maybe movies didn't have therapists right either.

He released a breath. "She didn't seem like the kind of person to end everything. It makes no sense."

Vera's expression relaxed, corners of the eyes softened. At last he was talking. She nodded.

"I mean, I wasn't as close with her as my girlfriend Rayah or some others." Oh, Bel, he wondered how she held up with the passing of her baby. "But I'd texted her the morning of. She didn't hint at it, nothing like they talked about at the assembly this morning, all the suicide prevention warning signs."

Sucking in a breath, he stopped himself short.

He focused on the coloring book. The front cover featured a cat with intricate swirls and zigzags awaiting a crayon touch.

"I imagine that must've been hard to hear the news."

"Oh, I didn't hear it. I saw her moments after the fact. I was the one who reported it to Principal Ari the moment I saw it in the gym."

Vera blanched; seeming to forget herself, she blurted, "You were the student who vomited on the gym floor?"

"Anxiety issues. It was on the online form."

Smoothing her bun, the counselor cleared her throat and adjusted her badge, which had gone crooked. "I'll bet that was frightening to see that."

"No kidding, second time this year." Dagon, Danny, stop.

"Second time?"

"M-my roommate. I found him after Homecoming." He clamped his mouth shut, vowing not to speak another word. Downstairs, his bag contained a sheet from the morning assembly on what peers should do if their fellow students experienced mental health problems. I.e., major PTSD from traumatic experiences, signs of suicidal thoughts, etc.

1. Call the suicide hotline.

2. Report the student to the hospital.

3. Don't worry. The hospital, as with all brain problems, will send the student to the psych ward.

4. Tell the student to enjoy their stay. That particular ward isn't keen on letting people out early until they're fixed.

Of course, they worded it with more flowery language such as "caring for your fellow peer" and "doing your part to protect the lives of your friends." Rayah emerged from that assembly shaking and eyeing each of her friends with dark eyes full of suspicion. Perhaps one of them would turn her in at any moment for her flashbacks.

"I'm doing all right, all things considered," Danny added. "It just makes me sad to know a friend who showed no warning signs all of a sudden is gone."

A weak smile flashed up Vera's blush-laden cheeks. "Unfortunately, we don't have much time today because of the number of student walk-ins, but I'd love to leave you with a few handouts, if that's all right with you."

"Fine."

She gave him a business card and two handouts. The first, "How to Cope with the Loss of a Friend." Second, "Am I Suicidal?" The latter had a stapled sheet, a copy to give to one of his friends.

After Vera walked him through the two sheets, their fifteen minutes had expired.

"Follow the steps on those sheets, and they should be able to help you manage any symptoms of grief or trauma that accompany the event. You're scheduled with me in three weeks, but in an emergency, call the number on that card, or the hotline."

He managed a nod, hard to do with his shoulders tensing all the way to his ears. Would she report him to the psych ward after this?

She led him out of the office where he checked out with the front desk lady. A flash of green paper landed in his hand. Messy handwriting had scribbled something about his next appointment in December.

They couldn't force him to go to a hospital if they scheduled another time, could they?

Thanking him for visiting, the lady at the front called up the next student to meet with Vera. As he glanced back, he noticed dark circles underneath the counselor's eyes. It was two in the afternoon. Did she have a break all day?

Galumphing down the winding staircase, he peered over the side to find all the tables had evacuated. He zoomed to his table and retrieved his bag. Digging through the papers, he found the assembly schedule.

12:00 Lunch (Dining Commons)

Students can eat lunch during this hour. If a student is having a hard time eating (see eating disorders handout from earlier assembly) refer them to the counseling center (located upstairs from the Atrium).

1:00 Art Therapy Session (Atrium)

Students have the option to paint on canvases in the Atrium. Watercolor palettes and water cups will be provided. The dining commons staff has provided some baked goods. These will be available during lunch but can be provided to students who have an appointment during the lunch hour.

2:00 The Beautiful You (Theater)

Psychology teacher Mrs. Dido Pamine will walk students through how to build each other up to aid in suicide prevention. This talk is mandatory and will be taking place at 2:00, 3:00, 4:00, 5:00, and 6:00. The theater holds more than 1500, so students should be able to find a time to watch this talk. Those unable to attend will be required to watch a video of "The Beautiful You" within the span of 24 hours.

He crumpled the paper into his bag. "How the heck did they pull this thing together so fast? Were they expecting another student to end it all?"

Checking over his shoulder, he relaxed since no one had heard him. He dashed down the trees of columns and to the left toward the theater. Whisking himself up the stairs, he found himself at the back of the clump of students filing into the auditorium. He entered and perused the rows until he found his group at the far-right corner. They saved him a seat on the aisle, right by Rayah. She looked uncomfortable, the same way Vera did in the therapy session. Perhaps Michelle or Hannah forced her to sit there.

"Mind if I sit?"

Rayah jolted as he settled into the squeaky chair. A plume of dust lifted from it.

"How did your counseling session go?" Rayah stared at her shoes. They were kicking at a sticky clump stuck to the concrete steps.

"Good, I avoided getting sent to the hospital."

Rayah's face screwed into a severe look. She looked scary more than anything else. "Oh?"

"I know Principal Ari likes to get things done and solved, but today may be taking things too far."

Feedback from a microphone up front pierced their ears, even with the carpeted walls there to absorb most of the screeching. A woman in a sky-blue business suit and pants to match adjusted a pair of thick glasses, not unlike the ones Martin wore.

"Good afternoon. Welcome to 'The Beautiful You.'" She shielded her eyes with a hand. Her voice ran in hypnotic tones. "I'm pleased to see a full house in the audience."

They didn't have a choice, but OK.

"In this lecture, we'll cover ways to encourage and uplift your peers. This is important because you, yes you"—she pointed at someone in the front row—"are the main defense against suicide. You very well may be the last person a victim sees, talks to, texts."

Bile shot up Danny's throat. His fingers seized his abdomen as his knees lifted to his chest.

"Therefore, we want to practice some elevating exercises that you can implement the moment you walk out of this auditorium. Turn to the person to your side and introduce yourself."

He extended an arm and forced a smile. "Name's Zerubbabel."

Rayah frowned as she shook his hand.

"Now, tell the person a little about yourself. What are you most proud of? Even if you know each other, remind them."

"I'm an expert underwater basket weaver and am bilingual in Klingon."

"Danny, be serious."

Dido Pamine waited for the loud din of conversation to shush to mere mutters between students caught up in dialogues. "Good, now, I want you to tell the person next to you something encouraging. From something you've heard from them or something you've noticed about them."

Hannah launched immediately after Dido stopped speaking. "Half the time you don't annoy me, Michelle."

Muscles in his face went slack. His hands itched to grip Rayah's shoulder and squeeze it as a comfort. Instead, he balled fingers. "Ray, you're one of the strongest people I know. I can't imagine what you've been going through, and know you need space. But even if we don't end up together"—water glazed the bottoms of his lids—"I want you to know that you're a gem. Anyone who fails to see that is an idiot."

Expressionless, Rayah leaned forward. "Racism."

His blood ran cold. "Was it something I said?"

She shook her head. "We figured out a common pattern with the deaths and attempts. And not just the fact they all happened in the gym. I had an inkling before yesterday, but July's death followed the pattern. Besides Ned, they were all minorities. Bel comes from Asia. And July and Reuben were both black."

"What about Mr. Peterson? He wasn't a minority, from what I've seen in yearbook pictures."

"Maybe the murderer didn't target him. Maybe they're just targeting students."

"You think someone tried to off Bel too?"

"I think"—Rayah sucked in a rattling breath—"I think my skin isn't white, Danny. And there aren't a whole lot of minorities in rural Pennsylvania. If it was murder, I'm on a very small hit list."

Dido chirped something else into the microphone. But all that filled Danny's ears was a ringing.

Chapter Twenty-Five

RAYAH: Hi, Danny, I would've called but I didn't want to assume you wanted to talk right now.

RAYAH: I'm so sorry to hear about both Zai and your dad. I can't imagine what that must be like, all in two weeks.

RAYAH: My mom talked with yours, they seem to be becoming friends. She says your anxiety has shot through the roof and that you're throwing up a lot. I'm so sorry to hear this. I know this isn't the same thing, but whenever my dad ... whenever he comes home angry, I get flashbacks sometimes.

RAYAH: I don't know if it's called PTSD or what, but I sometimes forget how to breathe.

RAYAH: But then I hop on your Twitter, Zai gave me your username. Although it doesn't make all the flashbacks go away, it helps a little, a lot. Words can go a lot farther than most things, I think.

RAYAH: I see you haven't posted in two weeks. I know it's not my place, and I'm usually a shy person, but I really think you should keep posting, if not for other people, for yourself. You may have lost two lives of people who are very close to you, but trust me, you're helping save others.

RAYAH: You saved mine.

Students,

A fellow student council member has brought to my attention that the most recent suicide might have been provoked by a social media post. Although the student council member asked to leave whoever posted it anonymous, I have cause to believe that this post had a pattern with the previous two.

For instance, all the posts contained a religious verse and a malevolent prayer for said person. There have been multiple disputes on Twitter already about the effectiveness of "thoughts and prayers" posts. Most of the time, these appear to harm more than help, more so in this case.

Because we can find no other prevalent pattern in previous posts, other than radical religious sentiments, I have made the executive decision that **all intolerant, hate speech filled, or religious posts are henceforth banned from social media platforms.**

This includes wishing a person a prayer (especially when they're experiencing a tough time), posting quotes from outspoken leaders of a faith (not limited to Islam, Judaism, Christianity, Hinduism, Buddhism, etc.), posting of scriptural references (from any religious text), or even photos or memes that contain content that would fit into any of these categories.

Any student who is found posting content of this nature will face **severe punishment.**

Furthermore, if a student attempts to "post" via a physical platform such as passing notes with verses or mantras or prayers (anything of the like) or attempting to evangelize students, this will also be included. I understand it is harder to measure physical platforms. However, I have asked the student council members as well as the student body to remain vigilant and to report such instances to the main office. If you are uncertain if something falls into these categories, contact me directly. If I do not reply, err on the side of caution and DO NOT post it, say it, or do it.

I know this may seem like a form of censorship when I adamantly refused to legislate how to dictate students' actions online or in person. However, given the recent circumstances, we had to act upon the lowest common denominator. Students should keep in mind that many other non-religious institutions have discouraged or banned the use of prayers, religious texts, or other such practices within the school's walls. This is mainly to prevent any discrimination for those who do not exercise such beliefs.

The ban will last until Christmas break. Although said student council member asked for an extension, I kept it to a month. I figured the past three tragedies that have stricken King's occurred within the span of three months (a tragedy a month). We will use the time of the restriction to discipline all guilty parties and enlist preventative measures.

Once again, I thank you for bearing with me on this. It's not, how would you say, how I roll. However, sometimes administrations must place safety in front of personal freedoms.

Ari Kingsley

Michelle shoveled a spoonful of cauliflower down her throat as she scrolled through her feed.

"Mazda, I've posted articles on pro-life, less centralized government control ... Mazda, even one on censorship in journalism. She's going to come after me."

"OK, first, stop trying to make Mazda a thing." Danny slid his plate onto the table. Cauliflower juice spattered by the case of napkins. "It's Dagon, *Da-gon*. Second, you never post anything remotely close to what she was talking about in the email."

Michelle frowned. "I don't know. She gave someone a detention the other day for retweeting a Gandhi quote. It didn't even have to do with Hinduism."

"He was outspoken. You're probably fine and off Ari's hit list."

Rayah's hands shook as she reached for the pepper.

"Anyone have any idea who the mysterious person who posted on July's Twitter was?" Juice spilled down Michelle's chin. "I can't find anything except lots of hate from Valentina's friends."

Danny siphoned the spill with a napkin and pulled up his Twitter. He clicked on July's page. No kidding.

> @catlover40404 Shocker that the girl who posts something intolerant kills herself after someone posted something intolerant about her #sorrynotsorry

> @dennis_baylor444 Hope it's nice and toasty where you are now.

> @lioness4lifffe Honestly I do feel sorry for you. Your family raised you wrong. July, you could've been a decent person if you grew up with anyone else.

> @val_luvs_life July, I really wanted to like you and be friends with you. I'm just so sorry that our differences got in the way. I'm sure, if you were here, you'd feel sorry too. In that case, I completely forgive you girlie.

"Her poor parents." Rayah bit into an over-peppered broccoli and grimaced.

Danny snorted into his oozing mashed potatoes. "No kidding, her dad is probably heartbroken seeing all those things on her feed, and that's not going to help his cancer any. We can't even post that we're praying for them. I wish I had their numbers."

With lightning speed, he filtered through his contacts. Nope.

He sighed and slumped back so far into his seat he almost toppled over, but regained his balance. "Mitch, tell me this must be illegal. Can we break this rule like the pledge thing last year? I want to post something so bad. I have, like, ten excellent comebacks."

Protection Mode: Activated

Friend Needing Protecting: July*

*Yes, Protection Mode even worked for dead friends.

Michelle rested her cheeks on her fists, giving the appearance of the chipmunks who were about to start hibernation season outside. "I'm not sure, about anything really. I used to be so certain on gun control laws and censorship after being so invested in the news, but after doing extensive research on the law when we wanted to sue Ned, even the court system's messed up."

"You didn't find that out before?" Hannah gargled some sort of red drink.

"I don't think there's a scenario in this where you can win. So I would avoid posting."

His face flared with fire. "Even when people are posting that they're glad she killed herself?"

"She didn't." Michelle glowered at him. "And you could always just tell the people what you think in person."

He shook his head. "Nope, Ari said we can't do stuff like that in person this month. And most of the people who posted are Valentina's friends. It'll get back to Ari."

Pink filled Michelle's face as the vein in her forehead bulged. "I'm not sure what you want us to do, Dan."

"Something."

"This isn't the pledge Ned made us do!" She banged her fist against the table and rose. "This isn't a case where you have no choice. You can let it sit for a month. The truth will come out in a month." She tore open her bag and shoved a campus newspaper in his face. "I'll make sure of it."

He rose too, abdomen and veins in his neck about to burst. "When? In January? Did you forget about winter break? Because her story will sit a solid two months before anything can get written. By then, who cares? Trends don't last that long, you know."

He wanted to add that no one read the campus newspaper anyway, but everything else appeared to have an effect on Michelle already. She wavered for a moment as if stunned by a gunshot.

A tear trickled down Michelle's cheek as she sank into her chair. She buried her head into her arms and shook the table.

"Why do you care so much?" Her muffled voice bounced off the wood.

Danny eyed the staircase to the dining commons as Judah walked in with Faith clutching a baby on her right hip. She came to visit today. "She was a believer, right?"

"So?"

"So that makes her family."

Michelle sighed.

"And she was Emmanuel. We stick together, even after death."

Mascara cascaded in rivers down Michelle's chin as she lifted her head. Her lips quivered. "I just"—she choked on a sob—"I just can't be in a room on fire again."

She dropped her head and hiccupped into the table.

"Whoa, hello purple."

Bel craned her neck at Danny and slammed the top drawer of Duke's dresser. She tousled her fingers through her very short purple hair.

"If you're looking for your brother, I don't think he'll fit in there." Danny gestured to the dresser.

She stood and wiped her hands on a sweater with a purple dragon stitched onto the center. "Not looking for him."

"I don't know where he is." He snapped his fingers. "Oh, it's Friday night, probably has a date with Hannah."

Bel wasted no time in scrounging through Duke's desk drawer. Her bandaged fingernails pickpocketed through wrappers and broken mechanical pencils.

"Anything I can help you find?"

The dark sweater didn't do very well at hiding the charcoal circles under her eyes. "I'm looking for a scarf. Left it here last time I visited."

"What's it look like?"

"Pashmina with a Persian design."

He frowned at the landfill on the bed in the corner of the room. "Was that English?"

She sighed. "It's blue with a gold design, lots of swirly things on it."

Danny reaped through the pile on the bed, aluminum soda cans, beef jerky wrappers, Zebra Cake crumbs. "And you came all this way to campus just for a scarf?"

"I didn't know my brother had a date today. Thought he and I could talk. He's terrible at picking up his phone."

Really? Because he scrolled on it all the time.

"I'll bet that blue-and-gold scarf doesn't match the purple sweater you're wearing."

"It is my favorite scarf."

She'd moved on to crawling on all fours underneath the bunk bed. Danny held back a warning that pregnant women shouldn't overexert themselves. She didn't have a baby anymore.

Oh shoot, he'd forgotten about the other baby.

Faith, Judah, and baby Taylor had planned to visit Phrat River after dinner. He reached for his pocket to warn them not to come. He patted an empty patch of fabric. Must've dropped his phone in the pile of trash on the bed.

He shoved back bottles and crumples of paper to dig for it.

"OK, I don't like it that much. You don't have to get that into it." Bel's knees cracked as she unbent herself from the bed.

"It's cold outside. You need a warm scarf."

"Clearly you don't know Pashmina."

"Is she nice?"

A crackled giggle sounded from Bel. It almost reminded him of a broken bell, with the way it echoed in the windowless room. It was interrupted by the din of a ball hitting the outside hallway walls.

"Thought that was thunder for a moment." Bel giggled again.

"You get used to it. Guys in Phrat River think it's a fun thing to do at two in the morning."

"Sounds about right." She shoved aside a pile of the trash to make room for herself to sit.

A pink rubber ball rolled into the room and hit the heater on the wall. Dean staggered in. With a pointed sigh, Danny motioned to the corner where the ball had landed, but Dean ignored him and leaned on his arm in the doorframe.

"Look who's out of the nuthouse."

Bel stiffened but no emotion crossed her face. "Dean."

"They give you enough meds so you don't try to pop more pills again?" He chuckled into his arm. "That's ironic, isn't it? Pills to stop pills."

She pinched the fuzzy dragon on her sweater. "They give you plenty of pills all right. So many that you think you'll explode."

"The ball's in the corner, Dean." Danny rolled his fists and side-stepped to block Dean's gaze.

A smirk jutted up his cheek as he trundled to the heater to grab his ball. He remarked something about how it felt warm and went on his merry way out into the hall. Thudding noises commenced seconds later.

"Ignore him."

Bel shrugged. "I was expecting it. People keep asking me what it's like there. And if it's anything like what they read about. And people keep asking me if I actually killed myself or if July, my ex-roommate, did. They really like to put emphasis on that *ex* part."

"Oh?"

"Of course, I tell them they're all ridiculous. I tried to kill myself. You saw me with the pills."

Light died in his chest. So much for the racism thing. The murderer would need a third minority victim for a common pattern.

Maybe Reuben and July had truly taken their own lives.

"But you're feeling like you have it under control?"

She chewed on her lip, thumbed the dragon design. "You don't go to that place to get better. And after the baby—"

Soft knocking rapped on the door. Danny launched himself forward to shut it. It was probably Dean bouncing the ball too close again. But instead, he found Faith and Judah at the entrance with a child cradled in his father's arms.

Danny's chest froze. He'd forgotten to text them not to come.

He stretched himself in front of the door, blocking out whatever corners he could. "'Sup, guys? Wanna sit in that nice comfy lounge over there?"

Taylor screwed up his face and cried.

Judah rocked him. "We'd probably rather come in. We don't want little Taylor to get hit by the bouncing ball in the hallway."

"They can come in." Bel stared at her feet, which dangled off the bed. "I saw them on campus earlier. I figured they'd come visit you."

Danny leaned out of the doorframe as the family ducked in and found a spot on Duke's bed. Faith frowned at the pile of trash on the other mattress.

Taylor sniveled with snot trailing out of his nostrils. His little navy onesie read in bright-yellow letters *Chick Magnet.*

The other chick, Bel, found herself very interested in an empty syringe she found in the landfill pile. She set it down and continued to stare at the floor.

Faith, perhaps sensing the awkwardness, cradled the baby in one hand, who stopped crying in the transfer. She extended the other toward Bel. "I don't think we've met. I'm Faith."

"Bel."

Faith's hand shrank back for a moment. Oh yes, she'd heard of the girl who tried to commit suicide a few months back. Danny, standing in the gap between the beds, shuffled from one foot to the other.

"You may have heard of her from my summer job. Bel worked with me in the ice cream shop. She helped me eat all the mistakes."

"Mistakes?" Faith cocked her head ninety degrees.

Bel appeared to brighten at this. She sat up and met Faith's eyes. "Whenever we messed up an order, we would put it in the freezer. Sometimes it was ridiculous things, strawberry syrup instead of chocolate, rainbow sprinkles instead of brown ones. At the end of the day we could eat mistakes." She laughed softly. "Danny by far made the most mistakes."

"Lies, all lies." He clung to the corner of the top bunk and leaned out like a spider monkey. "At least I didn't forget to give the lactose intolerant lady the lactose-free vanilla instead of the actual one."

Happy tears sparkled in the corners of Bel's eyes as she laughed. Then she caught her breath and pinched her nose to imitate the woman. "I want a refund and the largest size you've got. No, I don't care that I ordered the kid's size before." She shook her head. "She hadn't even taken a bite out of the first one. I think she just had a Spidey sense or something."

Danny noticed that Judah's shoulders had relaxed. Perhaps he too had heard too much about Bel from the other students. After all, he had her in class only one day.

"I'll bet you had lots of horrible customers." He swung an arm around Faith and pressed her to his side. Faith wiped some spit-up from Taylor with a yellow cloth.

"Oh, don't even get us started. Can you remember them all, Danny?"

"I think we'd have to break them into categories."

"Customer One." She twirled her hair to imitate a child. At least, best she could do with the new boyish cut. "Can I try every flavor you have and *not* buy a single one?"

"Customer Two." Danny hunched over and raised his voice to sound like an elderly lady. "Why won't my coupon scan?" He waved his hand in a shaky motion and set his tone to vibrate. "What do you mean it's two years expired? Give me the free cone."

"Customer Three."

Bel's imitation of a large man asking for a refund on his fully eaten ice cream was cut short by a shriek from Taylor. Light faded from her face fast and she returned her gaze to the floor. Laughter died on Judah's and Faith's lips as they watched her hug her knees to her chest and suck in heavy breaths.

A panic attack overtook her, just as it had done with Rayah.

Danny rushed forward and placed his hand on her shoulder.

"Are you having a hard time breathing?"

Tears trickled down her cheeks as she nodded. He backed up to give her space, but right as he did, something thudded against his ankle. He glanced down. Dean's shoes met his as he stooped to grab the rubber ball. They met eyes.

"What's wrong with her?"

"She's fine. Go back to bouncing this in the hall."

"We're supposed to report anything like this to the hospital. She's suicidal."

"Go back to the hall."

"I'm reporting it."

Danny lunged forward and grabbed a fistful of Dean's shirt. "Since when do you care about following the rules?"

"Be careful, Princess." Alcoholic traces on his breath stunned Danny's nose. "If you didn't have Ari's protection, I'd report you too."

He shoved Danny back and lumbered toward the door. He checked himself once to toss a quick glance at Bel, who had pressed her hands to her temples. "Surprised she wasn't from Emmanuel. Anyone who went to that school deserves to go where she's going."

To Hell or the nuthouse?

Right as Dean slammed the door, he heard him dialing three numbers.

Chapter Twenty-Six

"TO POST OR NOT TO POST?"

Danny's mouse hovered over the green tweet button. The glow of his laptop stung his eyes. He'd been at this too long.

"Are you still on this?"

Duke squinted at him as his head peered out from the bottom bunk. Danny checked the time at the right-hand corner of his screen. Two in the morning, happy Sunday.

"Sorry, I can take it out to the lounge."

His roommate rolled his one good eye and slunk back into bed. "You might not want to do that."

"Why?"

"Dean doused the couches with a poop-scented spray. Got it at a prank store."

"'Course he did. I guess that answers the question, not to post." He slammed the laptop lid shut.

Duke's mattress groaned as he rolled out from it and toward the light switch. He groped the wall for a second before flicking it on. Now, Danny's eyes stung more than ever. He knuckled them to catch some of the moisture.

"OK, usually I don't care if students break the rules, but why are you so adamant about posting this?"

He flipped open his laptop again. It hummed as it purred on the sheets back to life. "You should've seen what people are posting on her wall. It's nonstop for two days."

"Can't you just say something like, 'That's not true.'"

"Because that worked so well for Martin."

Martin, the terrible PE running buddy who'd grown fed up with the numerous posts on Friday, posted late into the night about the weaknesses in the arguments and statements presented. Danny had no idea how close Martin had been to July, but apparently he was chummy enough to get irked.

> @ModernMartinLuther27 Why don't we realize that none of these arguments toward July are justified? They are not objective but are appeals to the emotions that manipulate the mind. We may never know the true July if our feed is clogged by these insults to injury. #justiceforjuly

Saturday brought an onslaught of injuries for Martin. Valentina, as later revealed by Dean in the restroom, had called the hospital early in the morning on him.

"She'd heard horror stories about his OCD." Dean sprinkled his hands in the sink. "About him washing his hands too much until they bled and how he had to rearrange his room so often his roommates begged the school to transfer them to another dorm." He moved to the hand dryers. "Glad they took him to the hospital. Hopefully they'll fix him up before next semester."

Danny had buried his head into his hands in the stall as the blow dryer drowned out the bathroom with a roaring din.

Duke shoved aside the trash heap on the bed and faced his roommate. "So why do *you* have to be the one to post it?" He sat.

"Because." He glanced at the back wall where a window should've been built. "Because I'm the only one who hasn't been trapped in a burning room."

Jaw tightening, Duke swayed to the side. "That doesn't make any sense."

"Listen, July wasn't close to many people except for Bel and a few folks from Emmanuel. No one I know is going to argue her case, especially not after Valentina shipped Martin off for saying something."

"Right, so why *you*?"

Groaning along with the heater, he kicked off the sheets, which had caused a coat of sweat to cover his legs. He twisted until he could face Duke dead on, legs dangling off the top.

"Remember when someone insulted Bel in the cafeteria last year? What did you do to that girl?"

Duke rubbed his face, failing to wipe off a growing smile. "I don't see what pouring dishwater on someone's hair has to do with it."

"When someone insults someone you care about, what do you do?"

"You protect them, but—"

"And how do you think July's family is feeling anytime they scroll through her feed? Even if it gets taken down, you know they saw it."

Chewing on his cheek, Duke hunched forward and clawed his spiky tendrils of hair. "Lion Tamer, I know you've got a good heart, but the risk isn't worth it. There are some times when you can't be the hero. When you can't protect everybody." He turned away for a moment. "Isn't there something about turning the other cheek?"

"Yes." Heat rushed to his face. "But there's also a good deal about seeking justice for those who are repeatedly being oppressed, especially when you have the power to say something."

Duke sighed and launched himself from the bed. "It's your choice. Keep in mind the best decisions aren't made at two in the morning." He plucked a syringe from the garbage pile. "I would know."

After flicking the switch, he stumbled back into bed. Danny returned to his post. Hand hovering over the mouse pad, he reread it.

> @dannyintheden456 Praying for July and her family. I knew her. She was a great friend. I wish I knew her more. This was her favorite verse: The Lord is a refuge for the oppressed, a stronghold in times of trouble.

She had posted that verse a lot. Had also told him the very same one during the Suanna fire.

He hesitated and closed his eyes as he pressed the keypad. Posted.

Hopefully Ari's protection could last a little while longer, until winter break at least. Maybe then he could explore options with a homeschool co-op. School with Jeremy probably wasn't as bad as it sounded, and by this point, an expulsion from King's probably wasn't either.

Light glowed from Duke's bed from his phone. "Well, Lion Tamer, at least you went out with a bang."

Judah elbowed Danny as he checked his Twitter feed under the kitchen table. He ignored him and watched as he received a notification for the one-hundredth like of his post. Comments ranged from death threats to notes of affirmation. "So happy someone said it! Thank you!" "I'll bet you're a misogynist homophobe too!" "I'm sure her family is glad to hear this during their time of grief."

He slid the phone back into his pocket, fighting the tingling sensation in his fingers and brain to keep refreshing. His mother passed him a bowl of steamed broccoli that smelled overcooked. To appease her, he put a spoonful on his plate.

"I'm happy we have these family lunches every Sunday." His mother sipped a green glass full of milk. "Lucky we have Judah working at your school, Danny, so he can take you here every Sunday."

"Think next year I could get a car for school?"

Her eyelids narrowed to slits. "Let's work on that parallel parking first."

Laughter stopped short in his throat as his phone buzzed in his pocket. He pulled it out and an unknown number blared on the screen.

"Put it on silent."

So he did. Curiosity pounded in his temples. He guzzled his milk, followed by the anxiety meds, and shoveled the broccoli down his throat. Even with the moisture from the drink, it took a great deal of effort to swallow. Clearing his plate, he grabbed his dishes and darted toward the sink in the kitchen.

"Wait until everyone has finished."

"Sorry, Mom, group project," he lied. "Gotta return the call."

He'd gotten a number of texts that day from classmates about the tweet. Even some of his teachers emailed him to say they thought the new school rule was stupid and admired his desire to fight it.

Still, he had to be cautious. Perhaps Ari had obtained his number and called to let him know she planned to expel him the next morning. Then again, the post was mild. What on earth could she ding him for? For calling July a friend?

He spattered the dishes in soap and lukewarm water and tossed them into the dishwater. Zooming up the stairs, he checked his phone again and found a voicemail from the mysterious caller. Slamming the door to his room and collapsing on his bed, he pressed play.

"Are you freaking kidding me?"

Valentina's voice screeched through the earpiece. He had to hold the phone a foot away.

"You literally could have waited thirty days, but no. You broke all of the rules."

The *Gladiator* poster hanging caught his eye. He tightened his gut. Grin and bear it. He'd expected pushback from Valentina. Bracing himself for her to tell him that she'd already called 9-1-1 on him, he glanced at his closet. Would he have time to pack a bag for the ward? What would they let him keep? No way he could fit a suitcase in one of those lockers.

"You know, I wasn't going to post the tweet you had put on July's wall. I'd promised Ari I'd just keep the screenshot, but you leave me with no choice. I'm going to expose you for who you truly are, Daniel Belte."

Whoa, full name, this *was* serious.

"You are *not* a hero, Daniel Belte."

Beep, beep, beep signaled she'd hung up after huffing. Ice pumped through his arms and neck. What screenshot did she mean?

He clicked on his Twitter app and the first thing that popped into his feed was a screenshot from Valentina. She'd commented.

> @val_luvs_life For those of you who are calling Danny Belte a saint, check out what he'd posted to July's wall the day she killed herself. He deleted it soon after. Wonder why.

He enlarged the screenshot and read the "tweet" he supposedly posted.

@dannyintheden456 The Lord is a refuge for the oppressed, a stronghold in times of trouble. July oppressed Bel and Reuben, good friends of mine. Let's hope she meets the same troubled fate she left for them. Praying for her family.

"Duke, believe me, I didn't post that."

His roommate grabbed a fistful of his hoodie and pulled him in. He slammed the door behind them. Duke exhaled two breaths that smelled of energy drink. "I know."

"You do?"

He released his grip. "No, actually I don't, but after what happened to Martin, I don't trust Valentina." With a sturdy kick, he launched a Monster can into the back wall. "Plus, you don't seem like the type to wish death upon people."

He wasn't wrong, but it still kept happening to everyone around Danny.

Duke shrugged. "I wouldn't worry about it." Duke rushed to the door as if reaching for a lock, stopped himself. Doors locked on the outside here. "She'd supposedly shown Ari the screenshot before. The principal didn't call you in at any time. Maybe she thought it was fake."

"There are apps for that, faking Twitter posts." Danny pulled himself up to the top bunk. "If she didn't believe it, why would she make the rule?"

Duke stooped to pick up the Monster can and placed it on the growing heap. "Maybe some parents complained. Maybe to get Valentina off her back. Don't know what Dean sees in her ... she's annoying as crap."

Stomach burning inside of him, he leaned back into his pillow and let the pillowcase absorb the beads of cool sweat. He'd expected fire. He'd expected Valentina. So why was his heart racing so fast?

"I mean, her choice in guys is awful." Duke slumped onto the floor and avoided cascading paper towel clumps. "First, she dates Dean when he's dating someone else. Then, she gets with someone from Emmanuel, when she freaking hated that school—"

Danny bolted upright in bed. Emmanuel. Something clicked in his head like a computer switch rumbling machinery to life.

"July and Reuben were from Emmanuel."

"I don't think she was into girls."

He swiped a clammy tendril that stuck to his nose. "No, I mean, July and Reuben were from Emmanuel. Bel didn't ever go to that school."

His roommate squinted at him. "Not following."

"The three suicides, and suicide attempts, came from those three. And the two that involved a gunshot involved July and Reuben."

"So?"

"So, we found a pattern in the murder of July and Reuben. They came from Emmanuel. Valentina hated that school."

Duke sprang up at rocket speed, almost tripping because he'd stood up so fast. "Whoa, Lion Tamer. You sayin' Valentina murdered July and Reuben?"

Thunderous beatings of his heart filled his ears. It sounded crazy.

"It sort of adds up. She was in the back hallway during the Reuben thing. She knew July was going to stop by the gym to pick up her government book."

Duke's nose wrinkled so high his cheeks almost covered his eyes. "Wasn't there a newspaper article that said Valentina was out with August during the first shooting?"

"You read the newspaper?"

"No."

"Maybe she lied about it? August did say she had the details mixed up. And the quote unquote eyewitnesses were close friends of hers on student council."

Shrugging, Duke slumped against the wall. He bolted forward when something like the sound of paper rattled the door. Leaning around a desk, he saw something and stooped to grab it. Unfolding the paper with fringes, he read it and crumpled it into a ball. Onto the pile it went.

"Another death note?"

"You're popular today. This one had it in red."

Danny swallowed, saliva tasting like dust. "Must've meant business."

"At least you've got Ari's protection." Duke let out a low whistle and stopped it mid-trill. "That why you ended up posting the tweet? I mean the real one, not the screenshot."

"Sort of. I'd hoped, since Ari likes me and all, that she'd go a little easier. But even without the protection, I'd still have posted it." Danny's lips twitched in a sheepish grin and returned to a thin line.

Another paper slid underneath the door. Duke groaned and tore it in half.

"You didn't even read it."

"You wouldn't like the words people are using." Paper shavings fell like snowflakes onto the carpet. "Emmanuel students don't say them."

Soon as Duke leaned to pick up the pieces and sprinkle them on the mound, a pounding shook the door. Groaning through his fists, he marched toward the door and cracked it open. "You've exceeded your death threat quot—Gabe?"

He inched backward and let the pale boy slip through. Gabe lifted a ceramic plate through the holes of the fence on the top bunk. Danny peeled off the Saran Wrap, and the aroma of fresh mashed potatoes and corn filled the room.

"Thanks, Gabe. You're—"

"An angel, yes, we've been over this."

Mashed potatoes oozed toward the edge of the plate. He tilted it to the left.

"Sneaked it from the dining commons. They're doing Thanksgiv-ing-ish stuff, so not too many vegetarian options."

Fire swirled in Danny's abdomen. He winced. "I don't know if I'd be able to eat much anyway."

"Better get in what you can. The cafeteria staff's strict about students taking any food out."

Danny stared at the plate and his Adam's apple bobbled against his tight throat. Never imagined his last meal would be this. Spoonfuls of potatoes slid down his throat. At least their warmness gave his stomach a hug.

His phone dinged, and he was almost afraid to pick it up. Perhaps the death notes had traveled from snail mail to email. Made sense.

An email from Ari Kingsley blinked on the screen. Remnants of potato clinging to his molars tasted of sawdust now. He slid it open.

Daniel Belte,

My office. 7:00 a.m. Tomorrow.

Ari Kingsley

"What is it?" Gabe had reached the door but stopped to peer up at his friend.

"Probably nothing good."

Chapter Twenty-Seven

"I CAN'T GO BACK ON MY WORD."

Ari paced in front of a counter, her purple dress so dark it could've been black in certain lights. She pressed her hands behind her back and clasped them as a sufficient hand-holding mechanism for single people.

He'd have to learn that if Rayah ever clued him into how their relationship was going, or if he made it out of this office alive.

"You have to believe me that I didn't post the one she screenshot."

She drew in a breath during a pause of Ashley's clattering on the keyboard. "I had wanted to. When she showed me it originally, I thought she'd forged it somehow. I've never excelled at technology, but I know there are certain apps that can recreate that sort of thing."

Pausing at a large hand-sanitizer bottle, she pumped a clump of clear liquid onto her palms and rubbed. "Perhaps you hadn't posted that one, but you did write the other one that appeared early yesterday morning, correct?"

"Yes, but that one meant no harm. I got lots of notes from people who were encouraged by it, some even from July's family."

Long breaths trailed from her violet lips. "Indeed, but we've also received dozens of emails from angry parents and students. You may have meant to help, as I'm sure some previous posts from other sources had in the past, but you caused a significant amount of harm."

"So what now?"

"You'll pack your belongings and be out of here by Tuesday morning."

He bolted from his bench seat. "So that's it. One tweet expelled me." He clenched his fists. Relax, he'd expected it … he knew this was a possibility. But Ari seemed more reasonable than Ned or August.

Maybe Rayah was right. There never was an end to a Ned. Each one simply had a different face.

"You will also participate in the food drive you signed up for today. I figure from now until five in the evening gives you plenty of time to pack. Whatever you don't finish can be completed after the drive." She sighed and rubbed the wrinkles on her forehead. "I suppose I could give a little leniency as to what time in the morning you may go. After all, we did receive a lot of donations thanks to your initiative."

She leaned against the wall, and her chest puffed up and down. She clenched her fists, unrolled them. How was this hard for her? She was the one expelling him.

"That's it?"

"That is all."

Danny collected his backpack and slumped it over his shoulder, wishing he hadn't packed all his heavy books for that day. Ari grabbed his shoulder on the way out and turned him.

"One more thing." She blinked away a shimmering glaze in her eyes. "You've lost my protection."

A soft knock on his door caused him to get his hand caught in the bedsheet. He removed it and glanced at the entrance. Rayah.

She opened her arms. He slid off the top bunk and fell into a hug.

"Didn't see your text until second period."

"Ray, go back to class. It isn't worth a detention."

Pulling away, she flung open his closet and tore shirts off hangers. She started folding them. "Figured you could use a little help."

"Thanks." He motioned to Duke's bed. "He pulled out some cardboard boxes for me. Feel free to stuff them in there."

"Need help carrying these downstairs?"

"I'll get them." With his left hand, he reached for a pair of keys on his desk. "Judah let me borrow his truck. He's driving me home first thing tomorrow."

Rayah nodded and returned to smoothing out a wrinkled oxford. She gave up and stuffed it into a box full of textbooks. *Ancient Near East Civilizations* sat resolutely on top. Knees cracking, Rayah rose to attend to several unruly pairs of pants on the top shelf of the closet.

"Any idea what you'll do for school?"

"Maybe I'll join Jeremy's homeschool co-op." He exhaled and tore the sheet off his bed. Dust flew in spirals. "I know it's a black mark to get expelled from here, but maybe that's not so much the case after Ned retired."

His girlfriend stood on her tiptoes to retrieve something from the closet. She pulled out a green plastic bird and cocked her head at it. Her fingers ran up and down the grooved wings.

"Oh, must've grabbed that from Ned's house on accident." His fingers seized the hairs on his scalp. "Do you mind splitting the time watching Obi with Hannah? I'd drive back and forth, but that's a lot of gas."

She nodded and placed the bird on the top bunk. It fell over. She readjusted it to sit straight. This time it stayed.

"Wonder who'll watch Obi over winter break." She was still eyeing the plastic bird, almost as if expecting it to spring to life. "Or Thanksgiving break for that matter."

"Ashley's got time." He forced a pillow into the top of a stuffed-full box. This caused the cardboard to bulge in odd places. "Worst case, Hannah'll set him free before any of the breaks. He'll be able to fly around the wilderness all he wants, no more cages."

"No more cages," Rayah echoed.

She ran her hand along the wood to the top bunk, around the corner, and all the way to the wall where the architect forgot to put in a window. "You know, Danny"—she released her palm from the wall and faced him—"maybe you getting kicked out of King's isn't all that bad."

"Oh yeah?" The tape made a loud noise as he stretched it over the box. He cut the end and smoothed it over the lumpy cardboard. "You planning to post something and get expelled too?"

"No." Her lips trembled. A single tear spilled down her cheek.

Returning to the top bunk, she plucked the bird and held it. "I'm saying they're no longer keeping you in a cage." She outstretched her arms. "Spread your wings, darling. Fly."

Lights shuddered alive as he entered the gym at five. Screeches on the girls' court in the other gymnasium, not far off, filled the echoing walls with as much liveliness as a basketball practice could bring. Bins lined the far end of the sidelines full of various canned items. Dean, or someone strong, must've heaved them from the prospective academic buildings.

Uncertain of what to do at first, he paced the side of the gym to see if Ari left behind any packets of paper for them to review. He found the instructions on the whiteboard.

Food Drive Member Volunteers
Sort the items as follows:
Fruits, vegetables, meats, soups, peanut butter and jelly, other.
Sort them into separate bins. There should be plenty of bins for the various categories. If you find several of an "other" item and believe it will fit into a bin by itself, do so if you have spare bins at the end.

The farthest container, and most stuffed one, rested underneath the bleachers right by the *WELCOME TO THE DEN* sign. For some reason, it appeared to be a deep red in the lighting. Windows at the far end that led to the outside world showed a winter sky already shrouded by darkness.

He glanced over his shoulder and then at his watch. He blinked to make sure his vision hadn't gone blurry. Five. Where was everybody?

Ah yes, Valentina and Dean didn't always show up to things on time.

Marching down the sidelines, he made his way to the farthest bin, wondering just how long it would take him to sort through all these containers. Even with two helpers, this could take him well until two in the morning.

The screeches from the other gym had stopped, perhaps because he'd gone too far to hear it or because practice had ceased. Without them, he was left alone in a gym full of the echoing din of buzzing lights. Why couldn't they have done the food drive in any other room?

Tipping over the first bin, he spilled half its contents onto the shiny slick floor. He crouched and began to sort through them. Tomato soup, soup pile. Three aluminum cans went in that direction. Canned green beans? Sounded like a good contestant for the fruit and veggies pile. Perhaps a separate pile for each?

Wondered what would happen if he got canned tomatoes.

Revisiting the pile, he found an expired package of Twinkies. Seriously, guys? He bet half the items in the pile on Duke's bed could've been contenders for the food drive. Should've suggested it.

The gym door swung open with a creak. Dean sauntered in with his large silhouette larger than usual in his hoodie. He stepped in Danny's direction and swaggered toward the bin at the other end. Stopping to peer in, he continued going until he hovered behind Danny.

"Hi-ya, Princess, you look like Cinderellie mopping the floors."

"Thanks, Dean. What do you think will be the fastest way to get through these? Maybe each of us takes a bin? Or one bin at a time."

"Valentina and I will take care of it."

"Oh really? Because I've made a decent way through this pile and—"

Something clicked behind him as a cold piece of metal was pressed to his head. "I said we'll take care of it."

His heart stopped as he slowly ducked and twisted around to find Dean with a handgun, a similar model as the ones Reuben and July held. It was all black with a plastic case, almost like a toy.

Danny lifted his hands as if surrendering. "Take it easy."

His eyes shifted to the exit. He could break for it, but that required a sprinting start from his sitting position on the ground. This close, and any squeeze of that trigger meant instant death.

"Valentina tried to convince me to let you just be expelled and all, but I figured Dad had three guns in his vault downstairs. Might as well make use out of all of them. They're all different, you know, the guns. All from different dealers."

Glad to know his father was keeping several local businesses afloat.

"Valentina was worried about what he'd do when he found out I took them. But I haven't seen him open the thing in years. By the time he finds out, I'll be in college or the police will've tracked it down to him."

"Valentina knows?" His crackling voice betrayed him. "Did she help you kill the others?"

"Reuben?" He shrugged, still aiming the barrel with scary precision. At least, it was hard to be imprecise this close. "Thought you read the papers. Doesn't your friend write them? She wasn't anywhere near him when he got killed."

"So Valentina *was* with August during the Homecoming incident?" Her story checked out. August had lied about her mixing up details.

Dean's arm shook a little. Perhaps the gun was heavier than it looked. It was now that Danny realized he was wearing gloves, smart.

"She didn't help me off him or July. I mean, we were in the same room where you told us about her picking up her book. Tricky getting out of here so fast and leaving the gun in her hand. If it wasn't so dark in here, you might've seen me slip out."

He nodded toward a staircase that led upstairs to the weight-lifting room.

Right beside that staircase was a door for an exit out the back end of the gym. If Danny could launch to his feet in time, he could sprint out of here no problem.

His mind reeled through all the superhero movies he'd watched. Dean was a villain. He had to get him monologuing.

"Just before you do anything. Tell me why."

"Why?"

"Why'd you kill my friends?"

Chapped lips tore up Dean's cheek like a knife. "Plain and simple. I hate Emmanuel."

Danny's chest froze. There was nothing more to the explanation? This bought him no time. "Anything else?"

"Yeah." He inched the gun right in the spot between Danny's eyes. "I hate you even more."

Danny bolted to his feet and rushed for the exit. A bang sounded behind him.

The Adventure Concludes in

Vision

Acknowledgments

FIRST AND FOREMOST, TO MY LORD AND SAVIOR JESUS Christ. When the day-to-day feels unsafe in our nation. When administrations grow corrupt and kids fear for their lives on Monday through Friday, you are watching over us. It pains you to see people hurting because you are a God of justice and mercy.

I want to thank anyone who has (whether intentionally or unintentionally) introduced a rather difficult trial in my life—the Neds of the world. Whether you meant to do so for evil or for good, God always turned it out for the better. I may not have come out of such trials richer, stronger, or even having a greater sense of peace. But they have taught me to become kinder, driven, and most importantly, more loving. I forgive you and also want to thank you. No one can get to this point without having gone through you.

To those who have stuck by my side when I encountered a Ned. To Alyssa, James, Carlee, Amanda's support group, Katie, my family, Tessa, Cyle, Mrs. DiPaolo, Linda Taylor, and anyone else who believed in me when I didn't. Which is just about always.

To the poor editor who had to go through this book. Looking at you, Kelsey. Editors are superheroes who can turn any lump of coal into a diamond. Thank you for dealing with my dangling modifiers, floating body parts, point of view flips, and love of ellipses and em dashes.

To Depression and Anxiety, you made this process ten times more difficult than it needed to be. I hope you burn up like Suanna, Emmanuel, and pretty much everything did in book one.

To my poor characters. This, by far, is the grittiest of books I have ever written. I put you guys through a lot. Sorry about that.

And of course, to the readers (the few and brave who made it to the acknowledgment section). I know this book is a harder one to get through. I had a tough time writing it. Something deep inside my gut had to write about these issues, even if it would result in major criticism or dishonor on me, my family, and my cow. Sorry for the cliffhangers and such. Sorry book two is seldom as good as book one. And thank you for sticking with me this far.

I hope the end makes up for all the anxiety I have caused.

Made in the USA
Monee, IL
29 July 2020

37180695R00166